Unanimous acclaim for William C. Dietz's

Legion of the Damned

"Th
act

"Sci
—Billie Sue Mosiman, author of *Widow*

"Unrelenting action." —*Kliatt*

"Buckle your safety harness and enjoy
—Steve P *er Drug*

"A tough, mo
Drake

"One that I reco ts of military SF."
—*Australian SF News*

Ace Books by William C. Dietz

GALACTIC BOUNTY
(previously published as *War World*)
IMPERIAL BOUNTY
ALIEN BOUNTY
McCADE'S BOUNTY
FREEHOLD
PRISON PLANET
DRIFTER
DRIFTER'S RUN
DRIFTER'S WAR
LEGION OF THE DAMNED
BODYGUARD
THE FINAL BATTLE
WHERE THE SHIPS DIE

McCADE'S BOUNTY

WILLIAM C. DIETZ

ACE BOOKS, NEW YORK

This book is an Ace original edition,
and has never been previously published.

McCADE'S BOUNTY

An Ace Book / published by arrangement with
the author

PRINTING HISTORY
Ace edition / December 1990

Cover art by Edwin Herder.

For information address:
The Berkley Publishing Group, a member of Penguin Putnam Inc.,
200 Madison Avenue, New York, New York 10016.

The Putnam Berkley World Wide Web site address is
http://www.berkley.com

ISBN: 0-441-52303-X

ACE®
Ace Books are published by
The Berkley Publishing Group, a member of Penguin Putnam Inc.,
200 Madison Avenue, New York, New York 10016.
ACE and the "A" design are trademarks belonging to
Charter Communications, Inc.

PRINTED IN THE UNITED STATES OF AMERICA

10 9 8 7 6 5 4 3 2

For Allison and
Jessica, with thanks
for their technical
advice and encouragement.

One

FOR THE BETTER part of two rotations the battle raged on and around the ice-world called Alice.

The pirates managed to destroy the planet's small navy during the first few minutes of battle.

Then, expecting an easy victory on the ground, they dropped into orbit. The force fields around their ships disappeared, as hundreds of assault craft spilled out and spiraled down toward the bluish white planet below.

It was a mistake, and one for which the invaders would pay dearly. Missiles rose from the planet's surface followed by man-made lightning. Caught with force fields down, two of the attacking ships were destroyed, and others were damaged.

Then, angered by the effrontery of their victims, the pirates unleashed a terrible fury. Mushroom-shaped clouds marched across the frozen landscape turning vast sections of ice and snow into superheated steam and radioactive glass.

But most of the important targets were located deep underground safe from the planet's harsh winters and pirate attacks. They survived and the battle continued.

The combatants had fought many times before and knew each other well.

On the one side there were the settlers, life-long losers most of them, driven, or drifting farther and farther from the center of the human empire until reaching its very edge. For Alice was a rim world, the last stop before the Il Ronnian Empire, and the great unknown.

Now the settlers eked out a precarious existence built more on hard work than the scarce resources of their planet. They were quirky, independent, and tough as hell when backed into a corner.

The pirates were as pirates have always been, the lowest common denominator, the link between animal and man. Once, years before, they'd been something better.

They were soldiers back in those days. Soldiers who fought valiantly for a cause they believed in. A confederation of planets, each represented in a star spanning democracy, each part of a greater whole.

But in spite of their heroic efforts to hold it together, the confederation had collapsed of its own weight, and given rise to the Empire.

The first Emperor was wise in his own way, and knowing he couldn't micro-manage each planet, he provided all of them with a measure of independence and full amnesty for the confederates.

Tired of war, and preferring order to anarchy, most of them agreed.

But some scorned the offer, choosing to fight a guerrilla war instead, waiting for the day when they would seize power and restore the confederacy. The day never came.

Time passed, and with it, the ideals they'd fought for. Raid followed raid, and death followed death, until the difference between "military" and "civilian" targets started to blur.

There were atrocities, each worse than those that went before, until minds grew weary and hearts became numb.

Now, many years later, they sought loot rather than liberty. Gradually, without realizing it, patriots became pirates and a cause disappeared.

The settlers' command center was deep underground. During the past two days it had survived attacks from air-to-ground missiles, smart bombs, and a flight of robotic subsurface torpedoes. They'd burrowed within one mile of the complex before they were detected and destroyed.

The C&C was large, lit mostly by flickering vid screens, and filled with the soft murmur of radio traffic. Smoke streaked the air, empty meal paks crunched underfoot, and a feeling of weary desperation pervaded the room.

Sara Bridger-McCade focused tired eyes on the surface of the tac tank. She hadn't slept for more than twenty-six hours and exhaustion had taken its toll.

Sara was beautiful, or had been once. Now a long white scar slashed down across her face. It was deathly white against her heat-flushed skin. A grim reminder of her first encounter with the pirates many years before.

Sara wore a plain gray jump suit, light body armor, and a blaster in a cross-draw holster.

Ignoring concerned stares from C&C staff she tried to concentrate. The tac tank was a swirl of color and movement. It was similar to a three-dimensional electronic chess board, in which the green deltas belonged to her, and the red squares to someone else.

But this was no game. These markers represented real flesh-and-blood people. Mothers, fathers, sisters, and brothers. Friends of hers. They were dying and Sara couldn't stop it.

Some of the population would survive as slaves but most would die. It was the pirate way. Take what you want, destroy the rest. Sara peered into the tac tank and looked for an answer.

Hills and valleys were outlined with green contour lines and marked with elevations. Surface and subsurface installations showed up as yellow circles. Civilian domes and factories were light blue. All of it looked so neat and orderly without the sprawl of dead bodies, the stench of burned-out homes, and the cold-blue stutter of energy weapons.

Without ships to bring help, and without FTL communication, the settlers had a single ally. The weather. Up above, on the planet's surface, a class-two storm raged. Nothing like an eight or, God forbid, a ten, but just enough to slow the pirates down. Sara had hoped for more, hoped the storm would defeat them in a way that she couldn't, but the pirates were well prepared.

They wore heatsuits, rode in armored crawlers, and knew what they were doing. Slowly but surely the red squares were pressing in, pushing the green deltas toward the underground command center, crushing anything that stood in their way.

Over there, about ten klicks short of Donovan's Rift, Riston's Rifles were still holding against a company of mechanized infantry. And there, just short of the main armory, Colonel Larkin was fighting one last battle.

But that was it, after two days of battle the pirates had come close to wiping the planet clean, and would soon be victorious.

Sara's vision blurred and she rubbed her eyes. Was there a way out? Something she'd missed? A weakness?

No, nothing. The knowledge lay heavy in her gut. The pirates would take Alice within hours. She'd failed. The battle was lost.

But why? Why such determination? Why so well equipped? Why Alice?

"Sara?" The voice was calm and gentle. She looked up to see a man and a woman standing on the other side of the tac tank.

There were five members of the planetary council. Sara, Colonel Larkin, presently defending the armory, Rico, off-planet with Sam, Professor Wendel, and Dr. Hannah Lewis.

Three qualifies as a quorum, Sara thought tiredly, though it hardly matters. There's nothing left to decide.

Professor Wendel smiled wearily. He was an elderly man with bright blue eyes and a white ponytail. "We did the best we could, child. Let's save what we can."

Sara looked at Hannah. She had an open face, beautiful brown skin, and a tight cap of kinky black hair. She had a diagnostic scanner strapped to her right arm and a stethoscope hung around her neck. There were bloodstains on her OR greens. The planet's main medical facility was a thousand yards down the main corridor.

"The professor's right, Sara. Release the remaining troops and let them slip into the bush. The pirates won't find them. Not on Alice they won't."

Sara knew Hannah was right. The locals were experts at cold-weather survival. They knew the terrain, and those fortunate enough to be some distance from the C&C would have a chance of escape. "And the children?"

Hannah looked at Wendel. It was he who answered. "They're gathered in the cafeteria. The pirates will take them as slaves."

Sara felt a terrible sadness roll over her. Which was better? To die? Or live as a slave? She knew what Sam would say, knew he'd want his daughter to live, knew there was no other choice.

Sara nodded. "I'll give the necessary orders." She activated her throat mic and began to speak.

And so the word went out. "Disengage . . . pull back . . . fade into the bush. Save who and what you can. Live to fight another day. Thanks for all that you've done . . . and good-bye."

Then it was over, a kiss on the cheek from Professor Wendel, a hug from Hannah, and a wave to her quickly departing staff.

Some, either because of skills or appearance, would have a chance to become slaves, but most, like Sara with her disfiguring scar, would not. They would tend to last-minute chores, say good-bye to loved ones, and meet at the main entry. There they would make one last stand.

Sara's heels made a clicking sound as she walked down the corridor. Normally it was spotless, with shiny floors and clean walls. Now it was dark and gloomy, stained with smoke, and littered with the debris of war. Lights buzzed on the edge of burnout, bloody dressings littered the floor, and odd pieces of clothing lay here and there.

A horn honked behind her and Sara stepped aside. An electric cart rolled by, loaded down with heat-suited people, headed toward the main entry.

Many of the people wore bloodstained bandages. The wounded, determined to make their deaths count, looking forward to taking some pirates with them.

One waved. Sara waved back. She couldn't remember his name.

The cafeteria was dark and somber. There were fifty or sixty children spread around the room, all were subdued, some were crying. Sara saw small huddles here and there, as parents said good-bye to their children. Many would never have that chance, for they were already dead, or dying somewhere in the cold.

Ten or twelve hard-pressed teenagers moved among the crowd, little more than children themselves, doing the best they could to bring help and comfort.

Some elderly men and women were in charge. One, a woman named Edna, bustled over to greet Sara. She had a wrinkled face and plump hands. Edna wore the same cheerful smile she always did, and Sara admired her courage.

"Hello, dear, come to see Molly? She's right over there.

Hurry now, we plan to sing some songs until they come to take the children away."

Sara smiled her thanks, and marveled at Edna's words. ". . . until they come to take the children away." As if "they" were nothing more than counselors taking the children off to summer camp. But Edna was right. It wouldn't do any good to dwell on the horror of it, to think of what Molly would face, to break down and sob as she desperately wanted to do.

Sara felt angry for a moment. Angry at Sam for being off-planet when the pirates came, angry at the Empire for leaving the rim worlds vulnerable to attack, angry at God for letting it happen. It wasn't fair, damn it!

"Mommy!" Suddenly Molly was there, arms thrown around Sara's waist, face pressed against her stomach. Somehow, much to Sara's pleasure and her daughter's chagrin, Molly had a mop of tightly curled, brown, almost black hair. It was soft and thick, strangely comforting to her fingers, a reminder of Sam.

Suddenly the anger was gone, replaced by a terrible sadness. There was so much she wanted to say and so little time to say it. Sara knelt and took Molly in her arms. They hugged and took comfort from each other. Then as they pulled slightly apart Sara looked into her daughter's eyes. They were big and solemn, filled with knowledge beyond her years, and brimming with tears.

"Things didn't go very well, honey, we lost."

Molly nodded sadly. "I know, Mommy. They told us. The pirates are going to take us away."

Sara forced a smile. "I'm afraid so, Molly. Do you remember how the pirates took me, and your grandmother?"

Molly nodded. She'd heard the story many times. How the pirates had stopped the liner, how Mommy fought them at the main lock, how Daddy unknowingly saved her life a few months later. "I remember."

"Good . . . because you must do as I did. Stay alive, help others, and remember the things Mommy and Daddy taught you." Tears began to roll down Molly's cheeks.

"Are you listening to me, Molly?"

"Yes, Mommy, I'm listening."

Sara scanned her daughter's face, determined to remember it, and take the memory with her. "Good. This is the most important part of all. *Never* give up hope. No matter where they take you, no matter how long it takes, Daddy will come. He'll hunt them clear across the universe if that's what it takes. Be ready. There'll be trouble when Daddy comes, and he'll need your help."

Molly sobbed and pressed her face against Sara's shoulder. "I don't want to go! I want to stay with you!"

Sara gently pushed her away. "I know, honey . . . I wish you could. But Mommy has things to do. You take care of yourself, and remember I love you."

And with that Sara stood, kissed Molly on the top of her head, and turned away.

By the time Sara entered the main corridor she could hear the sounds of distant battle. The pirates were forcing their way in and the command center staff was making one last stand. Tears rolled down Sara's cheeks as she pulled her blaster, checked its charge, and headed for the entry. The bastards would pay.

Two

THE ROOM WAS small and heavily hung with rich fabrics. Perfume misted the air and shadows filled the corners as the two men regarded each other across the surface of the expensive desk.

The merchant straightened his robes, pouted his lips, and rubbed his chin. The likeness of a serpent wound itself around the merchant's bald skull and terminated at the center of his forehead. The merchant waved his hand and light winked off a golden pinky ring. "One hundred and thirty-five thousand imperials, and not a credit less."

Sam McCade took the cigar out of his mouth, examined the soggy end for defects, and shoved it back in. He had gray eyes, strong even features, and a two-day growth of beard. "You're out of your mind. I'm here to buy fertilizer, not diamonds. I'll pay one-twenty, and not a credit more."

The merchant shook his head sadly. "McCade, you are a crude man. I will lower my price just to be rid of you. A hundred and thirty."

McCade blew foul blue smoke toward the other man's face. "A hundred and twenty-five."

The merchant coughed and pushed a terminal across the surface of his inlaid desk. "Done. Collect the tanks from my private loading dock and never darken my door again."

McCade grinned, tapped in the amount of transfer, and added his personal code. His leathers were worn and stained. They creaked as he stood. "Thanks, Corrus. You're a thousand laughs. See you next time around."

Corrus waited till the other man was gone, sprayed the air with perfume, and allowed himself a big grin. He liked McCade. Only Sol knew why.

Rico waited outside. He was a big man, with a head of unruly black hair and a beard to match. His eyes were small and bright. He wore a loose-fitting shirt, a leather vest, and a pair of black trousers. Like McCade he was armed with a low-riding slug gun.

"Well? Did ya purchase the poop?"

McCade frowned. "Yes, and since it cost Alice more than a hundred thousand credits, I'll thank you to refer to it as 'liquid fertilizer.' Come on. Let's find Phil."

Rico grinned and followed McCade up the corridor.

The asteroid had a little spin but not much. The men moved carefully. Without much gravity it would be easy to bounce up and bang your head against solid rock.

Like most of the passageways within Rister's Rock, this one was courtesy of Rister himself.

Rister had lived on the asteroid for more than thirty years, and during that time, he'd bored tunnels in every direction.

Not because he *had* to, or was looking for minerals, but because he *wanted* to.

It seemed that Rister enjoyed the process of boring tunnels, and, more than that, believed the finished product was a work of art.

The fact that no one else agreed with him didn't bother Rister in the least. He went right on boring tunnels till the day he died. In fact, Rister had been dead for years by the time they found him, a dried-out mummy in a beat-up space suit, grinning like he understood the biggest joke of all.

Now Rister stood in the back of Meck's saloon, where he served as a sometimes hat rack and surefire conversation starter.

But regardless of Rister's intentions, the asteroid had been put to good use. Located as it was on the very edge of the asteroid belt, and close to a hyperspace nav beacon, the planetoid made a handy spot to do business.

In fact, Rister's Rock had a pretty good rep, but still attracted all kinds, and McCade watched as they passed by. There were the roid rats, striding the halls in beat-up armor, and spacers, bored-looking men and women, hunting for something they hadn't tried, and merchants, some as colorful as peacocks, others drab and boring, all watching one another with the wary look of potential combatants.

There were aliens too, not many, but a feathery, scaly scattering of Finthians, Lakorians, and Zords, plumage waving, tentacles writhing, feet stumping along.

From long habit McCade sifted the crowd for fugitives. They could be of any shape, size, or species, sentients who'd committed a crime, or been accused of one, and were on the run.

Pragmatic soul that he was, the first Emperor had decided to rely on bounty hunters, rather than ask his hard-pressed citizens to foot the bill for an empire-sized police force. And like many of his ideas, this one worked.

Most worlds had a police force, but its jurisdiction ended in the upper atmosphere, and that was fine with them.

Once someone fled the planet they were assumed to be guilty. A bounty was placed on their head, so many credits dead or alive, and they showed up in public data terms all over the Empire.

All a bounty hunter had to do was access a terminal, scroll through the possibilities, and select those he or she wished to pursue.

Then, for a very small fee, the bounty hunter could buy a hunting license and track them down.

It had been a long time since McCade had stepped up to a terminal and purchased a license, but he felt sure there were some fugitives in the crowd.

Loud ones, hiding behind carefully constructed false identities; quiet ones, doing their best to escape all notice; and the fortunate few, who by dint of biosculpture and organ transplants, had re-created themselves from the ground up. They'd be hard to catch.

McCade smiled. Well, they were safe from him. His bounty-hunting days were over. Now he was a part-time cop, a part-time purchasing agent, and a full-time husband. It would be good to get home.

McCade's thoughts were interrupted by a racket up ahead.

As the two men stepped out of the tunnel and into the circular area where a number of passageways came together, they found themselves in the midst of a crowd. There were numerous shops, but the largest was Meck's saloon, and people were looking in that direction. McCade craned his neck to see what the excitement was about.

There was an inarticulate roar followed by a loud crash as a spacer came flying through the front of the saloon to land in front of the crowd. Thanks to the light gravity, the man was able to roll over and shake his head. Friends picked the man up and dusted him off.

McCade turned to the roid rat on his left. He was a big man with a hooked nose and a walrus-style mustache. "What's going on?"

The man nodded his head toward the bar. "We were in Meck's having a drink when this bear-thing comes in. It orders a beer and sits at the bar. Then a spacer says 'I don't drink with freaks,' and all hell breaks loose."

The roid rat gestured toward the dazed spacer. "That guy tried to jump the bear from behind."

McCade looked at Rico and the other man shook his head. "Phil's gettin' less tolerant all the time. Must be gettin' old."

McCade sighed, pushed his way through the crowd, and entered the bar. Rico was right behind him.

The place was part saloon and part curiosity shop. Besides a mummified Rister, it boasted other wonders as well, including a cage full of alien birds, miniature landscapes made from human hair, a pickled something that no one could identify, a chunk of rock said to have strange healing powers, and much, much more.

The place was completely empty except for Phil, the man he was lifting over his head, and a distraught bartender. Broken furniture and shattered glass littered the floor.

Phil stood about seven feet tall, weighed in at more than three hundred pounds, and looked like a bear. He had brown eyes, a short muzzle, and thick brown fur. He wore a kilt of his own design, carried a machine pistol as a side arm, and wore a twelve-inch knife strapped to his right leg.

Originally human, Phil had been biosculpted for work on ice-worlds and liked Alice for that reason. Phil was not only a qualified biologist, but a one-variant army, with infrared vision, amplified muscle response, and razor-sharp durasteel teeth.

He could also go into full augmentation for short periods of time, a state that burned tremendous amounts of energy and left him completely exhausted.

In this case however the variant hadn't even worked up a sweat. This was partly due to the asteroid's light gravity but mostly because of his enormous strength. Phil was holding a man over his head and lecturing him at the same time. The man looked scared and, as McCade knew, had every reason to be.

Meanwhile the bartender, or perhaps Meck himself, danced around Phil and begged him to stop. It did little good. Phil had something to say and said it.

" . . . So, you can understand how I felt. No one likes to be singled out, identified as different, and subjected to verbal abuse. Especially by low-life cretins like you. Though generally a proponent of positive reinforcement, I think punishment has its place as well, which explains why I'm going to throw you through that wall."

Fortunately for the man in question this particular wall was made of lightweight plastic with a fire retardant foam core. He went through it with no problem at all. As luck would have it, however, there was nothing but solid rock on the other side. He hit with an audible thump.

McCade winced. Some of the crowd had filtered back in and lifted the unconscious man from the debris. He was alive but would spend the next few days in the rock's infirmary.

Phil ran an experienced eye over the damage, reached into his belt pouch, and produced five gold imperials. "This should cover the damage with something left over. Agreed?"

The bartender, a middle-aged man with radiation-burned skin and a sizable potbelly, nodded. He had no desire to engage Phil in protracted negotiations. "Agreed."

Phil smiled and revealed rows of gleaming teeth. "Good. Now, if it's all the same to you, I'll finish my beer."

So saying Phil hoisted his beer, poured it down in one swallow, and slammed the mug onto the surface of the bar. Tiny bits of foam and droplets of beer flew in every direction.

Phil belched and wiped his muzzle with the back of a hairy paw. "Ah! That hits the spot. Hello, Sam, Rico. Ready to go?"

McCade looked around and grinned. "Ready if you are. Sure you want to leave the place standing?"

Phil waved a dismissive paw. "Just a slight misunderstanding. You have the nutrient solution?"

Rico chuckled. "We've got it all right. More'n a hundred thousand credits' worth o' poop."

Phil frowned. "Rico, you're hopeless. It's not 'poop.' It's a specially formulated nutrient solution for use in our hydroponics tanks. Now, if you'd spent as much time looking at the planet's population curve as you do on hunting trips . . . "

Phil lectured Rico on hydroponics, demographics, and planetary ecology all the way up to the planetoid's surface. Once there they dodged a small army of vendors, paid an exit tax, and retrieved their space armor from rented lockers.

With space armor on and checked, they stepped into one of four large locks that served Rister's Rock, and waited for it to cycle them through. Five minutes later it did, and they stepped out on the asteroid's rocky surface. A good-sized landing zone was nearly filled with shuttles and smaller ships, while farther out, the sun made a line of jagged light across the top of a low-lying ridge.

All asteroids looked pretty much the same to McCade's eyes. As he bounced toward the shuttle McCade wondered what had made this one so special to Rister. He'd never know.

The shuttle, like the ship it belonged to, was of military design. Both had been gifts from a grateful Empire after McCade's last ship had been lost while searching for the Vial of Tears.

The Vial, a religious artifact sacred to the alien Il Ronn, had been stolen by a renegade pirate named Mustapha Pong.

The Il Ronn had sworn to regain the Vial no matter what the cost, and faced with the very real possibility of interstellar war, the Emperor had requested McCade's help. But that was history and something he'd just as soon forget.

The shuttle was a squat wedge-shaped hunk of metal, built to haul heavy loads and survive atmospheric landings under combat conditions. It had a blunt nose, a boxy fuselage, and short extendable wings. The shuttle crouched on retractable landing jacks and looked more like a primeval bug than a ship.

McCade punched a series of numbers into the key pad located on the shuttle's belly. A line of light appeared and expanded into a rectangle. Stairs slid down, found the ground, and stopped.

The three men made their way up the stairs, waited for the lock to cycle through, and took off their suits. They attached the suits to wall clips and entered the crew quarters.

Farther back, and almost full of goods and equipment, there was a cargo compartment. It could be pressurized to carry additional passengers or left unpressurized as it was now.

Passing between curtained bunks, through the tiny galley-mess area, and into the control room, McCade dropped into the pilot's position. Rico sat on the right, with Phil one seat back, in one of the two passenger slots.

McCade fired the shuttle's repulsors, got a clearance from the rock's computerized traffic-control system, and danced the ship toward the glare of greenish loading lights.

The loading docks were unpressurized and, outside of one or two space-suited figures, completely automated.

Auto loaders wove complicated patterns around one another, tall spindly robots stepped over and around piles of merchandise, and computer-controlled crawlers towed trains of power pallets toward distant ships.

Acting on a string of radio commands McCade skittered the shuttle over to loading dock seven, opened the main cargo hatch, and watched via vid screen as an auto loader positioned two silvery cylinders in the middle of the cargo bay.

The auto loader had four headlights, and as they swung away, a number of smaller robots scampered through the hatch to lock the cylinders in place. As soon as they were finished the robots left as quickly as they'd come.

McCade sealed the hatch, ran an auto check on all systems, and fired his repellors. The shuttle lifted and dust fountained up from the asteroid's surface. Then, with the ship safely aloft, McCade engaged the main drive.

Seconds later they were free of the asteroid's light gravity and headed out toward the area where the *Void Runner* and some of the other large ships drifted miles apart.

The *Void Runner* had originally been a Destroyer Escort and, as such, was twice the size of McCade's previous ship *Pegasus*.

Although still small enough to negotiate planetary atmospheres, and therefore streamlined in appearance, the *Void Runner* was more ship than one person could comfortably run by himself.

The ship had carried a crew of eight back in her military days, but McCade had modified her to operate with a crew of four, and could fly her single-handed in an emergency.

So, Rico and Phil had come along to keep McCade company and crew the ship. They chatted with each other as McCade sent *Void Runner* a recognition code, countersigned the return password, and slid the shuttle toward the lighted berth on DE's port side.

There was another similar berth on the starboard side presently occupied by a four-place speedster. More toy than tool, McCade justified it as a lifeboat and ignored Sara's disparaging remarks.

Easing the little ship into its bay, McCade fired the shuttle's repellors and lowered it onto the durasteel deck. The outer hatch slid closed shortly after that, air rushed in to pressurize the bay, and a pair of snakelike robo tubes slithered out to connect themselves to the shuttle. The tubes pulsed rhythmically as fuel flowed into the shuttle's tanks.

McCade, Rico, and Phil left the shuttle the moment the bay was properly pressurized. The argrav was adjusted to Alice normal and felt good after Rister's Rock.

Bright lights threw hard black shadows down against the durasteel deck. All around the three inner bulkheads, tools, torches, and hand testers were racked and waiting for use.

McCade tapped a code into the lock and waited for it to iris open. The lock was necessary so that a loss of pressure inside the shuttle bay wouldn't affect the rest of the ship.

McCade still felt a sense of pride when he stepped out of the lock into his ship. *Pegasus* had been comfortable and fast, but nothing like *this*. The *Void Runner* was larger, roomier, more heavily armed, and even faster than *Pegasus* had been. She was three years old, but she still smelled new, and McCade took pleasure in walking her corridors.

As McCade made his way toward the ship's bridge he passed the hundreds and hundreds of items that mean little by themselves but taken together make a warship.

There were com screens, remote status displays, zero-G handholds, navy gray bulkheads, damage-control stations, equipment panels, warning labels, first-aid kits, access doors, radiation detectors, patch paks, ventilation ducts, weapons lockers, maintenance ways, crash kits, miles of conduit, and, yes, brass that did little more than look good.

McCade scrambled up a short flight of metal stairs and entered the bridge. The overhead lighting was subdued. Hundreds of indicator lights glowed red, green, and amber.

There was a command chair located toward the center of the room, fronted by three control positions, one for the pilot, the copilot, and the weapons officer.

McCade dropped into the captain's chair and touched a button. "Maggie? You there?"

A screen came to life. It showed a middle-aged woman. She was all torso and no legs. Both had been horribly mangled during a drive-room explosion and scissored off by her self-sealing space armor.

For reasons only Magda Anne Homby could understand, she'd refused stim growth replacements *and* prosthetics, settling for a custom-designed argrav box instead.

But legs or no legs, Maggie was still the best damned engineer for a hundred lights in any direction, and knew it.

Maggie blew a stray strand of red hair out of her eyes. "Of course I'm here. Where the hell did you think I'd be?"

McCade grinned. He knew from experience that Maggie was impossible to please. In fact it was Maggie's personality rather than her handicap that kept her from more lucrative employment on a freighter or a big liner. "My mistake. I'll need the drives about five from now."

Maggie nodded curtly and the screen went black. Though welcome on the bridge, she preferred to ride where she worked, in the drive room.

Rico ran a manual preflight check, while McCade tapped instructions into the ship's navcomp, and Phil sharpened a durasteel claw. Although the variant was a lousy pilot, his keen brain and amplified reaction times made him a crackerjack weapons officer.

With all systems green, and a gruff "go ahead" from Maggie, McCade fired the *Void Runner*'s standard drives. The DE would reach the nav beacon in a few minutes, enter hyperspace, and exit about three standard days after that. A short run later and they'd see Alice.

McCade allowed the seat to make him comfortable and delegated control to the navcomp. He couldn't wait to get home.

Three

THE SHIP'S SCREENS blurred momentarily as the *Void Runner* slipped out of hyperspace. McCade felt the usual moment of nausea and scanned his readouts for signs of trouble. Nothing. All systems were green.

Phil tapped a series of keys. Sensors reached out to probe the surrounding vacuum for indications of heat, metal, or radiation. Passive receptors listened, scanners watched for signs of pulsed light, and vid cams searched for movement against the stars.

Phil growled in the back of his throat as the skin along the top of his muzzle formed a series of ridges and his fangs appeared.

Something was wrong. Although Alice couldn't afford remote weapons platforms, she did have deep-space robo sensors, and based on their warnings the *Void Runner* should've been challenged by now.

Phil opened a com link, tapped in a frequency, and spoke into his mic. "This is the *Void Runner*, Delta Beta, six-niner-two, requesting a planetary approach vector. What the hell's wrong with you people? Wake up and smell the coffee."

Silence.

Phil's chair whirred as he turned toward McCade. "I'm worried, Sam. No challenge so far, and no response."

McCade frowned. Maybe there was some sort of equipment failure.

"Try 'em again, Phil, and run a diagnostic routine on our

gear. There's always the chance that some equipment went belly up."

Phil tried again and got the same result. He ran an auto check on the ship's com gear. Nothing. The variant turned toward McCade and gave a shrug.

McCade lifted a protective cover and pushed a red button. A klaxon went off and called a nonexistent naval crew to battle stations. The ship's defensive screen went to full military power, weapons systems came on-line, and a three-dimensional tac tank appeared in front of McCade's chair.

The tac tank was empty of movement—outside of symbols representing Alice, her sister planets, and the sun itself. There were no warships waiting to pounce, no fighters vectoring in, no torpedoes flashing through space. Nothing.

The intercom bonged. Maggie appeared on-screen. She scowled. "You're starting to piss me off, McCade. What's all this battle stations crap? You hit the wrong button or something?"

McCade fought to keep his temper. "We can't raise Alice and we're not sure why. They should be all over us by now. Strap in and stand by."

Maggie nodded and the screen flashed to black.

McCade took another longer look in the tac tank. Still nothing. A hard lump formed in his throat. Where were the robo sensors? The usual tramp freighters? The planet's five-ship navy?

McCade swallowed hard. "Rico, full power. Phil, keep your eyes peeled. I've got a bad feeling about this."

It took twelve long, frustrating, tension-filled hours to close with Alice. Hours during which there was plenty of time to worry, to think about Sara and Molly, to imagine all sorts of terrible calamities. But nothing, not even McCade's worst imaginings, could compare with what they actually found.

Alice half filled the view screens when Phil spotted the first wreck. "Sam, Rico, take a look at this."

Phil's claws made a clicking sound as they hit the keys. A magnified image appeared on the main view screen. It was a ship, the remains of one anyway, tumbling end over end. Light and dark, light and dark, over and over again. Torpedoes had taken a terrible toll, ripping huge holes in the vessel's durasteel hull, gutting the interior.

Rico's fist made a loud bang as it hit the control panel. "Damn! That's the *Free Star*!"

"It *was* the *Free Star*," Phil corrected grimly. "Wait . . . there's more . . . "

McCade bit his lip. The *Free Star* had been a reconditioned destroyer, the flagship of the planet's small navy, crushed like a child's plaything. Who had done this? Pirates? The Il Ronn? It was impossible to tell.

By the time the DE swung into orbit around Alice the crew had seen more smashed ships, a ruptured habitat, and four or five burned-out satellites. Taken altogether the destruction meant hundreds of lives lost.

McCade thought about Sara and Molly. A muscle in his left cheek began to twitch. He had to get dirtside, had to find them, had to make sure they were okay. But what if they weren't? What if . . . Phil interrupted McCade's thoughts.

"Hold it! I've got something on VHF!"

Alice shimmered and disappeared as a new image formed on the main view screen. The shot showed a man, a nice-looking man, with a fleshy something on his shoulder. Was it blue? Purple? The thing shimmered like iridescent cloth. The man smiled.

"Hello. This message is intended for Sam McCade. Everyone else can open the nearest lock and suck vacuum.

"As for you, McCade, I sincerely hope you're dead. But if you survived . . . here's something to think about: 'Do unto others as you would have them do unto you.'

"Or, how about, 'What goes around comes around'?

"Or, the ever-popular, 'Screw with me and I will rip your goddamned lungs out'?

"Take your pick. Just remember. You stuck your nose where it didn't belong, and I chopped it off."

The screen snapped to black.

Rico's chair whirred as he turned toward McCade. "Okay, sport . . . who the hell was that?"

McCade's mind raced. Who the hell was that, indeed? Like most bounty hunters he was good at remembering faces. Yet McCade was sure that he'd never seen the man before. But that didn't make sense. The man had a personal grudge, a grudge so big he'd attack Alice, so surely they'd met. Wait a minute . . . the voice . . . there was something about the voice.

"Play the last part again."

Phil tapped some keys and the man reappeared. " . . . and I will rip your goddamned lungs out.

"Take your pick. Just remember. You stuck your nose where it didn't belong, and I chopped it off."

McCade slammed his fist down onto the arm of his chair. "Mustapha Pong!"

Now it made sense. Pong was the renegade pirate who'd unknowingly stolen the Il Ronnian Vial of Tears a few years earlier. In an attempt to avoid an interstellar war and pocket a sizable bounty, McCade had tracked the Vial to Pong's secret base. Shortly thereafter a combined human–Il Ronnian fleet had destroyed the base and almost all of Pong's ships. That explained the grudge.

And although McCade and Pong had spoken with each other by radio on one occasion, they'd never met face-to-face.

Rico nodded his understanding. "So what's the weird-lookin' thing on Pong's shoulder?"

"I can answer that," Phil said grimly. "The 'weird-lookin' thing' as you call it is a Melcetian mind slug."

McCade frowned. "A Melcetian what?"

"Mind slug," Phil replied evenly. "I read a paper on them once. They're nonsentient symbiotic creatures who rarely leave their native planet but have the capacity to amplify human brain activity."

"Amplify brain activity?" McCade asked. "As in think better?"

Phil nodded. "Better, faster, and more creatively."

Rico raised an eyebrow. "Oh, yeah? Then how come I never saw one before?"

Phil smiled, and given his durasteel dentition, it was a terrifying sight. "Because everything has a price. In this case the price involves allowing the slug to tap into your spinal cord, filter your blood for nutrients, and feed you addictive chemicals."

McCade shuddered as he hit his harness release. "Sounds horrible. It makes a certain kind of sense though. No wonder Pong's so good at what he does."

A few seconds later all three of them were headed for the shuttle. Although McCade was the only one who was married, both Rico and Phil had significant others, plus a raft of friends.

And as a member of the planetary council, Rico felt a special responsibility to the entire population.

They all hoped for the best but feared the worst.

McCade paused outside the shuttle bay access lock and touched a button. Maggie appeared on-screen. He knew without asking that the engineer had kept abreast of developments via the drive-room intercom and view screens. Maggie didn't talk much but she always knew what was going on. "We're heading dirtside."

Maggie nodded. "It didn't take a genius to figure that out."

"Are you coming?"

Maggie gave him a twisted smile. "No, I don't think so. I haven't got any people down there, and besides, who'd watch the ship?"

McCade had expected something of the kind and was secretly grateful. He hated to leave *Void Runner* unattended. "Thanks, Maggie. I'll call you from dirtside."

McCade was just starting to turn away when Maggie cleared her throat. "McCade?"

"Yeah?"

"I'm sorry."

McCade looked in Maggie's eyes and knew she thought Sara and Molly were dead. It was a logical conclusion but one he refused to accept. A lump formed in McCade's throat and he forced it down.

"Thanks, Maggie. Keep a sharp lookout. There's always the chance that they'll come back."

Maggie nodded silently and the screen faded to black.

The trip dirtside was a dark and somber affair. Heavy winds buffeted the shuttle as it entered the atmosphere and snow fell at lower altitudes.

McCade brought the shuttle down through the lowest layer of dark gray clouds and sent it skimming over pristine whiteness. He flew low and slow. Rocky hills swelled here and there, bare where the wind had scoured them clean, their sides covered with low vegetation.

Then the hills were gone and the shuttle entered the mouth of a long, low valley. Days of snow had hidden most of the damage, with only wisps of smoke and a higher-than-usual radiation count to indicate damage had been done.

McCade knew that to the north and east a number of low-yield nuclear devices had exploded, each destroying a surface-to-space missile battery, but leaving the underground population centers untouched. At least *that* strategy had worked.

Now, as the shuttle neared the capital city of New Home, the damage became more apparent. Shattered domes, covered with a dusting of new snow; wrecked crawlers, sitting at the center of fire-blackened circles; half-blasted radars, still searching the skies for targets long disappeared; and here and there, the pitiful huddle of someone's last stand, now little more than bumps under a shroud of white.

McCade bit his lip and glanced at Rico. The other man's feelings were effectively hidden behind his beard, but his eyes were on the view screen, and they were as cold as the land below.

All was not death and destruction however. Here and there signs of life could be seen. Fresh vehicle tracks in the snow, a hint of underground warmth on the infrared detectors, and the vague whisper of low-powered radio traffic. There was life down there, less than before, but life nonetheless.

McCade stuck an unlit cigar between his teeth. "Run the frequencies, Rico. Someone's talking. Let's see who it is."

Rico flipped some switches and ran the freqs, starting with commonly used civilian bands and working his way upward. "Rico here . . . anybody read me?"

The response was almost instantaneous. A surprisingly cheerful male voice said, "Pawley here, Rico . . . nice of you to drop in."

Rico grinned. "Pawley? What the hell are you doing here? I thought you were down south working the G-Tap."

McCade knew, as did all the planet's citizens, that "G-Tap" stood for "geo-thermal tap," and was a project to harness the energy resident in the planet's core. A lot of effort and a lot of tax money had flowed into that project, and Brian Pawley was the G-Tap team leader.

"We were lucky," Pawley replied soberly, "either they missed us, or thought us unimportant. In any case we survived and came back to help. Everybody's pitching in. Ranchers, miners, you name it, they're all lending a hand."

McCade saw the landing pad up ahead. Two piles of snow-dusted wreckage marked where a ship and a shuttle had been caught on the ground. Energy weapons had cut a confusing hatch work of dark lines into the ground. McCade cut speed and prepared to land.

"We're about to land," Rico said. "Where should we head?"

Pawley was silent for a moment. When he spoke there was a forced cheerfulness to his voice, as if he felt one way, and was saying something else.

"Stay on the pad . . . I'll pick you up."

McCade killed the shuttle's forward motion, fired repellors, and settled gently onto the pad.

A huge cloud of steam billowed up to obscure the view. As the wind blew it away McCade saw a crawler roll out onto the pad, its white and gray camouflage useless against the burnt area behind it, twin rooster tails of snow flying up behind it.

It took McCade and Rico a good ten minutes to pull on their heat suits and enter the lock. Phil was already there, sans suit, with a big grin on his face. Thanks to his thick layer of fur the variant could stroll through winter snowstorms that would kill Rico or McCade in a few short minutes.

The lock cycled open and they left the protection of the ship's hull. McCade had opted to leave his hood and goggles hanging down his back. The cold cut into his face like a thousand tiny knives. He removed the unlit cigar from his mouth and threw it away.

Unlike Sara, Rico, and Phil, McCade hated the cold, and would've preferred a warmer planet. Sara . . . Molly . . . the names were like spears through McCade's heart.

Their boots made a crunching sound as they approached the crawler. A door hissed open and released a blast of warm air. McCade scrambled inside, closely followed by Phil and Rico.

Pawley was at the controls. He turned sideways in his seat. Though normally clean-shaven, Pawley wore a two-day growth of beard. He had short hair, a crooked nose, and thick rather sensuous lips. "Welcome aboard, gentlemen."

Pawley's words were followed by an awkward silence. Rico was the first to break it. "No offense, ol' sport . . . but let's go straight to the bottom line. Who made it and who didn't?"

A cloud came over Pawley's face. "I'm sorry, Rico . . . Vanessa was killed. She died defending the fusion plant."

Rico nodded, and looked out through scratched plastic at the bleakness beyond. Tears ran down his cheeks and into his beard.

Pawley looked at Phil. The variant stared back, trying to read the scientist's eyes, steeling himself against the worst.

Pawley ran his tongue over dry lips. "We just don't know, Phil . . . Deena's unit went off-air more than a day ago . . . she's missing in action."

Phil gave a grunt of acknowledgment. Missing rather than dead. There was hope at least.

Now it was McCade's turn to look Pawley in the eye. "Well?"

The word sounded harsh, and McCade wished he could pull it back, but there was no need. Pawley understood.

"Good news and bad news, Sam. The good news first. Sara was wounded but she's alive. Doc Lewis says she'll be fine in a couple of weeks."

"And Molly?" McCade croaked the words out. If Sara was the good news, then . . .

Pawley swallowed hard. "They took her, Sam . . . along with sixty or seventy other children."

McCade let his breath out in a long, slow exhalation. At least she was alive. Frightened, lonely, but alive.

McCade's fingers curled into hard fists. First Molly, then Mustapha Pong. Not for money, not for empire, but for himself. McCade's Bounty.

Four

MOLLY MCCADE BIT her lip and refused to cry. She'd done a lot of crying during the last few days and it didn't do any good. The pirates didn't care, and the other girls were just as scared as she was. She didn't know where the boys were and hadn't seen any since the attack.

Molly rolled over, careful not to wake anyone who might be asleep. Sleep was a precious commodity for the children. It was a time of much needed rest and escape from the horror of the ship's small hold.

The girls were packed into four-foot-high sections, with cold metal gratings under their backs, and very little room to move around.

They were allowed to leave the hold twice a day. First came the scramble up ladders to the pressurized launch bay, then a bowl of tasteless protein mush, followed by fifteen laps around the hangar. Then they were forced through a bank of over-used chemical toilets, an antiseptic spray, and returned to the gratings.

And since everything was done in alphabetical order, there was no hope of a better position on the gratings.

Poor Susy Zobrist. She was stuck on the bottommost grating and cried all the time.

Some kids threw up a lot, others had to go to the bathroom all the time, and whoever lay just beneath them took the brunt of it.

But some dribbled past, and ended up at the very bottom of the hold where it coated everyone and everything.

From the pirate point of view it was an extremely efficient low-cost way of transporting a lot of people at once. Not only that, but when the gratings were removed, the hold could still be used for more conventional cargoes.

Looking up through the dark crisscross of metal gratings, and the black sprawl of supine bodies, Molly could see the glow of a single greenish light.

It reminded her of the night light in her room on Alice. As long as the light was on nothing could sneak up and hurt her. There had been two greenish lights originally, but one had gone out two cycles earlier, and now Molly feared that the other one would too.

"Oh, please, God," she prayed, "don't let the light go out. And if Mommy's with you, tell her I miss her, and I'm trying to be good. And, God, if Daddy's coming, tell him to hurry."

Five

THEY USED HAND blasters to cut down through the permafrost. After that the robo shovels moved in, their drive wheels squeaking in the cold, their scoops biting into frozen dirt.

Steam rose from the temporarily warmed earth, eddied around the mourners like strands of errant ectoplasm, and was whipped away by a steady breeze. It came from the south and made the minister's robes swish and pop. His words were feeble and small against the vast backdrop of frozen wilderness and gray sky.

" . . . And so it is that we lay these valiant souls to rest, secure in the knowledge that their essence lives on, looking forward to the time when we shall see them again . . . "

McCade felt Sara shift her weight from one leg to the other. Her right leg still hurt where the slug had ripped through her thigh. It was a miracle that she was still alive. Twenty-seven men and women had defended the main entry. Three had survived.

McCade thought Sara should be in the hospital, but between the pressures of office and her own stubbornness, she'd been up and around for a day now.

McCade tightened his arm around Sara's waist and pulled her even closer. He gloried in the feel of her, and had Molly been there beside him, he would've been secretly happy.

But she wasn't, and that, plus the guilt McCade felt for putting his own family first, pulled his emotions down.

At least Phil was alright. Deena had been found and was recovering in the hospital.

The minister paused, turned a page in the tattered book, and intoned the ancient words. " . . . Ashes to ashes . . . dust to dust . . . "

Sara leaned her head against his arm. She was crying.

McCade watched Rico as the coffins were lowered into the grave. They were all that remained of a full section. The rest would never be found. The second belonged to Vanessa. As her coffin disappeared from sight, Rico whispered a prayer and threw something in after her. McCade caught the glint of gold.

When the last coffin had been lowered into the grave, and blasters had rewarmed the earth, a robo shovel filled the trench.

Then, their shoulders covered with a dusting of snow, the mourners crunched their way back to the line of waiting crawlers. One had been set aside for Sara, McCade, Rico, and Phil.

It dipped and rolled through broken ground to waddle out onto the landing pad. The elevator mechanism that normally lowered ships below the frozen surface was still under repair, but both of the burned-out hulks had been pushed aside, and another shuttle sat beside his own. It was old and extremely beat-up.

A tramp freighter had dropped into orbit the day before. After all the death and destruction it seemed hard to believe that life would go on, that the rest of humanity was still going about its business, but the shuttle proved it. Things, outer things that didn't mean much, were returning to normal.

Somewhere, deep in space, a message torp was on its way to Imperial Earth. There wouldn't be much that the Emperor could do but it was worth a try.

Rico and Phil were quick to buss Sara on the cheek, say their good-byes, and head for the shuttle. The door opened and closed with a rush of cold air.

McCade glanced toward the driver but saw that the connecting hatch had been tactfully closed. Not for him, but for Sara. After all, she was head of the planetary council and a person of some importance.

McCade cupped Sara's face with his hands and used his thumb to remove a tear. "Don't cry, honey, I'll find Molly and bring her back."

"And the rest of the kids too."

McCade nodded solemnly. "And the rest of the kids too."

Sara bit her lower lip and nodded. He no longer saw the scar. She looked so pretty it made his heart ache.

"Be careful, Sam. Pong hates you so much he's willing to destroy entire planets. The possibility of losing Molly is bad enough . . . but if I lose you too . . . "

McCade put a finger over her lips. "It won't happen. Molly's got a good head on her shoulders. She'll hang in there and we'll do the rest."

Sara nodded slowly, her eyes searching every aspect of his face, as if committing it to memory. "Keep a close eye on Rico, Sam, he's hurting, and God knows what he might do."

McCade answered with a kiss, a long one that kindled memories and desires as well. When it was over Sara smiled.

"You'd better get out of here, Sam, or the driver will have a racy story to tell her friends, and I'll never live it down."

McCade laughed, kissed her on the tip of her nose, and keyed the door. It opened and he didn't look back. He was afraid to. Afraid he'd break down and start babbling what he felt. Conflicting things that didn't make sense and were all jumbled together.

That he should've been dirtside when Pong attacked. That he shouldn't leave Sara alone on Alice. That he should've started the search yesterday.

McCade was halfway to the shuttle before the cold cut through his thoughts and chilled his skin.

Every search has to begin somewhere and Lakor seemed a likely bet. A somewhat primitive planet, featuring a mishmash of high and low tech, Lakor was best known for its slave markets. Ugly, sprawling places, filled to overflowing with miserable sentients, they provided a much-needed source of foreign exchange.

In fact, Lakorians claimed the dubious distinction of being the biggest slave traders in all of known space, a claim disputed by the Zords, but probably true.

McCade, Rico, and Phil knew Lakor rather well, since they'd spent some rather unpleasant time there and weren't eager to return.

Still, knowing that pirates generally unload slaves as quickly as possible, Lakor was a logical place to go. After all, maybe they'd get lucky and find the children right off the top.

It could happen . . . especially if Lif came to their assistance.

While searching for the War World some years before, McCade had been dumped on Lakor by a rather unfriendly Il Ronnian naval officer and taken into slavery. McCade was rescued by Rico, but Sara wasn't so lucky. Together with Phil the two men set off to find her. During the journey they encountered the then Baron Lif, entered a conspiracy to overthrow King Zorta, and eventually did so rescuing Sara in the process.

This had positioned Baron Lif to take the planetary throne, and assuming he had, they might be eligible for some royal assistance. They could hope anyway.

Most of Lakor was obscured by a thick layer of clouds. The same clouds that dumped vast quantities of rain into the planet's swamps, filled its rivers to overflowing, and created two rather large oceans.

Having received clearance to land, and having left *Void Runner* under Maggie's surly care, McCade, Rico, and Phil rode the shuttle down through Lakor's cloudy skies. They couldn't see a thing and were totally reliant on the ship's instruments.

Even though the shuttle jerked and bucked its way down through the atmosphere it still felt comfortable compared to McCade's last trip.

Along with Sara, and a marine named Van Doren, McCade had been forced into an unpadded cargo module and dropped from orbit. The combination of Lakor's gravity and unpredictable winds had beaten all of them unconscious.

The shuttle dropped out of the clouds over a large bay. Beneath them a fleet of wooden fishing boats left tiny white streaks against the blue-green water. Their lateen sails were bright orange and pushed the boats along at a pretty good clip.

There were hovercraft as well, brightly colored rectangles, dashing here and there without regard for the fishing nets or their owner's safety.

Then the boats were gone, left miles behind as the shuttle flew over quickly shallowing water and a large swamp. Beyond the swamp was a river, a twisting, turning ribbon of reflected light, heavy with debris and brownish silt.

Thick jungle grew down to touch the river on both banks, filling the V-shaped valley with verdant life, much of which was dangerous as hell.

Dropping down so that the valley's steep walls reached upward from both sides, McCade took pleasure in the twisting, turning course. He loved the skill required, the feeling of speed, the hint of danger.

The valley started to widen out. McCade killed speed, missed the look of relief on Phil's face, and followed a series of flashing beacons in for a landing.

The shuttle had no more than touched down when four armed crawlers roared out onto the scorched duracrete followed by a company of mounted soldiers.

The crawlers were of standard imperial manufacture but the cavalry were quite extraordinary. First came the Lakorians themselves. Squat-looking humanoids with greenish skin and stumpy legs. They wore orange uniforms with dark brown trim.

Then there were the Lakorian mounts. Huge six-legged reptilian animals, carrying three riders apiece and wearing bright blue trappings. The lead riders carried lances from which long green pennants flew. Seated behind them were two more soldiers, each armed with an energy weapon and a mean expression. The shuttle was completely surrounded within seconds.

McCade could still lift, but in doing so he would kill some of the riders, and call in whatever navy the planet had. That would not only foreclose any possibility of finding the children but might be fatal as well.

Rico shook his head in pretended amazement. "Sam, ya never cease ta amaze me. We haven't even left the ship and someone's pissed! How the hell do ya do it?"

"By flying too damned low," Phil said sourly.

McCade initiated an auto shutdown sequence, released his harness, and stood up.

"Thank you for the vote of confidence. But as you are about to learn, things are not always as they appear. Where *you* see a group of soldiers bent on hanging me from the nearest tree, *I* see a guard of honor, sent by King Lif to escort us to his palace."

Rico looked at Phil, Phil looked at Rico, and both of them shrugged.

Five minutes later the outer hatch cycled open, McCade stepped out, and a horrible sound rent the air.

The source of this terrible noise was a stout-looking Lakorian noncom with a long-dead animal tucked under his right arm. By blowing air in through the poor creature's nostrils and squeezing its inflated body, he was able to produce a sound somewhat akin to a tortured house cat.

Realizing this was Lakorian music, and suspecting that it might be Lif's anthem, McCade popped to attention. Seeing this Rico and Phil did likewise.

The caterwauling went on for some time, rising and falling to the subtle manipulations of the steadfast noncom, finally ending in an earsplitting screech.

It was at this point that a much-bemedaled officer stepped forward, bowed formally, and said, "On behalf of King Lif, defender of the realm, protector of the innocent, and gift from the gods, I greet you. I am Major Rola. Please accompany us that we might take you into the presence of the king himself."

Like most Lakorians Rola spoke excellent standard. The slave markets drew an unending flow of off-world visitors, and that, plus the Lakorian fondness for things human, meant that the upper class spoke standard as fluently as Lakorian. Some even preferred it, much to the dismay of traditionalists.

McCade turned to Rico and Phil, raised an eyebrow as if to say "I told you so," and turned back to Major Rola. He bowed deeply. Lakor had a strong feudal tradition complete with fancy titles and courtly manners.

"Thank you, Major. We are honored. Please lead the way."

"The way," as it turned out, involved a crawler, and the axiom "that the shortest path between two points is always a straight line."

With their crawler leading the way, a convoy was formed and headed toward the northeast, with the cavalry following along behind.

During the brief moments when McCade wasn't being thrown from one side of the vehicle to the other, he took time to look out the viewports and observe their surroundings. Things were much as he remembered.

All Lakorian dwellings were built on pilings. This made them immune to the comings and goings of the water below them.

Most were circular and had domed roofs. Sections of the roofs were hinged so they could be opened during rare moments of sunshine.

All-terrain vehicles were very popular. McCade saw them all over the place. Brightly colored creations with huge balloon tires and lots of dents. Half roared this way and that, while the other half were parked, often right next to the rotting boats that they'd replaced.

The streets were haphazard. They followed the path of least resistance most of the time, or ran along beside sections of the old canal system, now choked with garbage and weeds.

This did not intimidate their driver however, who, true to his straight-line philosophy of navigation, splashed through all but the very deepest canals.

In addition their route carried them down busy thoroughfares, through residential backyards, across at least one swamp and out into a large clearing.

At its center stood a log palisade, and within that, the largest log structure McCade had ever seen. It was huge, boasting thousands of square feet, and like everything else was up on pilings. A pair of gates swung open to admit the crawler.

"Well, here's the palace," Major Rola said proudly as the crawler jerked to a sudden halt. "Unbelievable, isn't it?"

McCade looked out at the muddy courtyard, the domesticated animals rooting in one corner of the palisade, and nodded his agreement. "It sure is," he said dryly. "Don't the taxpayers complain?"

"Naw," Rola replied confidently. "Why should they? The money comes from slaves, not them."

The Lakorian's comment served to jerk McCade out of his role as tourist and remind him of his mission. Molly. Molly and the other children.

The door hissed open to admit some tired, soggy air. McCade stood. "Thanks for the ride, Major. Let's see the king."

After a short walk across the muddy courtyard they passed through a large door and entered a reception area. It was huge and, outside of the muddy floor, quite spotless.

Three guards flanked each side of the hall. They snapped to attention as a rather junior officer stepped forward.

"The humans will surrender their weapons. The hairy thing also."

McCade took a moment to look the Lakorian up and down. He didn't like surrendering his slug gun, especially on a slime ball like Lakor, and especially to some jumped-up clown in a fancy uniform.

But he did want Lif's cooperation, and even the most generous monarch might resent the loss of his bodyguard and find ways to express his displeasure.

Seeing the human's insolent gaze and correctly interpreting the lack of respect it conveyed, the officer went for the nerve lash secured to his belt. Five strokes would put the human in his place and restore the lieutenant's dignity.

Major Rola was just opening his mouth to object when another voice was heard. "As you were, Lieutenant!"

The officer came to rigid attention.

The Lakorian who stepped out into the reception area was splendidly clad, about a foot shorter than McCade, and by the standards of his race quite handsome.

He had a prominent forehead, intelligent eyes, and a wide, thick-lipped mouth. It was turned upward in a rather human smile. "Greetings, Sir Knight. Squire Rico, Squire Phil, welcome to my humble home."

Lif frowned as he turned to the unfortunate lieutenant. "While I appreciate the zeal with which you carry out your duties, I would recommend a good deal more tact, especially when dealing with humans like these. Any one of them could have killed you and all of your troops long before you pulled that silly nerve lash from your belt. These are not serfs for your abuse! Report to your quarters and give it some thought."

McCade thought he saw some looks of enjoyment pass between the enlisted males as the lieutenant left the room.

Moving in closer Lif shook their hands human style and lowered his voice. "Again, welcome. Imagine my surprise and pleasure when orbital control informed me of your wish to land."

Lif saw McCade's questioning look and waved a negligent hand. "Yes, some visitors are brought to my personal attention, and you among them. I owe you much. I apologize for the actions of my nephew Hora, but he is young and will eventually learn. But enough of that. Come! We must eat and drink. Then we shall speak of many things."

Lif led them into a sumptuous dining room, hosted them to

an enormous dinner, and did his best to drink them under the table. While appearing the genial host Lif liked to lubricate his guests as quickly as possible. It gave him the advantage.

Knowing that from past experience, all three of the humans had managed to swallow inhibitors during the early stages of the meal, and were only slightly drunk by the time it was over.

"So," Lif ventured, squinting through the haze of blue cigar smoke that circled their heads, "what brings you to Lakor?"

McCade tried to concentrate. The vak was clouding his thoughts. "A personal quest, sire. Pirates raided our planet. They came in such force that we couldn't stop them. When they left the pirates took more than sixty of our children with them. One was my daughter, Molly."

Lif shook his head sadly. "I'm sorry, good knight. The fault is partly ours. As long as we rely on slavery as a source of foreign exchange we will be partners to such horror. I hope to reduce our dependence on slavery but these things take time. In the meantime you came to Lakor wondering if the children had passed through our slave markets."

McCade nodded. The motion made his head swim. "Exactly, sire. We had hoped for your help and assistance."

"And have it you shall." Lif clapped his hands and an elderly Lakorian appeared from behind a large tapestry. McCade wondered how long he'd been there. He was slightly stooped over and clad in a long orange robe.

"Sire?"

"Murd, this is Sir Sam McCade and two of his squires. Sir Sam is searching for his daughter and sixty other children taken from his native planet. It is possible that they were brought here. Search all of the slave markets and report to me."

Murd bowed. "Yes, sire. It shall be as you say."

He turned to McCade. "Tell me, good knight, would you have a holo pix or other means of identification by any chance? Our markets are large, and there are many cubs."

Rico scowled at the thought and reached inside his vest. He removed a data cube and handed it over. "Photos, descriptions, it's all on this."

Murd bowed once more. "Thank you, squire. Work will begin immediately." Then he backed toward the tapestry and disappeared.

Lif hoisted a pitcher and filled their mugs with more vak.

"So, my friends, let us drink to Murd's success, after which I will seek your advice and counsel."

McCade lifted his mug and took a small sip. Here it comes, he thought to himself, the price for Lif's cooperation. Chances were Murd wasn't doing a damned thing and wouldn't until Lif made it clear that he should. Lakorians were shrewd bargainers, one reason why they'd been so successful as slavers, and everything had a price. He decided to move the process along.

"Advice, Your Highness? Surely you have advisors more qualified than we?"

Lif chuckled indulgently. "Yes, good knight, on things like taxes, crops, and fertilizer. But when it comes to matters of war, my advisors lack imagination. Surely you remember this from our campaign against the despot Zorta?"

McCade *did* remember. Though brave, the Lakorian officers tended toward all-out frontal attacks, and were something less than innovative.

Nonetheless, McCade was careful to avoid acquiescence, and an indirect insult to the Lakorian general staff. After all, if Murd liked to hang out behind the tapestry, there might be others as well.

"A successful campaign as I recall, Your Highness, and one in which your forces performed admirably."

Lif laughed. "Your tact does you credit, Sir Knight. But enough of this dancing around. Chances are it will take Murd a few days to check all the slave markets. In the meantime I have a small problem and would appreciate your help and advice."

McCade blew smoke toward the distant ceiling. Lif had set the trap. There was little he could do but jump in and hope for the best. "Of course, sire, we would be happy to help. What's the nature of the problem?"

Lif picked up a carving knife and waved it like a wand. "It's my brother, Bulo, the now Baron Lif. He has taken over a town outside of our ancestral lands and refuses to leave."

"I see," McCade replied with a growing sense of dread. "And how can we help?"

Lif brought the knife down hard. Two inches of the durasteel blade penetrated the wood. It wobbled back and forth as he let it go.

"That should be simple, good knight. Go into the town, find my brother, and do what has to be done."

Six

MOLLY AWOKE FROM a fitful sleep as a hatch swung back on its hinges and hit the ship's hull with a dull clang. The woman they called Boots let go of the ladder and dropped the last few feet to the first level. The gratings shook with the impact.

The nickname stemmed from the way the woman looked from below, like a large pair of combat boots, topped by a black blob. Of course the children saw her at meals as well, a beefy woman with her hair in a bun, but the name still seemed to fit.

Acting on impulse Molly made a rude noise. There was deathly silence for a moment, followed by giggles and laughter. It was the first time anyone had laughed since the attack on Alice.

Boots stamped a gigantic foot. The grating rang in response. "Who did that?"

Silence.

Boots spoke again. "Give me her name, or lose your next meal!"

Molly was afraid now. They received so little food that meals were extremely important. Most of the kids would protect her, but one was all it would take to give her away. She didn't know what Boots would do and didn't want to find out.

But there was only silence.

Boots climbed the ladder and closed the hatch. The children

had sacrificed a meal but gained a measure of self-respect.

Those closest to Molly whispered their congratulations and asked what she planned to do next. Accidentally, and without forethought, Molly had become a leader.

Molly knew Mommy was a leader, and a good one too. She chaired the council that ran Alice. And Mommy said Daddy was a leader as well, the kind you want to have when there's trouble, or when people start to give up.

All of Molly's life she'd heard them talk about politics, about people, about how to get things done. What would they say about this situation? What could she do to help herself and those around her?

Molly could almost hear her mother's voice. "Basics come first. Nobody wants to talk about freedom and justice until their stomachs are full."

Molly winced. Rather than give them food she had taken it away. Sure, the incident had granted her some temporary popularity, but that wouldn't last long. Hunger was stronger than loyalty.

First she must find a way to fill their bellies and improve their living conditions. Then it would be time to discuss things like freedom, which in this case meant escape.

Hours passed. Finally it was mealtime once again. The hatch opened and hit the hull with the usual clang. Boots dropped to the grating.

"All right, any wise comments this time?"

Silence.

Boots grunted her approval. "Good. All right, you little hold rats, time for din-din, top grating first. Hurry up, I don't have all watch."

There were the usual rattlings and clankings as the topmost layers of children crawled toward the ladder and climbed upward. Boots administered an occasional kick to the slower ones urging them to "hurry up or forget the whole damned thing."

Forcing herself to ignore the pain caused when her filth-encrusted clothes came in contact with the open sores on her arms and legs, Molly tried to think, tried to imagine a way in which she could use this brief moment of comparative freedom to better their living conditions. Try as she might nothing came to mind.

The children blinked as they left the darkness of the access way and entered the brightly lit hangar. As usual there was a row of shuttles and interceptors along the far side of the bay, attended by a small scattering of maintenance bots, and some ship-suited technicians.

The mess line cut the space in half and the A's, B's, and C's were already going through it. Molly could smell the yeasty slop and her stomach growled in response.

Shuffling forward when the line did Molly forced herself to look around. She must remember to think. What could she do to better their circumstances? Wait a minute, who was that?

A rather pleasant-looking man with some sort of lump on his shoulder. What was that thing anyway? Molly had never seen anything quite like it. Whatever it was looked kind of pretty, all shiny and shimmery, like the fabric in Mommy's best dress.

In any case, the nice-looking man was talking to someone else, a man who looked anything but nice. He was big, like a weight lifter, and wore a heavy leather harness instead of a shirt.

Without thinking, without considering the consequences, Molly left the chow line and walked toward them. They were in charge, she could tell that from the way they stood, and the other crew members shied away. She had thirty or forty feet to cover. It looked like a mile.

What was it Daddy had told her? If you're doing something you shouldn't, act natural, look relaxed. People see what they're conditioned to see. So Molly walked when every fiber of her body wanted to run.

And it worked. Molly was only five feet away from the two men when she heard a yell of protest and the sound of running feet.

The nice man turned, laser blue eyes locking onto hers like range finders, a smile touching his lips. The slug thing shimmered wildly and seemed to ooze a few inches to the right. The man didn't seem to notice.

"That's close enough, child. You smell like the bottom of a recycling vat."

Molly stopped and drew herself up straight. "Exactly, sir. Are you in command?"

The man gave a slight nod. "Yes, I am."

Loud footsteps came up behind her and a heavy hand fell on Molly's shoulder. She knew who it belonged to without turning around. Boots sounded half angry, half scared. "Come here, you . . . I'll teach you to disobey my orders!"

The man held up a hand. "Hold. I want to hear what she has to say."

"But, sir . . . I . . . "

"Silence. Let the child speak."

Molly's heart beat wildly in her chest. The blue eyes were cold and empty of compassion. What could Molly say that would move a man like this? Her voice quavered slightly.

"Sir, if you are in command, then we children are your property. It seems safe to assume that you plan to sell us. Yet we receive only two meals a day, no medical care, and spend most of our time on bare metal gratings."

Molly held out her arms. They were covered with infected sores. "Look at the condition of your property. Our value falls further with each passing hour. Eventually some of us will die."

"Is that it?" The man's voice was hard and unyielding.

Molly swallowed hard. "Yes, sir."

The man looked up over Molly's head. The meaty hands disappeared from her shoulders. "The child makes sense. Feed them three times a day. I will send the medical officer. Arrange for clean clothes. See to their quarters." He gestured toward the blond man. "Raz will inspect them once per cycle."

Molly felt Boots stiffen behind her. "Yes, sir!"

The man nodded and turned away. A few seconds later he and Raz were in deep conversation.

A hand fell on Molly's shoulder. It guided her away from the chow line to where some cargo modules were secured to tie-downs in the deck. As soon as the modules hid them from view Boots spun Molly around, grabbed the front of her ragged shirt, and pulled her in close.

"Listen, brat . . . and listen good! You think you're real smart, real slick the way you conned Pong, but you forgot one thing. *He* spends most of his time on the bridge . . . and *I* spend most of my time with you."

And with that Boots slapped Molly across the face. Then came more slaps followed by hard fists and huge boots. Darkness came as a welcome relief.

Seven

THE HOVERCRAFT BUMPED and shuddered through a series of small rapids throwing the tightly packed serfs left and right. Adults swore, children cried, and a variety of domesticated animals growled, hissed, and squealed their objections.

It was bad enough for the passengers in the main cabin, but for McCade, Rico, and Phil, as well as the Lakorians assigned to assist them, it was part of a long, boring hell.

They'd been locked in the forward hold for two days now, unable to see out, and constantly thrown about.

Light came from a couple of high portholes and some tired chem strips. And like most holds this one came complete with cargo, some unpleasant life forms, and plenty of strange odors. Their table was a cargo module, crates stood in for chairs, and odds and ends took care of everything else.

At the moment Rico and six of the Lakorian troopers sat around the table, playing poker and swearing prodigiously.

One of the Lakorians was named Ven, a crafty type who'd risen a couple of ranks since McCade's first visit years ago, and commanded the rest.

Ven folded with an expression of profound disgust and pushed the small pot in Rico's direction. The human raked it in.

It was good to see Rico having a little fun. He'd been dark and gloomy of late, something he denied, but the others recognized for what it was . . . grief. Vanessa's death had hit him hard.

McCade climbed up on a box and tried to look out through one of the small slitlike portholes. It was a waste of time. Between the spray thrown up by the hovercraft's fans, the rain that never seemed to stop, and the vessel's erratic motion, he could see little more than a gray-green blur.

McCade climbed down and lit another cigar. The air was already thick with smoke and moisture, but what the hell, it was something to do.

Phil opened one eye, didn't like what he saw, and turned over. The variant had built himself a bunk on the top of some packing crates and spent most of his time in it. The warmth and humidity made him miserable so he was sleeping through as much of the trip as he could.

There was a narrow open space along the port bulkhead. McCade used it to pace back and forth, cigar clenched between his teeth, smoke issuing forth in small puffs. At some point during the next hour or so the hovercraft should arrive in the village of Durn. Then he'd know what they were up against.

The whole thing sucked but there wasn't much McCade could do about it. Without saying so directly Lif had made it clear that the situation in Durn was directly linked to Murd's efforts on behalf of the children.

It seemed that Lif's younger brother Bulo had always been something of an embarrassment, spending most of his time chasing after females, and gambling away his share of the family fortune.

When Lif became king, Bulo had expected his brother to elevate him to an appropriately lofty post. Something lucrative but not very demanding.

So, when the post failed to materialize, and Lif refused his requests for favor, Bulo took drastic action.

Picking out a village, apparently at random, Bulo invaded using his entourage of toadies and young toughs to overwhelm the local police force.

Lif had received the predictable protest from Duke Isso, Lord of Durn and a powerful politician, not long thereafter.

Just as Bulo had intended, Lif found himself in a difficult position, forced to choose between a member of his own family and an important ally. If he used force against his brother, it would be the same as finding him guilty of a crime, and by Lakorian tradition, that guilt would extend to

Lif's entire family including Lif himself.

And if the king didn't move against Bulo, Duke Isso would use the issue to make serious trouble in the House of Nobles, possibly leading to war.

Of course he could give Bulo what he asked, and forget the whole matter, but Lif knew better than that. Bulo would want more, and more, until the entire planet groveled at his feet.

No, that would never do. So the answer was to have someone else perform his dirty work for him, someone Lif could deny if necessary, someone like a group of itinerant aliens.

McCade dropped the cigar butt on the deck and ground it out under his boot.

Yes, the whole thing was more than a little transparent, but effective nonetheless. Lakor was a big planet, home to many slave markets, and only by securing Lif's cooperation could they be sure of checking them all.

That meant they'd have to find Bulo, snatch him out from under his army of butt kissers, and get him back to so-called civilization.

McCade was thrown forward as someone cut the power too fast. He caught himself on a cargo module and heard feet thump as the crew ran to get bumpers and boat hooks.

Now McCade was thrown in the opposite direction as the captain ordered full speed astern. Thanks more to luck than skill, the hovercraft hit the pier with a gentle thud and came to a stop. Then the power was cut and the vessel settled down onto her inflated skirts.

McCade scrambled up to the porthole, wiped away the condensation, and peered out. Minus the spray, and with only a slight misting of rain, McCade could see most of the dock. It was surprisingly well made and in good repair. A testament to Duke Isso's provident use of tax money.

He saw some ragged-looking serfs drag the gangplank into position, lift it up into the air. He heard, rather than saw it hit the hovercraft's deck.

At this point some passengers started to disembark but the staccato cough of an automatic weapon sent them fleeing back up the gangplank.

A brand-new group of Lakorians was starting to board. Although heavily armed, they acted more like civilians than soldiers, sauntering up the gangway as if boarding a yacht.

McCade turned slightly, pointing toward the doors and overhead hatch. The Lakorians, all members of Lif's personal bodyguard, took up positions opposite the two main entrances. Phil aimed his machine pistol up toward the cargo hatch and Rico waited with a blast rifle cradled in his arms.

McCade looked back just in time to see the Lakorian dandies disappear from sight. He bit his lip and strained to hear what was going on.

There was a good deal of incoherent shouting as Bulo's followers asserted their right to search the hovercraft and the vessel's skipper told them to shove it.

The skipper had received a rather generous subsidy to carry the aliens in his forward hold, and to do so in complete secrecy. He could double-cross them of course, but that would mean double-crossing King Lif as well, a rather unhealthy thing to do.

The problem was finally resolved with a Lakorian-style compromise, in which the dandies were allowed to search the upper decks, while the holds remained sealed.

This saved face all the way around, and inconvenienced no one, except the peasants, who were more worried about getting enough to eat than notions of personal honor.

Satisfied that they'd carried out their duties, the bullies left the ship and headed for the inn that doubled as Bulo's headquarters.

The next hour or so was spent unloading supplies from the aft hold and loading a hundred bales of noxious weed. McCade's Lakorian troopers swore the stuff was a rare delicacy handpicked in jungle swamps and served in all of the finest restaurants. If so, McCade decided to avoid those restaurants at all costs.

Shortly after the weed was loaded they heard some confused shouts, the splash of a poorly handled bow line, and the loud roar of the hovercraft's twin engines. A few minutes later and they were skimming upriver.

An hour passed and the light started to fade. Then, right at that magic moment when the evening light granted the jungle a soft beauty, the engine noise dropped off and the hovercraft slowed.

"This must be it," McCade announced. "Let's gather up our gear and get ready to bail out of this floating coffin."

There was a loud banging on one of the doors. Rico unlatched it and stepped back with blast rifle leveled.

The captain entered, hands held up in protest. He was short, wrinkled, and solid as the deck he stood on. His standard was something less than perfect.

"Shoot me don't! Friend am I. Arrived have we. Come."

McCade took a look around to make sure they had everything. The soldiers were shouldering backpacks filled with food, medical supplies, and ammo, plus a lethal array of weapons.

Rico wore a backpack com set and Phil carried a flamethrower with two tanks of fuel.

That left a big black duffel bag that was made out of some sort of waterproof material and equipped with shoulder straps. McCade picked it up. The damned thing weighed a ton. It was tempting to leave it on the hovercraft, depend on plan A, and forget the backups. Tempting but stupid.

"Everybody ready?"

There were grunts of assent.

McCade nodded and they followed the captain up on deck. The passageways were filthy, the stairs were encrusted with dried mud, and the serfs were as tightly packed as ever. A good many had disembarked at Durn, but even more had trooped aboard, so conditions were little improved.

A child ran out in front of McCade. She wore one of the complicated sarongs that Lakorians loved to lavish on young females. She squealed with joy and headed straight for the gangplank. There was a shout of protest as her mother tired to intervene.

McCade scooped her up and smiled. The little female reminded him of Molly, of all the hugs he'd missed while traveling between the stars, of what he must find.

Frightened by the alien face, the child started to sob. McCade handed her to a grateful mother, shifted the duffel bag to a more comfortable position, and led the way onto the gangplank.

Once they were ashore the captain wasted little time on "good-byes." He gave a curt wave, shouted some orders, and disappeared into the wheelhouse.

The hovercraft made a loud roaring sound as it backed away from the bank and turned upstream. For a moment it looked big, with black skirts, orange hull, and a streamlined deckhouse.

Then it grew suddenly smaller as spray flew and the water flattened out around it. Seconds later the hovercraft was gone, disappeared around the next bend, heading upriver.

Something took a bite out of McCade's arm. He slapped it and swore. He wasn't looking forward to the stroll through the jungle, but if they wanted to sneak up on Baron Bulo Lif that's what it would take.

McCade lit a cigar and hoped that the smoke would discourage the rather numerous insect population.

"Sergeant Ven, put your two best troopers on point. Phil, you're next, with scanners running full bore, and the flamethrower on standby. Then comes Ven, myself, and, last but not least, Rico and the rest of the troopers. We shouldn't run into any trouble, but if we do, let's win. Any questions?"

No one had any questions so they set off down the trail. The trail followed the course of the river and had once been heavily traveled. Now, what with hovercraft service and all-terrain vehicles, the path was seldom used. By Lakorians that is.

As they moved down the trail Ven pointed out broken twigs, piles of green dung, and a wide variety of animal tracks.

When asked to comment on these signs, Ven would simply shrug his shoulders and say "very dangerous, very dangerous."

Then Ven would check his auto slug thrower, peer into the jungle, and shake his head sadly as if disaster would almost certainly strike.

McCade took it seriously at first, remembering some of the fauna he'd seen during his first stay, but time passed and he started to relax.

Knowing Ven could be less than truthful he even questioned the Lakorian's veracity. Chances were that the twigs had been broken by passing herbivores, the dung had been deposited by peaceful ruminants, and the tracks had been left by cute little furry things.

Yes, McCade decided, Ven's trying to scare us humans. Chances are he has some sort of elaborate bet going with the troops. Trying to see which one of us will freak out first. Well, to hell with that!

So McCade proceeded to focus all of his attention on the slippery log bridges, the vines that grew across the trail ankle high, and the occasional pockets of deep mud. And that's why he was so surprised when the vebores attacked.

They came without warning, hundreds of leathery little bodies, all teeth and no brains. The vebores were about the size of a Terran gerbil and very fast. So fast that they were in and among the sentients before anyone could shout a warning.

McCade felt a pain in his right calf, looked down, and saw that a small animal had managed to sink its teeth into his leg just above the boot top. He shouted a warning but it was too late. The vebores were swarming out of the jungle and piling onto human and Lakorian alike.

McCade heard the boom of a slug gun and the whine of energy weapons. It was a waste of time. The vebores were too small to make good targets and there were far too many of them.

McCade forced himself to ignore the animal gnawing at his leg. "Cease fire! The river! Run for the river!"

The rest of the party heard and obeyed. At the moment the river was about a hundred feet to the right. A tiny bit of remaining sunlight shimmered across the surface of the water.

Seeing it, human and Lakorian alike crashed through undergrowth, leaped over fallen trees, and tore at the vines that blocked their way.

Twice McCade tripped and fell, and each time he got up there were two or three more vebores locked onto his flesh, their little bodies flapping this way and that as he ran.

Finally there it was, darkly flowing water, and over to the right a small point. McCade shouted to make himself heard over the roar of the river. "Over this way! The point! Get on the point with your backs to the river!"

They heard and, after crashing their way through the thick vegetation that grew along the edge of the river, joined McCade on the point. All except the Lakorian named Kreb.

McCade spun around. "Kreb! Where the hell's Kreb?"

No one answered so McCade started back into the jungle. Strong hands grabbed and threw him down. McCade struggled but Rico and Ven had a good grip on him.

Rico waved at Phil. "Cook 'em, Phil, and make damn sure the little suckers are well done!"

The variant nodded and turned toward the jungle. He got a good grip on the nozzle and aimed it straight ahead. There was a *whoosh*ing sound as he pulled the trigger and the flamethrower sent a long tongue of flame into the jungle.

Though moist, the vegetation was no match for liquid fire, and went up in a roar of displaced air. McCade could feel the warmth on his face as Rico helped him to his feet.

More than a thousand vebores were caught in flames and they made a horrible chittering as they died.

McCade felt a sudden pain and looked down to find Ven was grabbing his vebores one at a time, slicing through their necks, and throwing the bodies into the river.

Then, when all of the animals were dead, Ven used the point of his commando knife to pry their jaws open and free the ugly-looking heads. These too were tossed into the river where they made a small plopping sound and disappeared from sight.

There was a loud pop as Phil killed the flamethrower. Black smoke floated toward them, pulled by the breeze that ran with the river, and heavy with the smell of burnt vegetation.

There was a moment of silence as they thought about what had happened and the fact that they were still alive. Ven touched McCade's arm.

"I am sorry about restraining you, but Kreb went down early on. There was nothing you could do."

McCade shuddered. What a horrible way to go, swarmed under by hundreds of little bodies, literally eaten alive. He forced the thought down and back. The light was almost completely gone. Time to make camp for the night.

First came a big fire, both for the light it would provide and psychological comfort as well. Phil used the flamethrower to get it going, grinning happily as the pile of vegetation *whoosh*ed into flame, extolling the merits of technology over bush craft.

Then came a round of first aid, with everyone taking turns as both doctor and patient, cleaning and dressing their many wounds.

The shelters went up with relative ease, and a good thing too, because it began to rain. Big fat drops that hit the tents hard, exploded into a hundred droplets, and were reunited as they slid toward the ground.

All of them took turns standing guard with the flamethrower, but nothing attacked beyond the scope of their own dreams, and the flickering light of the campfire.

As McCade lay there, he listened to Rico snore and wondered what Molly was doing. Could she be right there on Lakor? Waiting for him to come? Going through God knows what? There was no way to know.

It took him a long time to fall asleep.

Eight

THE HOLD WAS still too small, but half of the gratings had been removed, and those that remained had been covered with thick cargo pads. Most of them smelled and were less than perfectly clean, but they still beat the heck out of bare metal.

Molly sat with her arms wrapped around her knees and rocked back and forth. She still hurt from the beating that Boots had given her. But the bruises had started to disappear, and thanks to the ship's medical officer, her sores were healing as well.

Molly looked around. The crew had rigged more lights, the girls wore clean clothes, cut-down ship suits mostly, and true to Pong's word, they received three servings of slop a day rather than the previous two.

That was the good news. The bad news was that Boots resented these improvements as if they came at her own personal expense and never stopped looking for ways to punish Molly for obtaining them. It was hard to believe that anyone could be so mean.

But Mommy said that some people are sick that way, holding other people down in order to elevate themselves, and it was certainly true that Boots was one of the lowest-ranking people in the crew.

Molly thought about her mother. Was she alive? Oh, please, God, let her be alive, and Daddy too. She bit her lip in order to stop the tears.

There was an intercom in the hold for use when loading and unloading cargo. It bonged twice. Molly looked up in surprise. They'd taken her wrist comp but her internal clock insisted that mealtime was still an hour or more away.

Some of the other girls were surprised as well and gave each other noncommittal shrugs. Whatever would be would be.

The children lined up and climbed the ladder one after another. By allowing the girl in front of her to get a ways ahead, and by climbing quickly past the platform on which Boots stood, Molly managed to escape all but a glancing kick, and a growled, "Hurry up."

Things proceeded normally once they entered the pressurized launch bay, except Molly couldn't escape the feeling that they were eating early, and noticed an unusual amount of activity around one of the larger shuttles.

It wasn't until the meal was over and the girls had lined up for their return that Molly learned the truth.

Boots walked about halfway down the line and stopped. She put her hands on fleshy hips. "All right, you little snots, listen up! At the present moment this ship is in orbit around a planet named Lakor."

Molly remembered the slight nausea all of them had felt about three meals back. Although the pirates hadn't said anything to confirm it, the girls had assumed that the ship was leaving hyperspace, and now they knew where.

Molly's heart leaped with excitement. Lakor! Her father had been there! And Mommy too. They'd helped Baron what's-his-name, Lis or something, and there was a chance that he'd help. Any chance was better than no chance at all! And that's what she had aboard ship.

Molly fought to keep the excitement off her face. She listened carefully.

Boots grinned evilly. "Lakor is well known for its slave markets, and guess what, some of you little creeps are going to see them firsthand. A few, twenty or so, will stay with us."

No one dared say anything but Molly felt the girls on either side of her stiffen. This was it, another step away from home and family, and into the terrible unknown. With the exception of Molly none of the girls wanted to go. They preferred life in the hold to the unknown horrors of Lakor.

"So," Boots continued, "Raz will choose. Those heading

dirtside will report to the shuttle on the far side of the bay, and everyone else will stay where you are."

As usual Raz looked like some kind of barbarian warrior, long blond hair hanging down his back, muscles rippling under bronzed skin.

Raz started with the A's and worked his way down the alphabet. He was utterly detached, as if dividing a shipment of robots rather than people, sealing their fates with a laconic "Lakor" or "stays here."

Boots followed along behind Raz with a smile on her beefy face. Whenever Raz said "Lakor," Boots nodded her approval and took pleasure in the girl's dismay.

Finally, after what seemed like an eternity, Raz was one person away. Molly could feel the pulse pounding in her head. She was afraid that he could hear it too.

Raz's voice seemed abnormally loud as he said "Lakor." The girl next to Molly gave a pathetic sob and ran toward the shuttle.

Molly tried to control Raz through sheer force of will. Make it Lakor, please make it Lakor.

Raz stopped in front of Molly, looked thoughtful, and spoke.

Nine

A SOFT RAIN fell. It hit the topmost leaves, slid off, and fell to the next layer of vegetation fifty feet below. Raindrops exploded upward as they hit, subsided into pools, and dripped downward to pitter pat around McCade.

A large drop of water found its way down past the neck seal of McCade's Class II Environment suit and trickled between his shoulder blades. It made him shiver.

Like the rest of the team McCade was tired from the hike through the jungle, wet from wading through a seemingly endless swamp, and sore from a long afternoon spent crouched on the hillside.

For the last hour or so they had moved down the slope in tiny increments, on the lookout for old-fashioned trip wires or, Sol forbid, the latest in surveillance technology. So far there was no sign of either one. Not too surprising, since Bulo's bullies spent most of their time in the inn, drinking and chasing barmaids.

Now McCade and his companions were hidden along the edge of the road where the jungle gave way to the village of Durn. Twilight had turned to night, leaving the village little more than a scattering of dark shapes and widely spaced lights.

It was difficult to see, but when McCade brought the night-vision device to his eyes, an astonishing amount of detail appeared. Buildings were transformed into ghostly green rectangles, windows became blotches of red, and power plants showed up as blobs of white. That's why McCade knew that the all-terrain vehicle parked next to the inn had been there for a relatively short period of time. The engine appeared as a ball of white radiance located toward the rear of a reddish haze.

Other than that, and the occasional movement of a blurry-looking guard, there was nothing worth watching. McCade put the device away.

A breeze blew in from the river. It made the vegetation rustle and swish. McCade made a face as the smell of Lakorian body odor hit his nostrils. When exposed to rain Lakorians exuded an oily substance that formed a microscopic layer of insulation between them and the water.

McCade took one last look around. There was no point in waiting any longer. By now Bulo's toughs should be either drunk or asleep. The perfect time to slip into the inn, grab Bulo, and make their escape. Or so McCade hoped.

McCade clicked his mic on and off. There were seven clicks in response. Gently, careful not to fall or make unnecessary noise, Rico made his way down onto the muddy road.

A single streetlight made a pool of sickly yellow light.

Beyond it the town was long and narrow, crushed between hill and river, with its most important buildings toward the center. Of these the inn was the largest, an impressive log structure with a stable on the ground floor and living quarters above that.

McCade watched approvingly as dark shadows flitted across the road to merge with the blackness beyond.

A domesticated animal squealed in protest as its litter mates shoved it up against a wall. McCade's heart pounded in his chest but nothing happened.

Now it was his turn to cross the road. The big black duffel bag seemed to weigh a thousand pounds as he slipped and slid the last few feet down the hill and sprinted across the road. McCade's boots made squishing sounds and his pack swayed back and forth as he ran. Then he was across and slipping between two of the many hovels that fronted the road.

"Over here." The voice belonged to Ven and came from his left. McCade moved with care trying to avoid the considerable garbage strewn between the huts.

Thick fingers reached out to grab his arm and pull him into the shadows. The smell of Lakorian body odor was extremely strong. Ven whispered in his ear.

"There are two guards just ahead, sire. I'll take the left, you take the right."

McCade nodded, realized the Lakorian couldn't see him, and whispered, "Understood. You're left, I'm right."

Ven faded into the darkness as McCade moved forward. There . . . about fifty feet away . . . something moved against the darker background of a building. A sentry.

McCade left his slug gun in its holster and pulled a knife. Silence was critical. One shot, one yell, and they'd lose the advantage of surprise.

Hugging a long, low wall McCade eased his way closer. Bit by bit the smell of Lakorian body odor grew stronger and stronger. There he was, a low blocky shadow with an energy weapon slung over his shoulder. Just a little bit closer . . .

The sentry gave a sudden snort, as if something really putrid had assailed his nostrils, and swung in McCade's direction. As he did so the guard reached for his weapon.

Damn! Either the body odor thing cut both ways . . . or the sentry had unusually good night vision.

Knowing that he'd never be able close the distance in time, and knowing that if he didn't some sort of sound was inevitable, McCade did the only thing he could.

He brought his arm all the way back, jerked it forward, and let go of the knife. McCade wasn't that good with knives, but he practiced every now and then, and hoped for the best.

There was a gurgle followed by the thump of a body hitting the ground. Not bad! Tiptoeing up to the body McCade was startled to find Ven already there.

Pulling a knife out of the sentry's throat the Lakorian grinned, wiped it on the tough's coat, and slid the weapon into his boot. He gestured to one side. "Your knife is over there, sire . . . sticking in the wall."

McCade looked, and sure enough, his knife had missed the sentry and embedded itself in a log wall. Light gleamed off the blade. Even though McCade couldn't see the Lakorian's face, he knew the alien was smiling. Ven would tell the story for many years to come. Assuming he survived, that is.

McCade returned the knife to its sheath and moved inward toward the inn. There should be at least one more cordon of guards, *would* be if *he* were Bulo.

Pausing to scoop up a rain-slippery rock, McCade rubbed it against his pants leg, and found a comfortable grip.

Determined not to repeat his sorry performance with the knife, McCade tiptoed forward, thankful for his rubber-soled boots. Maybe he'd smell this sentry as well.

But this sentry was sloppy and hit an empty vak bottle with his foot. It made a clinking sound as it rolled away.

Three quick steps and McCade was there, blindsiding the guard with the rock and easing him to the ground. A quick check assured him the sentry was still alive. Good. The less bloodshed the better.

McCade heard a low whistle and knew the rest of the sentries had been accounted for too.

With Ven close behind McCade slid along the side of the inn's stable searching for the rear entrance. He hadn't gone more than two or three yards when he heard a hissing scream. The entire wall shook as heavy bodies moved back and forth just beyond the log enclosure.

The reptiles! These were hunting mounts, trained for use in the jungle, and attuned to the slightest disturbance. Something, a slight noise, or the scent of alien flesh, had disturbed them. Another animal screamed, and another, until there was a cacophony of sound.

McCade swore and activated his mic. "Okay, team. So much for the subtle approach, go in and get the sucker!"

The words were hardly out of McCade's mouth when Phil kicked the door in, body blocked a surprised guard, and took the stairs two at a time. He had the flamethrower on his back and a machine pistol in his right paw.

Rico grabbed the now-unconscious sentry and dragged him outside, while Ven, two of his troopers, and McCade followed Phil up the stairs.

The inn had its own fusion plant, so lights started to come on, and there was a lot of confused shouting.

A heavily carved wooden door splintered under the force of Phil's boot and banged off an inner wall. He disappeared inside, closely followed by Ven and the troopers.

There were shouts of outrage, followed by the sound of breaking furniture, and the roar of Phil's voice. McCade had just arrived at the top of the stairs when the variant emerged and bowed formally.

"Greetings, sire. Baron Bulo is awake and receiving guests. Please excuse the broken furniture. The palace is undergoing repairs."

McCade grinned. "Thank you, squire. Excuse me while I hasten within. The royal yacht will arrive at any minute . . . and we mustn't be late."

McCade stepped through the door into a small vestibule, from there into a hallway, and from there into a richly appointed bedroom. Ven and his troopers were there pointing their weapons toward the center of the room.

Lakorians of all classes favor canopied beds because they provide excellent protection against leaky roofs and Bulo was no exception. In addition to the canopy his bed was hung with richly embroidered curtains and piled high with pillows.

Bulo occupied the center of the bed, with a presumably comely maiden to either side, and a princely frown on his not-so-noble brow. He looked like a weaker, dissipated version of Lif, especially when dressed in lavender jamies.

"Who are you? And how dare you break into my quarters! Guards! Guards! Kill these intruders and feed them to my mounts!"

McCade shook his head sadly, found a cigar, and stuck it in the corner of his mouth. " 'Feed them to my mounts'? Is that any way to treat guests? Well, I'm sure your brother will teach you better manners. In the meantime, get your royal ass out of bed. You're coming with us."

Bulo crossed his arms. His expression was defiant. "I am not! Run while you can, human. In seconds, minutes at the most, my guards will kill you *and* your traitorous assistants."

There was a loud pop to McCade's left. He turned to see fingers of yellow flame climbing up an embroidered curtain toward the canopy.

Phil waved the nozzle of his flamethrower. Smoke drifted away. "Ooops. Sorry about that. My mistake."

Bulo looked at the flames. His eyes grew big. "You wouldn't dare!"

The two females looked at Bulo, looked at the fire, and rolled out of bed. They were gone three seconds later.

McCade walked over, held his cigar in the flames, and puffed. Once the cigar was lit he blew a long streamer of smoke toward the ceiling.

"Oh, yes, he would. There's nothing Phil loves better than fresh meat roasted over an open fire."

Bulo looked at the variant, saw a mouth full of gleaming durasteel teeth, and turned a lighter shade of green. He was careful to stay away from Phil as he rolled out of bed. "Where are you taking me?"

"For a reunion with your brother," McCade replied. "Come on, let's go."

As they left the room the canopy burst into flames.

Phil led the way, with McCade right behind, and Ven, Bulo, and two troopers bringing up the rear.

They were halfway down the stairs when the front door crashed open and Rico dived in. An energy weapon stitched a line of diagonal holes through the door barely missing Phil's sizable feet.

There was a mad scramble to reach the bottom of the stairs and line up along the walls.

Rico stood by sliding himself up a wall. He shoved another power pak into the receiver of his blast rifle. "Time ta haul ya all."

McCade nodded. "Casualties?"

"One trooper dead . . . one missing, presumed dead."

"Damn." McCade had hoped to pull it off without any more casualties. "Any sight of the hovercraft?"

"Nope. Just a lot of bozos with more weapons than brains."

"See?" Bulo demanded shrilly. "My bodyguards are everywhere. Surrender while you still have a chance!"

There was a loud whump as Bulo's entire bedroom was engulfed by flames.

McCade shook his head in disgust. "Sergeant Ven . . . if his supreme effluence says anything more, gag him."

Ven grinned wickedly and slid the muzzle of his blast rifle into Bulo's left ear. The dead troopers had been friends of his.

McCade pulled his handgun and looked around. Everyone was here. No need to use his mic. "All right, everyone . . . head for the pier. Plan one is still operational. Okay, Phil, light 'em up."

Phil sent a long funnel of flame out the door to intimidate attackers and ruin their night sight. Then he released the trigger, shifted the pistol grip to his left paw, and kicked the door open. Phil fired three round bursts from his machine pistol as he headed toward the river.

Ven and the troopers went next, pushing Bulo along in front of them as a shield, firing around him.

Then came McCade and Rico, firing their weapons for effect, zigzagging toward the river.

Energy beams whined overhead, bullets threw up geysers of mud behind their heels, and a heat-seeking missile hit the inn with a loud boom. Rico was right. Bulo's rowdies had more weapons than brains.

McCade heard a roar of sound off to the right. Here came the hovercraft! Right on time and lit up like a Christmas tree! Against all instructions the captain had the vessel's interior and exterior lights turned on.

The hovercraft made a wonderful target. Unable to resist all of Bulo's retainers shifted their fire to the oncoming vessel. A heat-seeking missile hit the rear deck and blew up.

The explosion did very little structural damage, but did sever some control cables and caused both engines to race out of control.

The captain did the only thing he could and shut down both of his engines. Thanks to the swift current he was able to steer toward the middle of the channel. Mercifully the lights went out when the engines stopped.

Although the hovercraft wasn't able to pick them up, it did provide a much-needed diversion, and the entire group made it to the pier unharmed.

By now the hoverboat's captain had mustered a somewhat ineffectual damage-control party. They made dark silhouettes against the flames as they aimed an intermittent stream of water at the base of the fire.

McCade shook his head in disgust, removed the cigar from his mouth, and flicked it into the river.

"All right, everybody . . . so much for plan A. It looks like we're gonna get our feet wet."

"But I can't swim!" Bulo wailed. "I'll drown!"

"That would be nice," McCade said agreeably. "But if you shut up, and do exactly what Sergeant Ven says, maybe you won't."

"Company's coming!" Rico yelled, and sent a stutter of blue energy toward town. Two of the troopers took cover nearby and added their fire to his.

McCade shrugged his way out from under the black duffel. "Give me a hand, Phil . . . this thing's awkward as hell." Together they laid the bag out with the seal upward.

Rico yelled something incoherent and bullets screamed overhead.

Fingers fumbling, heart pounding, McCade broke the seal, found the T-shaped yellow handle, gave it a single turn to the right, and pulled.

The results were quite dramatic. There was a loud *whooshing* sound, followed by a series of pops as various air chambers filled, and a final hiss as the now-inflated raft vented a bit of excess air.

"All right," McCade yelled, "massed fire to keep their heads down, then grab the raft and jump together!"

Rico and the two troopers backed toward the river firing as they came.

Phil hit a quick release, dumped the flamethrower, and set it to explode sixty seconds later.

McCade unloaded his slug gun in the general direction of town and got a grip on the boat.

Ven handcuffed himself to Bulo and flinched as a stray bullet whapped through the raft right next to his leg.

"Grab on!" McCade ordered, and the moment they had, he yelled, "Run!"

With bullets zinging around them, and energy beams slicing the night into geometric shapes, they galloped to the end of the pier and jumped.

Then they learned a painful lesson. A well-inflated raft won't sink after a twenty-foot fall, but those hanging on to it will. The force of the fall, plus their own weight, ripped hands loose and pushed them toward the bottom.

The water was cold. McCade kicked toward the surface, unable to see through the blackness, groping for the raft.

Ven got a pleasant surprise meanwhile as Bulo demonstrated a sudden mastery of underwater swimming and towed him toward the surface.

Rico felt a trooper struggling nearby, grabbed his harness, and dragged him upward.

Phil struggled against the weight of his remaining equipment and water-logged fur, considered going into full augmentation, and decided not to. He would be completely exhausted afterward and that might be just as fatal as drowning. Slowly but surely, forcing himself to stay calm, he kicked his way upward until his head broke the surface.

Most of Phil's attention was centered on the vital process of sucking air into his oxygen-starved lungs, but a distant part of his mind was still able to register a ball of red-orange flame and the thump of a sizable explosion.

The flamethrower had exploded right on schedule taking twelve of Bulo's retainers and most of the pier with it.

McCade was the first one into the raft. As a side current pulled them out and away from shore, he helped others into the raft and urged them to hurry up.

Given the raft's low profile, and its dark color, the boat was almost impossible to see. That didn't bother Bulo's surviving retainers however, they were still firing, hoping for a lucky hit. The fact that they might hit Bulo hadn't occurred to them or just didn't matter.

"Welcome aboard, your wetness," McCade said as he helped Ven, then Bulo, over the side.

The Lakorian noble ignored him as he collapsed in the bottom of the boat.

McCade looked for the hovercraft. It had drifted downriver and out of sight.

Phil was the last one aboard, and as he fell gasping into the bottom of the boat, McCade realized there was a problem. The raft was sinking.

The raft had a number of self-contained air chambers so it wouldn't sink completely, but it looked as if they were in for a long wet ride.

McCade didn't say anything. He didn't have to. The boat told its own story as it sank deeper in the water and began to flood.

One by one they were dumped into the river and forced to find a spot around the raft's sides. Although they couldn't ride in it, the boat did provide flotation and something to cling to.

They talked at first, still high on adrenaline, or the Lakorian equivalent. But as time passed the obvious things were soon said and gave way to periods of silence. These grew longer and longer until conversation stopped entirely and was replaced by swishing, gurgling rhythms of the river. It had a lulling, soothing effect, and McCade drifted in and out of sleep.

Eventually he dreamed that he was far, far away, on a planet where it never snowed and never rained, where Sara and Molly were sunny and full of happiness.

Then a terrible night fell over the land. Molly disappeared into darkness. McCade searched for her, flailing around in the blackness, grabbing squirmy things and throwing them away.

Then a wavelet came and slapped him in the face.

The others were yelling, pointing downriver where the hovercraft was grounded on a sandbar, celebrating their good fortune.

But not McCade. His thoughts were farther downriver, in the slave markets that dotted the coast, with the little girl who might be waiting there.

It took the better part of a day for the hovercraft's crew to complete temporary repairs, and two more to reach the town of Riversplit. It was there that they said good-bye to Ven and his surviving troopers, gave Bulo into the custody of Lif's troops, and met up with Murd.

As before the king's advisor, or gofer, whichever he was, wore a long orange robe and looked somewhat fragile. But appearances can be deceiving as Murd demonstrated over the next few days.

It took a full day to reach the coast and the first slave market. Already tired from his activities in Durn, the trip sapped even more of McCade's energy and left him drained.

Not Murd though, when they arrived at the slave market he was as spry as ever, busy throwing his weight around and generally pissing everyone off.

McCade didn't mind though since Murd's efforts were in his behalf and did a great deal to get things moving.

Though a different slave market from the one McCade had experienced some years earlier, it was still quite similar.

Their all-terrain vehicle had no top. As a result McCade was able to smell the slave market long before they actually arrived.

It was horrible. The unbelievable stench that goes with open sewers and insufficient drainage, but something more as well, something part smell and part emotion.

A feeling of misery, of fear, of hopelessness. It made McCade sick to his stomach.

Then they rounded a bend and saw the stockade made of vertical logs. There were enormous gates that, with the Lakorian tendency to combine old with new, whirred open to let their vehicle pass.

Once inside the vehicle was swamped by a small army of functionaries all vying for the privilege of kissing Murd's ancient rear end.

Ignoring the mob McCade, Rico, and Phil got out of the vehicle and looked around. There was a large expanse of mud at the center of the market, an awning-covered platform where slaves were bought and sold, and rows of enclosed pens where they were housed.

Having spent some time in similar accommodations McCade knew they had dirt floors, a single water tap, and an open sewer that ran along one wall.

The thought that Molly might be locked inside one of those pens made his heart ache.

He turned toward the knot of gesticulating Lakorians. "Murd . . . tell them to bring out the children . . . and to do it now."

Murd, who was enjoying all the attention, considered telling the arrogant human to sit on something pointy but changed his mind. Yes, there was Lif to consider, but more than that the human himself. He had an obvious propensity for violence this human did, and seemed quite agitated.

Murd forced himself to perform a polite bow and issued a long string of orders.

Thirty minutes later the three humans sat and watched one of the most horrible sights they'd ever seen.

The slave market's entire population of human children, some thirty-three in all, were paraded by for their inspection. Little boys and girls, with bony, underfed bodies and hopeless expressions.

Under normal circumstances an auctioneer would be haranguing the audience about the children's virtues, extolling their sexual attractiveness, and reminding them that human fingers are extremely nimble as compared to the appendages found on many other sentient beings.

But this was different. The children trudged across the platform in weary silence, looking neither right nor left, numb to what happened around them.

All three of the men searched for familiar features, hoping, praying to see one or more familiar faces, but none of the children was from Alice.

When the last child had passed the men sat staring at the emptiness in front of them. McCade wanted desperately to buy the children, or simply take them, destroying anyone or anything who got in the way, but knew that was impossible. The three of them had neither the money nor the brute strength to get the job done. No, they must steel themselves against what they saw, and continue the search.

McCade looked at Rico and Phil. Rico had tears glistening on his beard, and Phil's lips were pulled back in a rictus of hate, durasteel teeth almost completely bared.

Murd cleared his throat. "Well, sire? Were any of the cubs yours?"

McCade stood. "No. Take us to the next market."

It was three days and two slave markets later before they found the children.

This time there was an actual auction taking place on the main platform, so they were seated inside a striped tent, watching a line of pathetic children straggle past.

Later it was hard to say who saw who first, but McCade heard Phil yell "Mary!" and heard a child say "Citizen McCade!" almost simultaneously.

Then there was total pandemonium as twenty-six of the twenty-eight children crowded around the three men, crying and talking all at the same time.

His heart in his throat McCade hugged little girl after little girl, calling those he knew by name, using "sweetheart" on all the rest.

Some of the girls were orphans and didn't know it yet, others would be reunited with anxious parents, but all would end up safe and sound on Alice.

After the first few frantic seconds McCade knew the truth. Molly wasn't there. A wave of grief rolled over him submerging the joy he'd known moments before. Molly was still out there somewhere, waiting for him, or . . .

McCade grabbed the nearest girl, a child named Cindy, and stared into her eyes so intensely that she started to cry. "Molly? Where's Molly McCade? What happened to my daughter?"

The words jerked their way out along with the tears. "Sshee's sstill on the sship."

McCade felt a wave of relief. Alive then. There was hope. McCade pulled Cindy to his chest, and as he apologized for scaring her, he saw something awful over her shoulder.

Two little boys had been brought in along with the girls, the little boys he'd never seen before, but were being led away by a Lakorian guard.

McCade stood up. "Wait! Bring those boys back! Look, Rico! It's John, and his brother Paul!"

Rico looked up from the little girl who was asking about her mother. "Huh? John and Paul?"

Then Rico saw McCade's expression. "Oh, yeah! John and Paul! Hey, boys, don'tcha recognize Uncle Rico? Come on over here!"

The younger boy looked momentarily confused, but the older boy put on a happy expression and dragged the little boy with him. "Uncle Rico, sure, I didn't recognize you with the beard!"

McCade smiled in spite of himself. The boy was smart. He'd do well on Alice. They all would.

Ten

MOLLY WAITED PATIENTLY for the other girls to fall asleep. The dim glow provided by two light switches was enough to see by.

Shortly after the other children had been loaded aboard the shuttle and taken dirtside, the twenty or so remaining girls were removed from the hold and assigned to adjoining compartments. It was a tight fit, but at least they had real bunks and adequate toilet facilities.

Molly still felt certain that she would've been better off on the surface of Lakor, but Raz had kept her aboard, so that was that.

Determined to escape, or at least pave the way, Molly had conceived a plan. A plan that relied on her increased freedom of movement.

Although significant portions of the ship were still off-limits, the girls were now permitted to roam through the rest.

Many of the girls saw their new quarters, and lack of confinement, as a change of heart by the pirates and said so during whispered conversations.

Molly disagreed, pointing out that shortly after they vacated the hold, it had been filled with some sort of cargo brought up from the surface of Lakor. In addition, Molly suggested, the pirates could have hidden motives for allowing them more freedom as well. What if it was part of a plan? A plan in which the girls would wind up colluding in their own slavery? At what point do prisoners cease to be prisoners, and join ranks with those who imprisoned them?

Some of the girls agreed, and were suspicious of pirate motives, but Lia, one of the older girls, was especially critical of Molly's ideas.

"Come on, Molly," she'd whispered, "you griped when we were in the hold . . . and you're griping now. Give us a break. Things are better, that's all. Quit worrying so much."

But Molly *did* worry, and planned to keep right on worrying, no matter what. The pirates had attacked Alice, killed innocent people, and sold children into slavery. Maybe the others could forgive and forget but not Molly. No, she planned to get free, and get even. No matter how long that took.

Because of her attitude Molly had fallen from a position of leadership into that of semi-outcast. She hoped Mommy wouldn't be disappointed, but Lia was wrong, and wasn't there a difference between popularity and leadership? Daddy said so . . . and Molly hoped he was right.

Time passed, and finally, when the last of the whispered conversations had died away, and everyone else was asleep, Molly made her move.

Slipping out from under the covers Molly tiptoed to the doorway and touched the softly glowing circle of red light. The circle turned green and the hatch hissed open.

Molly paused, searched the compartmcnt for signs of movement, and seeing none stepped outside.

Satisfied that she'd managed to slip out of the room undetected, Molly padded down the corridor, ready to claim a stomachache if she encountered a member of the crew.

It felt weird to wear the one-piece black body stocking in the corridor, but that's what the girls used for pajamas, so that's what she'd have on if truly on her way to the sick bay.

This would be her last trip to the S-4 damage-control station. She'd been there three times before, and didn't dare make any more trips after this one. Someone or something was sure to go wrong eventually and trip her up.

Intended for use during a full scale disaster, the station's computer console would provide backup access to the vessel's atmospheric and fire-control systems, allowing the crew to pump oxygen out of various compartments, dump fire retardant in, or selectively cut power to various locations.

As such the computer console located in S-4 had nothing to do with the ship's primary navcomp, or wasn't supposed to, but Molly had written a conversion program that linked both computers together. Or had *almost* linked them together, since she was still in the process of debugging the conversion, and had yet to actually access the navcomp.

By now Martha Chong, Molly's computer instructor back on Alice, would have been mumbling in frustration. The truth was that at least two of the other girls were better with computers than Molly was, but she couldn't trust them. They were friends of Lia's, and the older girl would make fun of the whole thing.

Assuming that she did gain access to the navcomp, Molly planned to obtain a cube dump of the ship's travels for the last month or so. By backtracking along the ship's course she could find Alice. Assuming she had something to backtrack in, which she didn't, but like Mom always said, "Take one thing at a time, Molly. Take one thing at a time."

Like all damage-control stations this one was unlocked. After all, in the case of major damage to the ship's hull, there would be scant time for access codes. Nor was there any way to be sure which crew member would use the station. So, like S-1, S-2, and S-3, S-4 was unsecured.

Molly took one last look around, saw nothing but empty corridor, and palmed the access panel. The hatch slid open, then closed behind her.

It was a tiny compartment with barely enough room for tool storage, a computer console, and an emergency patch kit.

Molly felt her pulse start to pound a little faster. While her stomach ache story might fly out in the corridor, it wouldn't do much good in here. She forced the fear down and back.

A rudimentary seat was held up against the bulkhead by a spring-loaded hinge. Molly pushed the seat down and sat on it. The metal felt cold through the thin body stocking.

Molly slid the keyboard out of its recess and turned it on. Under normal circumstances that would have activated one of the zillion indicator lights located on the bridge, but she had eliminated that function the first time out. Having spent hundreds of hours on her father's ships, Molly had a better-than-average understanding of how they worked.

Molly entered a multidigit code, checked to make sure that

no one had tampered with her program, and went to work.

Five minutes later Molly was completely lost in what she was doing. Bit by bit Molly felt her way through the last few interfaces, neutralized two security procedures meant to keep her out, and dipped into the navcomp's huge memory. Not bad for one of Chong's worst students.

Her first question was simple: "Where is the ship now?"

A long string of numbers flooded the screen.

Molly frowned and fingers flew over keys: "Request plain language description of the ship's position using nearest stars or planets as points of reference."

The reply was almost instantaneous: "Ship is en route from Lakor to Drang."

Molly nodded. The ship was headed for Drang, wherever that was. Okay, enough messing around. First she'd get a cube dump on the mathematical stuff . . . then she'd back out of the navcomp, erasing the conversion program as she went. In fifteen or twenty minutes she'd have everything she needed and no one the wiser.

Molly had just started to type when she heard feet scuffle outside. She whirled just in time to see the hatch open.

Lia stood outside, as did a smug-looking Boots and an angry Raz. Lia smiled and pointed a triumphant finger in Molly's direction.

"There she is, sir . . . just like I told you. Thank goodness you caught her in time! There's no telling what harm she might have done!"

Eleven

NEXUS. THAT WAS the name it had given itself, or had been given, depending on which story you chose to believe.

It made little difference to McCade. To him Nexus was a place, a place to look for Molly, or clues that would point in her direction.

At the moment Nexus just hung there, a vast amalgamation of interconnected spaceships, slowly spinning before a distant star.

The ships came in all shapes and sizes. There were tankers, freighters, tugs, yachts, liners, and Sol knows what else, at least a hundred of them, all hooked together in what looked like random order, their various shapes appearing and disappearing as dim sunlight moved across their combined hulls.

Taken as a whole, the ships and the computer that made the gathering possible were known as Nexus.

The purpose of the gathering was simple, to sell things you didn't need, and buy things you did. And to do so without the taxes, duties, laws, and other encumbrances that so often get in the way of free trade.

That's why Nexus was located out along the rim, beyond the jurisdiction of systemic or planetary governments, and a law unto itself.

Nexus was not without structure however, no, it was far too complex to function without rules, and that meant a guiding intelligence.

And that intelligence was supplied by a sentient computer, a machine of rather mysterious origins, which ran Nexus like a personal fiefdom.

There were two theories about the artificial intelligence. One held that the computer had escaped from some sort of governmental research project, while the other suggested that the AI was owned by a huge mega-corp, and provided it with a source of untaxed revenue.

McCade decided it didn't make too much difference which theory was true. Nexus pulled some heavy G's any way you figured it. More than that, Nexus knew the details of every transaction that took place within its sphere of influence, including what was traded by whom.

McCade stuck a cigar in his mouth and puffed it into life. The smoke floated upward and drifted toward a vent.

So, if Pong, or any of Pong's ships, had been here, chances were Nexus would know. In some ways it was a long shot . . . and in some ways it wasn't.

There were a limited number of places where one could sell stolen goods on a large scale, and because Pong had betrayed the pirates during the Vial of Tears episode, he was barred from the brotherhood's markets. The primary one being located on the fortified planet known as The Rock.

That meant he'd have to use one of the others, and there weren't all that many to choose from. There was Tin Town, a free-floating, wide-open, anything-goes habitat, a rather grubby planet called Seed, and a few others, the most famous of which was Nexus.

So, having made sure that all of the children were safely aboard the small freighter that would carry them to Alice, McCade held a council of war.

They listed alternative destinations, discussed the pros and cons of each, and came to a final decision. Nexus. It wasn't controlled by the brotherhood, was relatively close to Lakor, and played a significant role in the slave trade.

Shortly thereafter the group said good-bye to a smug King Lif, climbed aboard their shuttle, and lifted for space.

Once aboard *Void Runner* it was a quick jump into hyperspace and a three-day trip to the point called Nexus.

Most of them enjoyed the trip, or would have had their mission been different, the exception being Rico. He'd fallen into an ever-deepening depression. It was clear that Vanessa's death weighed heavily on his mind.

The activity on Lakor had provided a momentary distraction, something to occupy Rico's mind and body, but now, without anything to do, his emotions were spiraling down.

McCade remembered the glint of gold as Rico had thrown something into Vanessa's grave, and the comment Sara had made just prior to liftoff: "Keep a close eye on Rico, Sam, he's hurting, and God knows what he might do."

At the moment the big man was conning the ship, following orders provided by some tiny portion of the Nexus brain, heading for the point where *Void Runner* would become part of the ever-evolving whole.

For such was the computer's intelligence that it could calculate exactly where to place *Void Runner*'s additional mass, monitor some very complex transactions, and run the habitat all at the same time.

They were still fifty miles away from the mass of interconnected ships when Nexus ordered Rico to surrender control. Conscious of the fact that the computer controlled enough weapons to destroy a small fleet, Rico obeyed.

Numbers and schematics rippled across the command screens as Nexus assumed control, inventoried the ship's offensive and defensive capabilities, and drew the ship steadily in.

Now Nexus could be seen without magnification. The central construct was a globe, and reaching out from it were innumerable black tentacles, each one clutching a ship. The design reminded McCade of the cephalopods of his native Terra.

The comparison seemed even more appropriate when a tube came snaking out to make contact with *Void Runner*'s main lock.

Indicator lights flashed on and off as Nexus ran a final check on the ship's systems, locked out all of her weapons systems, and verified a positive seal with *Void Runner*'s main lock. Like any sentient being Nexus had a well-developed sense of self-preservation.

Somewhere at the hub of the metallic maze an order went out and the heretofore flexible tube turned hard as steel.

Thanks to the tube's rigidity the ship would be held firmly in place preventing the possibility of collision with the vessels that surrounded it.

Lights flashed and numbers vanished from the screens as Nexus withdrew all but a tendril of its intelligence from the ship and turned that part of its attention elsewhere. There were many things to do.

McCade activated the intercom. "Maggie?"

"Yeah?" The chief engineer's voice had an edge to it as usual.

"Meet us in the lounge please."

"Roger."

All four of them were gathered in the lounge five minutes later. It was large enough for twice their number and, thanks to the money McCade had invested in it, quite comfortable.

McCade dropped into a chair and felt it shift slightly to accommodate the shape of his body. Rico and Phil did likewise, while Maggie killed power and lowered herself to the deck.

"Well, here we are," Phil said cheerfully. "Now what?"

McCade checked his cigar, found it was getting a bit short, and stubbed it out.

"Now we take a look around. Find out where the slave market is . . . and look for the children."

Maggie gave a snort of derision.

McCade smiled patiently. "Yes, Maggie? You've got something to add?"

"Only that your plan is stupid," Maggie replied evenly.

"Don't be shy . . . say what ya mean," Rico commented dryly.

"Thanks, I will," Maggie answered, eyes flashing. "If the kids are here, you want to rescue them, right?"

"Obviously," McCade said, somewhat annoyed. "What's your point?"

Maggie met their eyes one at a time. "My point is that we should prepare for success. Think about it. Let's say you find 'em, there's what, twenty or so girls unaccounted for? And the same number of boys? What're you going to do? Take 'em out at gunpoint? If so, you'd better come up with a battalion of marines, cause I've been here before, and if the owners don't stop you, Nexus will.

"Or," Maggie continued, "maybe you plan to buy the children. Tell me, Sam . . . have you got a couple hundred thousand credits stashed under your pillow? Lif paid the freight on Lakor . . . but what happens here?"

There was a long silence while McCade got up and walked over to the autobar. He ordered a Terran whiskey and, when it came, took a thoughtful sip. When McCade turned around there was a grin on his face.

"Thanks, Maggie. I guess I'm so used to rolling over and through problems, I don't always think 'em through. From the sound of things we couldn't take the children by force, and no, I don't have two hundred big ones stashed under my pillow. So, if the children are here, we've got a problem, and if they aren't, we don't. How about you and Rico taking a look around? That way we'll know if we need the two hundred thousand or not."

Maggie found herself nodding in agreement. McCade made the whole thing sound so reasonable there wasn't much choice.

The *Void Runner*'s lock hissed closed behind them. The tube was about seven feet in diameter, slightly ridged along its inner surface, and off-white in color. A yellowish light seemed to ooze around them.

Maggie gestured Rico forward. The tube featured some tight turns and if Maggie made a mistake she'd do so privately.

Rico shrugged and walked away. Within seconds he disappeared around a curve.

Maggie followed, watching the turns, increasingly confident the farther she went. Then the tube straightened out and she saw Rico up ahead. By applying some additional power she was able to reach the main lock only seconds after he did.

The lock opened, they moved inside, and it closed again. A wall screen came to life. On it Maggie saw a softly rounded something with a head and shoulders but no face. It was silver and slightly reflective.

Where a human face would have eyes it had shallow depressions, and where there should be a nose, the thing had a bump. The black background gave it a dramatic look.

This was a new development. Whatever it was hadn't been there during Maggie's previous visit.

Her first impulse was to classify the thing as a robot, an intermediate step between the functional-looking machines used for most tasks and the more humanoid forms favored for domestic applications. But as Maggie was about to learn, this machine was different.

The machine's silvery face was motionless as it spoke, and its voice was neutral, sounding neither male nor female.

"Greetings, and welcome to Nexus. I am a remote, one of four hundred and sixty-three remotes scattered around the habitat, and the direct embodiment of the intelligence known as Nexus.

"I was created to answer your questions, to solve your problems, to make your visit to Nexus as pleasant and productive as possible. Please approach me whenever you need help.

"Before venturing forth, please listen to and memorize my laws: First, no one shall contemplate or take any action that could harm, damage, or incapacitate Nexus, its employees, remotes, or other representatives.

"Secondly," the remote continued, "no one shall possess or use projectile weapons while visiting Nexus."

"Kinda understandable," Rico observed. "Don't mess with the boss . . . and don't punch any unauthorized holes in the habitat."

"Violation of my laws," the remote added, "is punishable by death. Have a nice visit."

"Thanks, ol' sport," Rico said sarcastically, "let the fun begin."

The picture faded to black and the lock cycled open. Clever, Maggie thought to herself. You step into the lock, and presto! A captive audience.

"Come on," Rico said, "let's see the sights."

As Rico stepped out of the lock Maggie heard a tone, and a soft voice that said, "You are leaving lock seventy-seven. Please retain that number for future reference. Should you forget the number, or need other assistance, please approach a remote and ask. I will be happy to help. Have a nice vis it."

Maggie floated out of the lock and spun the hover box around. A huge super-graphic of the number seventy-seven covered the entire area around the lock. It should be visible from quite a distance away. Had that been there during her last visit? Maggie couldn't remember.

Rico touched her arm. "Come on, chief . . . the kids remember? We're supposed ta find out if they're here."

Maggie nodded and whirred along beside him. The hall was huge, and seemed to run straight ahead for a long ways, before taking a gentle curve to the right.

The habitat was enormous. And that raised questions larger than the origins of Nexus itself. Who constructed the habitat for Nexus? And why? There was no way to tell.

Except for a path that wound its way down the center of the hall, the corridor was crammed with a bewildering array of cargo modules, vending stands, miscellaneous equipment, and just plain junk.

Moving in and around these objects were humans, robots, aliens, auto loaders, pet animals, silvery remotes, power pallets, cyborgs, androids, and things Maggie wasn't sure of. This at least was as it had been during her previous visit.

Although there were formal venues for selling certain kinds of merchandise, they were in heavy demand and cost a lot to rent.

So the halls functioned as staging areas, and as secondary markets, since many of the merchants had offerings too modest to justify a presentation room.

Maggie looked at Rico striding along at her side. He was uncharacteristically silent. She knew why, or thought she did, and forced herself to make conversation.

"So tell me, Rico . . . why us? Why didn't Sam do this himself?"

Rico came to a sudden stop and turned on her. He looked angry. "Listen here, Maggie . . . I'm gettin' real tired of your crap. I don't know what Sam has up his sleeve. He'll tell us when he's good 'n' ready. Till then I suggest you keep a coupla things in mind.

"First, there ain't ten people on the whole rim that's as savvy as Sam is. You can take all the cheap shots you want, but if we find those kids, it'll be Sam that gets it done.

"Second, I don't know what your problem is, but you better back off, or by God I'll arrange ta leave your crotchety ass right here on Nexus!"

Maggie felt a variety of emotions. The first was anger. How dare Rico speak to her that way? Leave *her* would he? Not very damn likely! She'd leave him . . . and Sam too . . . there were plenty of berths for a good engineer.

Next came a more rational response. One that recognized

Rico's pain, and, more than that, recognized the same old pattern.

In place after place, ship after ship, Maggie had made herself obnoxious and been fired.

That way Maggie never got involved, never came to care, never got hurt. It began with the explosion, with the loss of her legs, and the deaths of her entire crew. But when would it end? A year from now? Two?

Maggie cleared her throat and looked away. "I have a big mouth sometimes. Sorry, Rico."

Rico searched Maggie's face, saw she was sincere, and shrugged. "The truth is that ya have a big mouth *all* the time . . . but what the hell . . . so do I. Shake."

Maggie's hand disappeared into Rico's giant paw and she smiled.

Twelve

MUSTAPHA PONG was lost somewhere between the past and present.

He sat as he always did under the vast canopy of stars projected on the overhead. The compartment was circular and, except for the pool of light that surrounded Pong, completely dark.

There had been a time many years before when the cabin would've been filled to overflowing with loot, the tangible symbol of his success, the living out of boyhood dreams.

Back then Pong had favored chests brimming over with gold jewelry, ingots of platinum stacked in the corner, slave girls who responded to a snap from his fingers. Raw, open manifestations of power.

But he'd been young and immature then. Raw clay still finding its final shape.

The compartment was different now. Open, nearly empty, boasting little more than a dais at its center, and the custom-designed power lounger that served Pong as both chair and bed.

The cabin was a symbol of what Mustapha Pong wanted to be. Open, centered, at one with the cosmos. A force great enough to move planets, to redefine the course of sentient history, to leave a mark so deep it would still be visible after a million years had come and gone.

The thing on his shoulder stirred and injected a mild stimulant into Pong's bloodstream. As usual the mind slug's thoughts were caustic and mocking.

"Bestir yourself, human, there is work to do, and you are lost in your own ambition."

His reverie broken, and annoyed at the alien's criticism, Pong punched a request for coffee into the arm of his chair. There was a whirring sound and a cup of coffee appeared at Pong's fingertips. The mind slug hated caffeine, and drinking it would serve both as a punishment and a reminder. Pong was in charge . . . and it would stay that way.

Now back to the problem at hand. Pong sipped his coffee. The problem was the one he always faced. How to overcome resistance and work his will on the universe around him.

The larger problem was necessarily subdivided into a series of tasks. Move ships over there, raid that particular planet, invest the profit in certain companies, buy more information, bribe . . .

The Melcetian interrupted. "You are drifting again, O conqueror of the universe. Focus on the problem at hand . . . and drink something else."

Pong frowned and tried to focus. The 56,827 were never satisfied. Now they wanted a full-scale planetary war to observe. A global conflict on a reasonably high-tech world, say level four or five, that would serve to demonstrate the latest in human tactics. Tactics they must overcome in order to enslave the human race.

Pong had laughed the first time they said that, and nearly lost his life.

But that was back before he knew them, when he'd responded to a mysterious but profitable summons, and agreed to function as their sole human ally. Now Pong knew the aliens could do what they claimed.

Not even he knew where the 56,827's homeworld was, but Pong had been to some of the planets they'd enslaved, seen those the aliens had destroyed. Black airless rocks burned clean of the life that had dared to defy them.

But relentless though they were, the 56,827 were cautious as well, carefully studying each race prior to attacking it. That explained their desire for a war, and more than that, their insistence that Pong participate in it. They would see a blade and test it prior to striking a blow.

Pong took another sip of coffee. Drang was the obvious choice since there was a war brewing there anyway . . . but which side should he take? That of the world government? Or that of the corporate combine that hoped to overthrow it? Both had advantages and disadvantages.

"Sir?"

Pong looked up and wondered how long they'd been there, standing on the edge of darkness, waiting for him to respond.

There was Raz, an ugly-looking female guard, and a little girl. The girl was a slave, one of those they'd taken on Alice, a skinny little thing with a mop of curly brown-black hair.

The girl looked familiar, but Pong couldn't place her. A trivial problem most likely . . . but important to the crew. It never seemed to end. If the 56,827 weren't after something, then his crew was.

"Yes, Raz, what is it?"

Raz kept it brief knowing Pong's distaste for unnecessary detail. "Thanks to a tip from another slave, this female was found making unauthorized use of the damage-control computer console located in station S-4."

Pong frowned. "So? Why bring her to me? Can't you people handle anything by yourselves?"

Boots had started to tremble but Raz was unaffected. "There is more, sir. The slave wrote a conversion program that allowed her access to the ship's navcomp via the damage-control console."

Pong sat straight up in his chair. "Really? How interesting. I didn't know such a thing was possible. Let me see her."

Boots gave Molly a shove and she stumbled into the light. The girl looked very familiar, but Pong still couldn't place her.

The mind slug made a tiny secretion and the memory came flooding back. Pong found himself standing in the launch bay, looking down at the girl's ulcerated arms, listening to her arguments. It was all there. The smell of her unwashed body, the echo of a tool hitting the deck, everything.

It took a fraction of a second for the entire conversation to flash through Pong's mind. He smiled.

"So, we meet again. Tell me, child, what's your name?"

Molly felt her lower lip start to quiver and fought for control. "Molly McCade, sir."

Adrenaline surged through Pong's body. It was strong, too strong, and the mind slug worked to buffer it. Pong was jubilant.

McCade! Could it be? Could this be Sam McCade's daughter?

He worked to hide his excitement.

"Molly McCade . . . a pretty name . . . a familiar name. Is your father named Sam by any chance?"

Something, Molly wasn't sure what, told her there was danger here. But what kind? And was it real? After all, her father knew a lot of strange sentients, and considered many to be friends. Could this man be one? If so, she should tell him the truth; besides, Lia would if she didn't. "Yes, sir, my father is named Sam. Do you know him?"

Pong shook his head, and the mind slug shivered a thousand rainbows. "No, child, although I once spoke with him over a com link. Tell me, was your father dirtside when the ships attacked?"

Molly squinted upward into the light. The man looked nice enough, but she was frightened of the thing on his shoulder. Molly wanted to say that had her father been home, the attack might have gone differently, but she resisted the temptation. It wasn't true for one thing, and might make the man mad for another. "No, he wasn't."

Pong slumped back in his chair. So, it was just as he'd feared, McCade was alive. How unfortunate. Hatred welled up from deep inside. Hatred for McCade, for the damage he'd done, for the loss of irreplaceable time. The one thing no one, not even Pong, had enough of.

But hatred would get him nowhere. He must think, he must plan, he must put petty problems aside and focus on Drang.

Raz was waiting, and so was the ugly guard. They didn't care about Drang, they wanted him to pass judgment, to punish the girl in a way that would make their jobs easier.

The problem was that Pong *liked* Molly McCade. It was strange but true. He liked her intelligence, her courage, and her unwillingness to bend.

He'd known a little boy like her once, a boy who grew up hungry in the ghettos of Desus II, a boy named Mustapha Pong.

Besides . . . the girl was Sam McCade's daughter, and there

was something delicious about having her under his control.

Pong gestured to Raz. "Who's in charge of the slaves?"

Raz looked at a terrified Boots and back again. "She is, sir. The slaves call her Boots."

Pong nodded. "Give Boots some brig time. Maybe she'll be a little more zealous when she gets out."

Boots flushed red and tried to say something, but a glance from Raz shut her up. He didn't say anything but she got the message just the same. "You may think *this* is bad but it could've been a lot worse."

Pong ignored the byplay. "As for the girl, she'll remain here, where I can keep an eye on her."

He looked down at Molly and smiled. "I could use someone to run errands. Tell the security officer to give her an L-band."

Raz nodded curtly, took Boots by the arm, and marched her to the hatch. It hissed open and closed.

Molly was alone with Mustapha Pong.

Thirteen

AN AUTO LOADER beeped and Maggie hurried to get out of its way. The markets ran in cycles, and with the fourth cycle about to begin, there was a lot of coming and going.

"You've been here before," Rico said, "where do we go? Where's the slave market?"

Maggie shook her head doubtfully. "Sorry, Rico, Nexus has changed. It's bigger and more complicated than when I was here. Maybe we should ask a remote."

"And maybe we shouldn't," Rico replied with a frown. "Call me paranoid, but the less we tell ol' binary brain the better I'll feel. Come on."

Maggie followed Rico back in the direction they'd come from and over to a vending stand. The electronic reader board said, "Robo guides, by the minute, hour, or day. Fully guided sex tours, market information, ship arrivals . . . "

The vendor was a birdlike Finthian, with saucerlike eyes and a translator hung around its neck. It looked this way and that with a nervous sort of twitch.

"Hello, gentle beings, step right up and get your robo guide. These are the best, the brightest, the . . . "

"Cut the crap and give me one," Rico interrupted.

The Finthian looked disappointed but did as Rico asked.

Maggie saw credits change hands and watched a tiny robo guide scamper up Rico's arm to perch on his shoulder.

The machine was globular in shape, had three spindly legs,

and a single sensor that stuck up periscope fashion above its body. There was a tiny whine like that of a mosquito when the sensor moved.

"Hello," the robot chirped, "I am robo guide thirty-two. My main purpose is to provide you with navigational assistance within the confines of the Nexus habitat. However, my programming includes a wealth of incidental information and commercial messages that I will be happy to share upon request. Where would you like to go?"

"The slave market," Rico replied, "and pronto."

"You are in luck," the robot replied cheerfully. "Cycle four will start soon. Proceed down the hall to lift tube B, go up two decks, and exit to the right."

Rico and Maggie followed the robo guide's direction, and were soon among a crowd of sentients walking, gliding, hopping, and sliding into a circular room.

The programmable seats could accommodate 87.6 percent of known sentient species and were mounted on an incline so that everyone had a good view.

Spotlights washed back and forth across the pit, as if it were a stage and a play were about to begin. But this was no play. This was real. Maggie lowered her hover box next to Rico's seat and waited for the auction to begin.

It didn't take long. For some reason Maggie expected a live auctioneer, a human perhaps, all dressed up like the ringmaster at a circus.

But like most employers, Nexus hired in its own image, and the master of ceremonies was a machine.

A flying machine, that looked like a ball of pulsating energy and arrived with a blare of trumpets. It buzzed as it flew, skimming the crowd, coming within a foot of Maggie's head.

Then with a dramatic display of aerobatics, and the strobe of carefully placed lasers, the machine came to a sudden stop. The robot hung over the pit like a miniature sun and its voice came from everywhere at once.

It came as no surprise to Maggie that this, like most other things on the habitat, was another manifestation of Nexus.

"Greetings, I am Nexus. Welcome to slave cycle four. Being a machine myself, I believe that machines have an important place in the universe . . . but I value natural sentience as well.

"In fact, from a machine's point of view, you sentients are a good buy. You are reasonably intelligent, work hard when properly motivated, and are always eager to replicate yourselves. That's why I own a few sentients myself."

There was laughter from the humans, and a variety of noises from the other sentients, which might have been anything from an amused chuckle to a cry of outrage. Maggie assumed the former.

"Now," the MC said, "let's get down to business. As usual, cycle four will center around oxygen breathers so if you're looking for something more exotic, try cycle five or six.

"So, let's get things started with a nice group of Tillarians."

As the MC spoke six proud-looking Tillarian males were herded into the center of the slave pit. They stood back-to-back, eyes scanning the audience, as if daring the crowd to attack.

They were completely naked, and, with the exception of the bony ridge that bisected their skulls, very humanoid.

Or, Maggie thought to herself, we are quite Tillaroid, depending on your point of view.

In any case the Tillarians would be quite useful on any Earth-normal planet, and were soon sold to a Zord wholesaler, who would parcel them out to a network of retail traders.

During the transaction the robo guide would occasionally chirrup potentially useful information into Rico's ear, like the average price for Tillarian slaves over the last thousand cycles, and the minimum annual cost for maintenance.

And so it went, group after group, race after race until Maggie felt numb inside. Maybe that's how it works, she reflected. If you see something long enough, no matter how horrible it is, the thing becomes commonplace. Bit by bit your emotions grow less intense until eventually you feel nothing at all.

It was Rico who brought her back to the present. "Maggie! Look! Those boys! Aren't they some of ours?"

Maggie looked in the direction of Rico's pointing finger, and sure enough, there was a group of ragged-looking boys standing in the center of the pit. Here and there you could see brothers, or best friends, standing side by side, hoping that some sort of miracle would keep them together.

Outside of Molly McCade, and a few others, Maggie knew hardly any of Alice's children. She spent very little time on the planet's surface. But the expression of joy on Rico's face was all the confirmation she needed.

"I think you're right, Rico . . . what now?"

Rico held a finger to his lips. "Let's listen."

"So," the MC continued, buzzing the perimeter of the slave pit, "here's lot forty-one, a group of twenty-three juvenile humans, recently taken off some slush ball along the rim. They are ice-world acclimated, in good health, and a bargain at ten thousand credits apiece. Do I have a bid?"

Bidding began, and because it was done using the key pad built into each chair, it was impossible to see *who* was taking part.

The Nexus MC provided a running commentary on how much was being bid, but that was beside the point at the moment, and Rico tuned it out.

He turned toward the robo guide on his shoulder. "Can ya tell who's bidding?"

"Of course," the robot replied cheerfully, "it's on freq four. There were five or six bidders a moment ago, but it's down to a couple now, and they're going at it hot and heavy.

"One group is on your right, two rows back, and six seats over. Zords, I think, although it's hard to see with the crummy two-credit vid pickup they gave me.

"The others are over there, on the far side of the pit, the Lakorian in light body armor."

Rico resisted the impulse to look at the Zords but could see the Lakorian without difficulty. He was nothing special, a middle-aged male, dressed in well-worn armor.

Rico spoke from the side of his mouth. "How 'bout the seller? Does Nexus own the boys . . . or is it someone else?"

The robot was silent for a moment as it sorted through a variety of electronic signals. "No, Nexus doesn't own them, and yes, the owners are here. In seats G5, G6, G7, G8, G9, and G10 to be exact."

It took Rico a moment to locate them off to his left, four men and two women, all dressed in ship suits and heavily armed.

Maggie was getting concerned, things were moving quickly, and she didn't understand what Rico was up to. "Rico . . . "

"I have fourteen thousand . . . do I hear fourteen five? Going once, going twice . . . "

Rico ignored Maggie as his stubby fingers danced over the

chair's key pad. "Not now, Maggie . . . it's time ta buy the boys."

"But, Rico . . . we don't have any money!"

"Wait a minute, gentle beings," the MC said with calculated enthusiasm, "we have another bid. I have fifteen, do I hear fifteen five? No? Going once, going twice, gone to bid number C-487912!

"Now our next lot consists . . . "

A bored-looking Cellite, with muscles on his muscles, herded the boys out of sight.

"Rico . . . " Maggie started, but stopped when she saw his fingers still moving over the key pad. A minute passed while queries appeared on a tiny screen and Rico tapped in the answers. Then he punched one last button and gave a sigh of relief. "Got 'em."

"But how?" Maggie asked, completely mystified.

"Easy," Rico replied, "I borrowed three hundred and forty-five thousand credits from Nexus, agreed ta pay ten percent interest compounded every thirty-six cycles, and used the boys, plus *Void Runner*, as collateral."

"But that doesn't solve anything. We still have to pay off the loan."

"Right," Rico said patiently. "But it *does* keep the boys here on Nexus. Got it?"

Maggie not only got it, her respect for Rico went up a notch as well. "So what now?"

"So now we follow them," Rico said grimly, nodding toward the group of humans now getting up to leave. "I want a word with that bunch."

A whole cacophony of alarm bells went off in Maggie's mind. "I don't know if that's such a good idea, Rico. Let's find Sam, tell him about the boys, and come back later."

Rico got to his feet. "Sam already knows about the boys, he authorized the lien on *Void Runner*.

"But that's a good idea," Rico said distantly, "you give Sam a hand, and I'll be along after a while."

Something about the way Rico said it, and the look in his eyes, scared Maggie. So she whirred along behind, wishing she could stop him, knowing she couldn't. Deep down Maggie knew this was something personal. Rico would never admit but this had something to do with Vanessa.

The six humans left the venue, laughing and joking, happy with the profit they'd made. Even after the ten percent that went to Nexus, and another ten for Pong, they were still doing very well indeed. Now it was time for a little celebration.

Rico and Maggie followed the pirates down one level and into a recreational zone. There were all sorts of drug dens, sex shops, bars, and restaurants. The pirates turned into the first bar they came to.

Rico followed with Maggie trailing along right behind.

Rico waited until the pirates had seated themselves at a table, selected a booth nearby, and sat down to wait. Maggie did likewise.

The pirates made fun of the blast-burned woman who took their order, used their combat knives to play tic tac toe on the tabletop, and downed their first round of drinks in five seconds flat.

That's when Rico stood up, removed the robo guide from his shoulder, and set it on the tabletop. It scuttled away.

Then Rico walked over to the pirate's table, produced a big smile, and said "Hi."

Most of the pirates snickered, but one replied. He had long lank hair parted in the middle, carefully plucked eyebrows, and a once-broken nose.

"Hi? Don't you mean 'Hi, sir'? That *is* what you meant, right, rimmer?"

Rico nodded. "Yes, sir, that's exactly what I meant, sir."

"Good," the man answered. "Now tell me, rimmer, what the hell do you want?"

"Just a little information, sir. Someone attacked a planet called Alice a while ago, and I wondered if you were there."

Maggie swallowed hard and moved away from the booth. The bar was completely silent. The tension was so thick you could cut it with a laser.

The pirate's eyes narrowed. "Oh, you did, huh? Why's that, rimmer? You from Alice by any chance?"

Rico smiled slowly. "Why yes, sir, I have that honor. Now I'd appreciate an answer."

A woman spoke this time. She had hard eyes, a dope stick hanging from the corner of her mouth, and a whippet-thin body.

"Yeah, rimmer, we were there, the dirties put up quite a

fight, but we waxed 'em good. How'd we miss something as big and ugly as you?"

It was the last thing she ever said. Maggie had never seen anything so fast. One moment Rico was standing there, arms hanging loosely by his sides, and the next there was a blaster in his hand.

The first bolt of energy took the woman right between the eyes. She fell over backward.

The next hit the man sitting beside her in the center of his chest, punched a hole through the back of his chair, and turned a neuro-game into a collection of fused circuit boards.

The air felt like quicksand as Maggie slapped the right side of her hover box, heard the panel pop open, and felt the spring-loaded blaster jump into her hand. As the weapon started upward Maggie wondered if it would arrive in time.

Meanwhile, the second woman shouted something incoherent as she put a bolt of blue energy through Rico's shoulder, and died a fraction of a second later.

One of the men stood and brought a blaster into line with Rico's chest.

Maggie fired. Her bolt took the man's hand off at the wrist. It made an audible thump as it hit the deck.

The man screamed and died as Rico put a bolt through his head.

Maggie fired again, saw a man try to cover the hole in his throat, and felt herself fall as raw energy sliced through her hover box.

She didn't see the last man die from her vantage point on the floor, but she heard the scream of energy bolts and saw Rico's boots appear in front of her face.

A second later his face was visible too, full of concern, asking how she was. Maggie saw a wisp of smoke drift away from the hole in Rico's shoulder.

She didn't get to answer, because a bunch of blaster-toting remotes picked that particular moment to show up, but Maggie knew what she wanted to say.

She wanted to say that it felt good to have friends.

Fourteen

THERE WAS AN observatory tucked away far above the ship's bridge, a tiny place where the navigator could get a star fix in an emergency, and the chief engineer could visually inspect thirty percent of the ship's hull. The observatory was hardly ever used and had become Molly's secret hideaway.

At the moment there was nothing to see since the ship was in hyperspace. Still, it was comforting to have a space of her own, where she could think and, if necessary, cry.

She sat on the circular bench, arms around her knees, and stared at the opposite bulkhead.

The headband was tight around her forehead, a constant reminder of Pong and what he could do to her.

The security officer had been a small man, with a shaved head and a walrus-style mustache. As he pulled the loyalty-band around Molly's head and locked it in place, he described how it would work.

"Most o' the time it ain't nuthin', just a headband like ya might wear to keep the hair outta your eyes. But ya try to take it off, or do somethun' the Pong don't like, and blamo! You're history.

"Yasee it's full o' OS-3, carefully shaped ta explode inward, liftin' the top of *your* head off, but keepin' everyone else neat and tidy! It all works off that ring on his right pinky."

The security officer thought he was doing Molly a favor, warning her so she wouldn't mess around with the band and get herself killed, but his lecture had given her regular nightmares.

Every time Molly went to sleep she had the same recurring dream.

It began as she stepped off a shuttle. She could see Mommy and Daddy on the far side of the landing pad. They were alive! Then she ran across the pad, shouting her happiness, waiting to feel their arms around her.

And then, when she was only feet away, something horrible would happen. She would see the bands around their heads, hear Pong laughing, and wake up crying.

It was horrible and caused her to stay awake as long as she could.

But if the headband was terrifying, it conferred benefits too. Molly was allowed to go anywhere she wanted. By order of Pong himself she was accorded the respect shown a junior officer.

She thought it was a joke at first, a strange way to tease her, but now she knew it was real.

On three different occasions she'd given orders and they'd been obeyed. It had been a thrill at first, to suddenly have power, but that feeling quickly disappeared. Now the power troubled her . . . and she didn't know what to do.

Her first impulse was to help the others, but thanks to their already improved circumstances, there wasn't much she could do.

Still, she did what she could, and was able to get them some nicer clothes and holo cubes.

The girls seemed to appreciate Molly's efforts at first, until Lia told them she was a spy, and they turned against her. Now they wouldn't even talk to her.

And that had led to a strange and disturbing encounter. During each twenty-six-hour cycle it was Pong's wish that she spend two hours with him.

Molly didn't see the point of this, because he spent most of the time working and rarely even spoke to her. But her presence seemed to give him pleasure, and Molly had no choice in the matter, so that's how it was.

This particular cycle Pong decided to inspect the ship, an activity he usually left to others, but sometimes did himself.

So with Molly at his side, and the Melcetian mind slug

riding his shoulder, Pong started in the bow and worked his way toward the stern.

Most of the inspection was a long succession of worried-looking faces, boring conversation, and trips into odd nooks and crannies.

Molly spent most of the time eyeing the signet ring on Pong's little finger. The ring that gave him the power of life and death over her.

But then something strange happened. They were walking down one of the ship's main corridors when they encountered Lia. She was on hands and knees, polishing the long metal strip that ran along the point where bulkhead met deck. There was no one else in sight.

Later, Molly would wonder *how* Lia came to be in that particular place at that particular time, and *why* Pong would know her name. But it seemed natural at the time and she accepted it.

Pong stopped. Lia looked frightened and polished twice as fast as she had before.

"So," Pong said, "this is Lia."

Molly looked from Lia to Pong. What was he doing? Why the sudden interest in Lia? Did it have anything to do with her?

"Correct me if I'm wrong, child," Pong said thoughtfully, "but Lia's the one who turned you in. Not only that, she did so without any knowledge of what the consequences might be. For all Lia knew, I might torture you or have you killed."

Molly struggled for an answer. Pong *knew* Lia had ratted on her, so why ask the question? And given the fact that Lia *had* acted without any thought for the possible consequences, why protect her? Emotions surged. Come to think of it, Lia was still doing everything she could to isolate Molly and make her life miserable.

Still, to confirm Lia's guilt seemed disloyal somehow so Molly said nothing.

Pong nodded, as if he understood exactly what had passed through Molly's mind.

"Loyalty. A fine quality when deserved. But ask yourself the following question. Does Lia deserve your loyalty? What would *she* say if your positions were reversed?"

Molly had a pretty good idea what the answer to that was. Lia would condemn her without a second's thought.

Lia knew too, and had forgotten to work, staring upward in abject terror. Her eyes pleaded for mercy.

"Right," Pong said as if Molly had spoken. "She would betray you in a second. Not just now, but later too if she gets the chance. She's jealous of you, and wants to dominate the other girls.

"So, here's the problem. Should you forgive her? Knowing that she'll betray you if given the chance? Or kill her, and remove the threat?"

Lia made a mewing noise and started to back away.

Molly felt resentment bubble up from deep inside her, resentment at what Lia had done, *would do* if she got the chance.

Molly's emotions demanded one thing, and her mind another. Her mind won. "No, killing Lia would be wrong."

Pong nodded agreeably. "I understand, and might agree if you were home, dealing with childish squabbles.

"But remember, child, you aren't home anymore. It's unlikely that you'll ever see your mother and father again. I know what that's like . . . I too lost my parents at an early age.

"So the decision is up to you. What do you want of life? What it gives you, or what you can take? Will you be victim or victor? The choice is yours. Just say the word, and Lia will die."

And with that Pong had continued on his way, running a finger along a piece of conduit looking for dust, whistling through his teeth.

Molly had followed, looking backward over her shoulder at a terrified Lia, not knowing what to do or say.

And now Molly felt horrible, because she knew that for one brief moment, Lia had been very close to death.

Fifteen

McCade leaned back, left one foot on the deck, and placed the other on the bulkhead behind him. Phil stood a few feet away tapping numbers into his oversize wrist comp.

Four major passageways spilled people and machines into the intersection in front of them. Some paused for a second, looked around, and resumed their journeys. Others knew where they wanted to go, and worked their way through traffic with the determination of fish swimming upstream.

McCade found half a smoked cigar in his breast pocket, stuck it into the corner of his mouth, and puffed it into life.

The bounty hunter had mixed emotions. On the one hand he was glad that Rico had found the boys, but there was no sign of the missing girls, or of Molly. He couldn't help feeling disappointed.

Nexus wouldn't allow them to speak with the boys until they were paid for, but McCade figured they'd been on an entirely different ship, and hadn't seen the girls since the raid.

Well, there was nothing he could do except free the boys as quickly as possible and resume the search for Molly.

McCade removed the cigar, flicked some ash toward the deck, and stuck it back in his mouth. "So what's the tab?"

Phil punched a few more keys, gave a low whistle, and looked up. "Well, what with the three hundred and forty-five that Rico borrowed to pay for the boys, damage to the bar, medical treatment, interest, and a whole bunch of service charges that Nexus tacked on, we're looking at a grand total of five hundred and thirty-six thousand credits. Not counting the money we're spending now."

"A substantial piece of change," McCade said, eyeing the crowd.

Phil nodded. "Yeah, *real* substantial. Do you think we can pull it off?

"Sure," McCade answered, sounding more confident than he felt.

"There must be a couple hundred sentients wandering around this place with a price on their heads. All we have to do is round 'em up, sell their bounties at a ten-percent discount, and let some enterprising soul haul 'em in. What could be more simple?"

"Training rath snakes to make coffee," Phil growled in reply.

The variant didn't mean it. The idea made sense. Well, not sense exactly, but it might work anyhow.

The alternative wasn't that great either. Sell *Void Runner*, use the proceeds to pay off their debts, and walk home.

"So," McCade said. "Is the holding tank ready?"

"Ready and staffed," Phil replied. "I hired some rather nasty Zords to act as guards."

Smoke dribbled from the corner of McCade's mouth. "Good. How 'bout the scanner?"

"Up and running," Phil assured him. "Both it and the computer are hidden behind the clothes racks across the way."

There was a vendor on the other side of the hall. He sold clothes, accessories, and a scattering of cheap jewelry.

McCade looked, and sure enough, he could just barely see a lens peeking between a couple of leather jackets. The operator was a fourteen-year-old pickpocket. He'd seen Phil, assumed the variant was a rim rube, and tried to bump and dip him. A serious mistake for which he was now paying.

"And the escorts?"

"Some mercenaries on leave. They're about fifty yards up corridor. We call, and they come running."

"Okay," McCade said, pushing himself away from the wall. "It's time to open up shop." He dropped the cigar and crushed it under his boot.

Phil pulled the tiny boom mic a little closer to his mouth and whispered something.

On the other side of the hall the pickpocket flipped a series of switches and settled down to wait.

The scanner panned back and forth as it fed images into the computer. The computer took the images, compared them to those McCade had obtained from a public terminal, and notified the boy of a match. At that point the pickpocket would alert his employers and they'd do the rest.

The pickpocket had instructions to lay low after that.

His name was Dawk. He had blond hair, bright blue eyes, and a snub nose.

Dawk was resentful at first, but when Phil explained how the scam would reduce competition and increase profits, the boy became downright enthusiastic. Now he paid close attention as the scanner panned the crowd and waited for a match. It came with surprising speed.

Dawk heard a soft buzz from his earpiece. His heart thumped with excitement. The computer screen split itself into one, two, three equal sections.

Heads filled all three sections, rotated 360 degrees, and squeeze zoomed into the upper right-hand corner. Data flooded the now empty space below. Name, description, crimes, weapons, it was all there.

Dawk fingered a switch. "Dawk here. I've got three positives coming down corridor three. Here's a peek." The pickpocket pushed a button.

McCade looked at his wrist term and swore. Why so many? Why not two, or one? Bad luck, that's why. Well, beggars can't be choosers.

McCade looked up, spotted the three of them right away, and wished he hadn't. They were big, *real* big, and looked very much alike.

McCade glanced down at his wrist term. Looked, hell, they were triplets! And wanted for everything from spitting on the sidewalk to cold-blooded murder!

He looked back up. Each of the triplets was seven feet tall, had a shaved head, and a bushy black beard. All were dressed in matching leather outfits and carried identical weapons. *Lots* of weapons, including blasters, force blades, and Lord knew what else.

Phil nudged McCade's arm. "It's now or never."

McCade wanted to say "never," but the triplets were worth

thirty thousand each, plus an extra ten if someone produced the matched set.

"Okay, Phil. Remember to cheat."

Phil grinned wickedly. "You can count on me!"

The two men sidled out into the intersection just as the triplets arrived and began to push their way through the crowd.

McCade went left, and Phil went right.

Then, just as the fugitives passed to the inside, both men turned and sapped the outer triplets from behind. The saps were little more than leather sacks filled with hundreds of tiny ball bearings. They worked extremely well. Both fugitives slumped to the deck.

Stunners had been the other option, but with so many sentients around it would be easy to miss and hit the wrong individual. The same went for blasters only more so.

McCade was still congratulating himself on how well things were going when the third triplet hit him on the side of the head with a ham-sized fist.

This time McCade was the one who hit the deck with a thump, and lay there, wondering what it would feel like when triplet number three jumped on his chest.

Fortunately Phil chose that moment to tap the giant on the shoulder. "Excuse me."

The triplet turned. "Huh?"

That's when Phil delivered a powerful uppercut. It started near the deck, accelerated upward, and hit the man's jaw with a solid thud.

Much to Phil's amazement, the triplet shook his head and moved in for the kill. He was surprisingly fast and had huge hairy hands around Phil's neck in nothing flat.

Phil brought both of his massive forearms up, broke the hold, and kneed the giant in the groin. The man gave a gasp of pain, doubled over, and fell as McCade hit him with a sap.

McCade held his blaster on the triplets while Phil called the mercenaries. They arrived a few seconds later, placed the still groggy giants in triple restraints, and hauled them off to Phil's makeshift holding tank.

With the show over the now-substantial crowd had started to move again. Many were looking at the two bounty hunters and talking among themselves.

McCade knew that word would spread, and knew that fugitives would get harder and harder to find. But that would take time. Five-hundred and thirty-six thousand credits' worth if things went as planned.

Of even more concern however was the fact that three or four remotes had witnessed the incident and relayed what they'd seen to the central processing unit. What did Nexus think of the situation? Did it care?

There was no way to tell, but McCade planned to run the trap as long as he could.

A full hour passed before the computer produced another positive match and notified Dawk. It was a single fugitive this time and not much of a catch.

Her name was Lorina Dep-Smith. She was about two hundred pounds overweight, surrendered with nothing more violent than a loud belch, and swore a blue streak when she understood the situation.

According to the computer Dep-Smith had embezzled some money from a New Britain-based shipping line, and, judging from the paltry five-thousand-credit reward on her head, hadn't escaped with very much.

Still, every credit counts, and Dep-Smith was led away to join the triplets in holding. McCade wondered how the four of them would get along.

The next six hours were quite productive. No one had ever tried bounty hunting on this scale before, and because of the habitat's lawless reputation, there were plenty of fugitives.

They nabbed a twenty-thousand-credit bank robber, a fifty-thousand-credit drug smuggler, a pair of thirty-six-thousand-credit organ runners, and four petty thieves worth seventy thousand total.

Fortunately the triplets were atypical, and with the exception of a minor scuffle or two, all of them surrendered without a fight. The trap was so unexpected that most of the fugitives didn't understand what was going on until it was too late.

Then, just when it seemed as if things couldn't get any better, along came a cyborg with a suitcase full of cash.

The borg was wanted for fraud, and had a paltry thousand-credit price on his head. But the suitcase contained almost a million in cash, and in accordance with Imperial law, the bounty hunters were entitled to a ten-percent recovery fee.

The saps proved completely ineffective on the cyborg's metal brain case but a flying tackle did the trick.

In retrospect the trap had worked better than McCade's wildest dreams, and according to Phil's math, they were only a hundred and eighteen thousand credits short of their goal.

About forty-five minutes passed before the next score came along. It was a big one this time, a psychopath named Hassan, who'd demonstrated his dislike for the elders of his church by blowing them up.

The Empire was offering forty thousand for Hassan dead or alive, and that plus the fifty that had been raised by the membership of the church brought his total value up to a nice round ninety thousand.

There was something about Hassan, something about the twitchy way he moved, that told McCade the man wouldn't surrender easily.

Hassan had a slender build. He was dressed in a high-collared cloak with matching skintight trousers and knee-high boots. While there weren't any weapons in plain sight there could be an entire arsenal concealed under the man's cloak.

McCade nodded to Phil and they moved out into the traffic. Phil circled around behind Hassan while McCade waited in front. A muscle twitched in his left cheek.

When the fugitive was about fifteen feet away, McCade pulled his blaster, gave startled pedestrians a moment to scurry out of the way, and yelled, "Hassan! Hold it right there!"

Hassan didn't even flinch. He pointed a finger at McCade. Something warm brushed past the bounty hunter's left cheek and hit a maintenance bot somewhere behind him. It blew up with a brilliant flash of light.

Hassan had some sort of energy weapon hidden up his sleeve! Whatever the weapon was, it was unusually powerful, and must use a lot of energy. Maybe it would run out soon.

Still, one more shot like the last, and McCade would be little more than a scorch mark on the deck.

Phil tried to club Hassan from behind, but was blocked by a hysterical merchant who threw himself at the variant's feet and screamed, "Save me! Save me!"

The blaster was lighter than the slug gun McCade usually carried and generated no recoil.

Blue light sliced down and across the front of Hassan's cloak. Nothing! The son-of-a-bitch was wearing armor!

Hassan grinned. God protects her own. Now the bounty hunter would pay the price for his impudence. Idolators must die!

Hassan moved his arm a hair to the left and aligned the custom-designed energy tube with McCade's chest. The trigger was a small black ball that Hassan held in the palm of his right hand. His brain told his hand to squeeze the ball but it was too late.

Hassan blew up. Although *he* was armored, his power supply *wasn't*, and McCade hit it. The result was loud and messy.

Disentangling himself from the sobbing merchant, Phil came over to join McCade, still flicking little bits of Hassan off his kilt. "Nice going, Sam. How do we get a reward with nothing to turn in?"

McCade slid the blaster into its holster. He'd been lucky, *damned* lucky, and his hands were shaking. He tried to smile.

"The Empire is quite liberal about such matters, Phil. They'll accept retinas, a full set of teeth, or fingers with prints attached. See what you can find.

"In the meantime I'll help Dawk tear the equipment down. We've pushed our luck far enough."

Phil checked to make sure McCade was serious, saw that he was, and walked away mumbling to himself.

Twenty minutes later a crew of maintenance bots had just finished cleaning up the mess, Phil had one of Hassan's hands in a stasis bag, and McCade was helping Dawk to dismantle the scanner system. He didn't hear the remote approach.

"You will accompany me now."

McCade turned. "Excuse me?"

The remote's face was completely devoid of expression as always. There were six remotes altogether, all armed, all equally featureless.

"You will accompany me now. I wish to speak with you."

McCade knew the "I" was Nexus, and that there was no point in resistance since the AI was all powerful. The computer wanted to talk and, for reasons known only to it, didn't wish to use a remote for that purpose.

There was little doubt as to what Nexus sought to discuss. When Hassan blew up, things had come perilously close to violating law number one, "Don't harm Nexus."

Chances were they'd get a "cease and desist" order. Okay,

McCade could live with that, as long as the machine didn't try to block them altogether.

McCade forced a smile and wondered if nonverbal communication counted for anything with Nexus.

"Of course. We'll be right there."

McCade turned. "Dawk, drop Hassan's hand off at our holding tank, and take the computer gear to lock seventy-seven. Ask for Rico or Maggie. Drop by the tank later on. There'll be something extra in your pay."

Dawk looked surprised. "Pay? You mean I get paid?"

McCade looked at Phil but the variant was busy examining his durasteel claws. "Yeah," McCade answered, "no matter what my furry friend may have told you, *all* of our employees get paid. I'll see you later."

Dawk grinned and busied himself with the electronic gear.

McCade turned to the remote. "Okay, we're all yours. Lead the way."

With three of the silvery remotes walking ahead, and three behind, the crowd seemed to melt away. No one wanted to mess with Nexus or get too close to the idiots who already had.

The procession wound its way through a labyrinth of corridors and into a lift tube marked, RESTRICTED—NEXUS ONLY. They stepped out into a large open space a few seconds later.

The first impression was of lights, thousands of them, covering the walls and dome-shaped ceiling, denser than any galaxy, but starlike nonetheless. They seemed to ripple outward in overlapping circles, like raindrops hitting the surface of a pond.

Suddenly McCade realized that all six of the remotes had retreated to wall niches. They looked like statues.

The deck, which had been a glossy black, was suddenly transformed into a vid screen. Video of the intersection appeared. A variety of shots followed, each covering a different angle, and representing what one remote had seen.

McCade and Phil watched as the triplets, Dep-Smith, and Hassan fell into the trap.

As the video disappeared the asexual voice came from everywhere and nowhere at once. "Explain."

McCade considered a number of lies but couldn't be sure that any of them would hold up. Nexus was no fool and had innumerable sources of information. No, it seemed better to tell the truth, and hope for the best.

McCade cleared his throat. "A few weeks ago the planet Alice was attacked by pirates. A number of our children were taken during the raid. My companions and I were sent to find the children and return them to Alice. During slave cycle four, we discovered that twenty-three of our children were for sale, and bought them using funds borrowed from you.

"We are presently engaged in an effort to capture individuals wanted by the Imperial government. We plan to sell their bounties at a discount, use the money to pay off our loans, and take the children home."

McCade turned to Phil. "Did I leave anything out?"

The variant shook his head.

Nexus was silent for a moment, as if thinking, or dealing with something or someone else. Then it spoke. "I disagree with your companion. There is something that you neglected to mention. One of the missing children is your daughter."

McCade looked up at the multitude of twinkling lights and wished the computer had a face. His heart beat like a trip-hammer. How did Nexus know about Molly? Was she here? Was this the end of his search? McCade fought to keep his voice under control.

"That's true. Do you know where she is?"

The answer was emotionless. Machinelike. "No, I do not. However, I do have a personal message for you."

"You have a what?"

Once again the deck transformed itself into a huge video screen. The man who appeared there had blond hair, blue eyes, and was known to billions of sentients across hundreds of systems. Loved by many, hated by some, the face belonged to the Emperor himself.

A man who might still be meditating high in the mountains of the Wind World, learning from the mystics who called themselves Walkers of the Way, if it weren't for Sam McCade.

Yes, Alexander owed McCade a debt of gratitude, but more than that considered the bounty hunter his friend.

And because McCade was untempted by the Emperor's power, uninterested in his wealth, and unimpressed by his rank, he was that rarest of all things, a man Alexander could trust.

The Emperor smiled. "Hello, Sam. I wish this greeting came

at a better time. I'm sorry about the raid, worried about Molly, and well aware that it was your service to *me* that put Alice in jeopardy.

"Most people think that I'm all powerful, capable of righting any wrong, but you know better. I'm painfully aware that it is beyond my ability to restore a life, to heal a broken body, or undo the damage done to Alice. Nonetheless I do what I can.

"Descriptions of the children have gone out to every naval base in the Empire, our ships have been alerted to watch out for vessels that belong to Pong, and Swanson-Pierce has his people working on it as well."

A sometimes friend, and sometimes enemy, Swanson-Pierce was none other than *Admiral* Swanson-Pierce, head of Naval Intelligence, and a member of Alexander's personal staff.

"Knowing *you* however," the Emperor continued, "I suspect you are already tackling the problem in your own way, and probably making more progress than we are.

"Still, it never hurts to have a friend in high places, so call on me if there's something I can do. Though not controlled by me, Nexus and I do each other favors from time to time, and it may be willing to help.

"Linnea sends her love. Please let us know when Molly is safe and sound." The picture faded to black.

Silence descended. Seconds became minutes. It seemed Nexus was thinking, or doing other things, or just didn't care.

Of the three McCade thought the last was most likely. There was plenty of Nexus to go around, and had the machine wished to, it could've held a conversation with them *and* covered everything else as well.

Finally, after a good five minutes had passed, Nexus spoke. It was as if no time had passed whatsoever. "So, Citizen McCade, it seems you have an unexpectedly powerful ally, and that will stand you in good stead.

"You will be interested to know that the imperial message torpedo arrived only hours ago. Were it not for the Emperor's intervention this conversation would have turned in a different direction. Your most recent activities threatened not only my personal well-being, but that of my customers as well, leaving me no choice but to discipline you.

"Fortunately you have captured a sufficient number of fugitives to pay off most of your debt. Given the fact that the

Emperor is willing to pay off the remaining balance, and given the fact that you are no doubt anxious to leave, I will order my staff to place the children in your custody.

"My staff will also take charge of the unauthorized prison that you and your companions have established on C deck. I will dispose of the fugitives as I see fit."

McCade raised an eyebrow. What did Nexus mean by that? Would the computer turn the fugitives in? Or turn them loose to maintain the habitat's lawless reputation? But as long as Nexus released the children he really didn't care.

The computer hadn't asked for agreement but McCade supplied it anyway. "Thank you. That arrangement will be quite satisfactory."

A section of lights rippled toward the top of the dome. "Have a nice visit."

McCade nodded and started for the lift tube. He was almost there when Nexus spoke again.

"Citizen McCade."

"Yes?"

"Before you turn the prisoners over to my staff you might want to interrogate the woman known as Lorina Dep-Smith."

McCade frowned. "Okay . . . but why?"

The computer paused as if for effect. "Because she commands the ship that brought the children to Nexus."

Sixteen

THE YACHT SLOWED. The vessel was a wedge of streamlined metal on the outside, and on the inside it was extremely comfortable.

Everywhere Molly looked she saw muted colors, subdued lighting, and carefully chosen fixtures. There was no way she could know, but this was the *Arrow*, the very ship on which Pong had escaped from her father.

Molly sat beside Mustapha Pong on the side opposite the mind slug. She was thankful, because no matter how much time Molly spent with Pong, the Melcetian still made her nervous.

Molly felt both excitement and guilt. Excitement because she liked doing new things, and guilt because she was doing them with Mustapha Pong, and he'd attacked her planet.

And what about the other girls? True, they weren't suffering, but they weren't happy either, and wouldn't be until they returned to Alice. And what had she done to free them?

Nothing, that's what, not since her attempt to access the navcomp, and the placement of the L-band around her head. Not that the other girls *wanted* any help.

Molly felt a sudden surge of anger. Ever since the incident in the corridor things were even worse than before. Lia still hated her, but now the older girl was afraid as well, and cowered when Molly was around. This had the effect of further distancing Molly from the rest of the girls and left her completely isolated.

Yes, Molly thought to herself. Pong's right about one thing. When people betray you it's stupid to give them another chance. Why should I try and help them? Let them stay with Lia! I'll find my own way out of here and leave them behind.

Pong touched Molly's arm. "Look, child, there it is."

Molly looked out of the viewport. The alien ship was huge, large enough to be mistaken for an asteroid, or an errant moon.

Where human and even Il Ronnian spacecraft looked like what they were, this one looked like a big rock. Sunlight moved steadily across its surface as the alien vessel rotated on its axis.

Surely the ship had weapons emplacements, solar collectors, and all the other hardware common to its kind, but Molly couldn't see them.

Molly had never heard of the 56,827 before. She thought that a number made a strange name for an entire race, but Pong had explained that it was the way the aliens saw themselves, as an aggregate comprised of individual numbers.

The total number, and therefore the name of the race, changed with each birth and death. Not only that, but individual names, and their entire social order, stemmed from numbers as well.

If for example someone was born number 32,105, they would forever be junior to individual 32,104, and senior to 32,106.

And, given a long average life span and extremely low birthrate, their relative social position would remain constant for years at a time. This made for a rigid and rather hierarchal social structure.

Because of this internal rigidity Pong explained, the more ambitious members of the race were encouraged to direct their energies outward, and that explained the ship. The aliens were on the lookout for new commercial opportunities.

When Molly asked where the 56,827 came from, Pong replied that they came from somewhere beyond the rim, beyond the limits of human exploration.

As the shuttle approached, the alien spaceship grew even larger. "Are all of their ships that big?" Molly asked.

Pong looked down at her, then out of the viewport. "No, child, as a matter of fact that's the only ship they have."

Molly looked up to see if Pong was teasing her.

The pirate smiled. "I'm serious. They claim one ship is all

they need. And what's even more surprising is that in spite of the ship's size, it carries only sixteen individuals, and they think it's crowded."

Molly thought about that for a moment. "They must be huge."

Pong laughed. "A logical conclusion, child, but false nonetheless. They are larger than humans, but not by much.

"No, I'm afraid it's more complicated than that. Due to conditions on their native planet the 56,827 are extremely territorial.

"From what they tell me that stems from the ancient need for individual hunting preserves. Vast lands where they could hunt. With the passage of time and the coming of advanced technology, competition has become more commercial and less carnivorous. The result is the same however. Each adult requires a large amount of personal space."

"And that accounts for the size of their ship," Molly finished for him. "They can't stand to be cooped up together."

Pong clapped his hands in approval. "Exactly, child! Correct as usual. Now excuse me while I deal with an incoming message."

Molly couldn't hear the message because it came in via the small plug in Pong's left ear. And due to the fact that the pirate subvocalized his reply, she couldn't hear that either.

Returning her attention to the alien ship, Molly saw she was right. It *was* more mechanical than it appeared. A section of the planetoid's surface had opened to reveal a spacious landing bay. A complicated latticework of laser beams reached out to touch receptors on the shuttle's hull and guide it in.

Fifteen minutes passed while the shuttle touched down inside the otherwise empty hangar, the outer door slid closed, and a breathable atmosphere was pumped into the bay.

Freed from her seat, Molly passed the time in the shuttle's control compartment, asking the pilot questions and playing with the vessel's external cameras.

The pilot, a humanoid-shaped cyborg, didn't like Molly messing around with the controls but was afraid to object. Like the rest of Pong's crew, the cyborg didn't understand her leader's relationship with Molly, and had no desire to test it.

Oblivious to these concerns, Molly activated a vid cam

located halfway down the shuttle's port side, and moved it around using a small joystick. It was fun to track the robots as they scurried hither and yon, fueling the shuttle and getting in each other's way.

Molly turned a knob that caused the vid cam to zoom in and out. As the robots became larger and smaller Molly noticed something strange. Many of the robots were extremely dissimilar. Startlingly so.

Take the matter of locomotion for example. Some of the robots walked, while others hopped, rolled, and crawled. Why so many variations? It was as though the robots had been created by different designers with wildly different ideas of how they should look and function.

As Molly watched the robots she remembered Daddy saying that mechanical artifacts vary tremendously from race to race due to environmental, physical, and cultural differences.

For example, human house bots tend to look humanoid, while their Finthian equivalents have a distinctly birdlike quality. Given that, which one of these machines looked like the 56,827?

Molly looked from robot to robot but still couldn't find many similarities. Of course form follows function where utility bots are concerned . . . so that might explain it.

Mustapha Pong interrupted her thoughts. "What are you thinking?"

Molly pointed at the screen. "The robots look different from each other. Were all of them designed by 56,827?"

Pong was startled. This girl never ceased to amaze him. Without realizing what she'd done, Molly had put her finger on the aliens' greatest secret, and their one weakness.

The truth was that the 56,827 hadn't built *any* of the robots, or the ship either for that matter, and were frightened of more technologically advanced races.

The ship was a good example. Pong knew that the 56,827 had forced another more sophisticated race to build and arm it.

Ah, but there was one thing the aliens did very well indeed, and that was fight. Pound for pound, tooth for tooth, they were among the most vicious carnivores in the known universe.

And even more importantly the 56,827 had the will to win, the absolute ruthlessness it takes to eradicate an entire race, and do so without compunction. That was the quality Pong found absent in so many humans and admired in his secret allies.

But none of this could be shared with Molly so Pong ignored her question and glanced at his wrist term instead.

"Come on, Molly, our host awaits."

Molly slid off the copilot's chair. The Melcetian mind slug quivered and color rippled across its surface.

Molly positioned herself on the opposite side of Pong's body.

"Our host? One of the 56,827?"

The pirate nodded. "Number 47,721 to be exact. You will be one of the few humans privileged to meet a member of the 56,827."

Pong almost added " . . . and survive," but decided not to.

They went alone, just Pong and Molly, down a ramp and into the bay. There was a lock set into the left side of the bay, and from the height of the controls, Molly judged the aliens were at least a foot taller than Phil.

The door whirred open, then closed. Pong whistled tunelessly while they waited. The pirate seemed preoccupied so Molly passed the time counting the number of rivets in a section of bulkhead.

Then the inner hatch slid open and Molly gave a gasp of surprise. Where she should be looking at a utilitarian corridor, or at most a reception area, there were rolling grasslands giving way to a distant forest. And where there should be gray metal, nearly invisible behind duct work, conduit, and pipe, there was a dim lavender sky. Everything looked dark and murky.

Pong smiled at her consternation. "Amazing, isn't it? A clever combination of carefully regulated biosphere and electronic trickery. As you can see the 56,827 are rather fond of their home planet and take a likeness of it wherever they go."

Molly nodded wordlessly and followed as Pong stepped out onto a dirt path and followed it up a slight rise toward a stand of strange-looking trees. Or was it "tree" singular?

Whichever it was had grown in a circle, with hard vertical trunks forming an outer stockade, and rich purple foliage hanging down into the center. They looked dark and foreboding.

They were about ten feet away from the grove when something stepped out from between the tree trunks and turned their way. Molly grabbed Pong's arm. She'd met three or four different types of aliens nose to snout, beak, or whatever, and seen holos of many more.

Over and over Molly's parents had told her that regardless of how strange another race might look to human eyes, regardless of how they sounded or smelled, what mattered was the way they behaved. Were they truthful? Ethical, by their own standards at least? Compassionate? These were the measuring sticks Molly had been taught to use.

But try as she might Molly couldn't suppress the overwhelming fear that burbled up from some primeval well deep inside her. This thing reeked of such raw unrepentant evil that it made her blood run cold.

Number 47,721 stood about seven and a half feet tall. Its head consisted of two distinct parts. A cigar-shaped section with eyes mounted at either end and, set at right angles to that, a pair of lethal-looking jaws. They parted slightly to show rows of teeth. A long rope of salivalike mucus dribbled out.

The alien had narrow shoulders, heavily muscled arms, and ivory, almost-translucent skin. 47,721's torso curved backward slightly, reminding Molly of the Terran insects she'd seen on study tapes, and was balanced on a pair of powerful legs. Each of its feet had three toes, each toe ending in a two-inch claw, each claw razor-sharp.

Pong gave Molly's hand a reassuring squeeze. "Greetings, 47,721. This numberless one comes seeking an audience."

Molly gulped as the alien looked her way. Now she saw that its eyes were huge, multifaceted, and probably much better at collecting light than hers. Molly noticed the translator hung around its neck. It spoke standard like a machine, free of accent, and without intonation. "I hereby grant the audience you seek. Is this one of the juveniles?"

Pong frowned as if hearing an undertone he didn't like. "Yes, this is a juvenile, but not one of those we discussed. This one belongs to me."

Molly looked upward at Pong. Juvenile? Discussed? Belongs to me? What were they talking about anyway?

Mucus drooped down from the alien's jaws. Its voice dropped an octave. "Careful, numberless one. *Nothing* belongs to you save that which the 56,827 grant you. But enough of this.

We have much to discuss. Leave the juvenile here. It will be safe enough as long as it stays near the trees."

Pong turned to Molly. "Stay here, child. 47,721 and I have business to discuss. Do as he says and stay near the trees. I'll be gone for an hour or so."

Molly nodded silently. Much better to stay here alone than go with the alien. It was even worse than Pong's mind slug.

Pong gave her a nervous smile and turned to 47,721. "The numberless one is ready."

The alien made an inarticulate grunting sound and turned toward the path. Moments later alien and human alike had disappeared around the side of a small hill.

Molly just stood there for a moment, staring after them, half hoping that Pong would reappear. When he didn't she walked a few yards away from the trees and sat down in the grass. It smelled good.

It was silent at first. But bit by bit sound returned as tiny insects buzzed around Molly's head and a breeze rustled its way through the grass.

Had the sun been brighter, it would have been enjoyable, sitting there on what seemed like solid ground after countless days aboard ship, feeling the sunlight on her face.

But the strange twilight that surrounded Molly made her shiver instead and wish that she'd brought a cloak.

Still, Molly started to feel bored after a while, and stood up in order to look around.

Surely she could explore the immediate area without running into anything dangerous. Though somewhat dark the countryside was peaceful and quiet.

Molly saw a pile of boulders downhill and to the left. There were holes in them, big round openings that looked perfectly symmetrical and might be fun to crawl through.

Molly made her way down the slight incline and was about fifty feet away from the jumble of boulders when a voice said, "Are you old enough to speak?"

Molly looked around. She saw nothing but gently waving grass, the boulders, and forest beyond. "Yes, I'm old enough. Who are you? Where are you?"

"Right here," the voice said, and a triangular-shaped head appeared followed by a skeletal-looking body. It stood erect, but looked more sauroid than human. It wore a complicated-looking vest with a multitude of pockets. Busy hands fluttered this way and that as if searching for something to do. The creature's leathery skin was the same color as the grass and made it hard to see. "My name is Jareth."

Now Molly remembered 47,721's warning and took a step backward. "I thought I was alone."

The creature snorted softly. "Not very damned likely. This ship is too small. You were headed for the rocks. That's a bad place to go."

"Why?"

"You see the holes?"

"Sure, they look innocent enough."

"Throw something toward one."

Molly bent over, picked up a loose stone, and threw it toward the boulders. Something black flashed out, snatched the rock from midair, and disappeared back into its hole.

Molly swallowed hard and took a couple more steps backward. "What was that?"

"Something bad," the creature said noncommittally.

"You speak standard."

The creature took a few steps forward. It made a sign with its left hand. In the same way that 47,721 seemed evil, this alien felt nice. Molly stood her ground.

"Yes, we runners are good at languages, and I met one of your kind before . . . bigger though and even more frightened. I learned your type of sound talk from him."

Molly thought about that. A grown-up even more scared than she was. It seemed hard to believe. "Where is he now?"

The creature swayed back and forth. "Death came. The you-thing ran. Death found it."

"Death?" Molly looked around. If black things were hiding in the rocks, then what else was lurking around?

"Yes, that is what we call them."

"We?"

"Runners. Those that look as I do."

"So you don't like them?"

Jareth blinked. "Who?"

Molly forced herself to be patient. "Them. Death."

"Not very damned likely," the runner replied. "Would you?"

"Would I what?" Molly asked, grinning when she realized she was doing it too.

"Like death, if it ate you," the alien said.

Something cold and hard tumbled into Molly's stomach. "They eat you?"

Jareth swayed back and forth for a moment before cocking its head to one side. "Yes, that is what we are here for. That, and repairing the ship. We built it, you know."

Suddenly Molly understood or thought she did. The spacecraft was a true biosphere and contained its own ecosystem. An ecosystem in which the 56,827 fed on the runners and used them to maintain the ship as well. "That's horrible!"

"Yes," the alien said calmly, "it is."

There was silence for a moment. Molly broke it. "So death ate the one like me?"

"Yes," Jareth replied. "Only the hard-supporting things were left. Do you want them?"

Molly shuddered. "No, it wouldn't do any good."

"No," the runner echoed, "it wouldn't do any good."

"Molly!"

Molly turned and looked toward the trees. Pong was there, looking in her direction, hands cupped around his mouth. The thing called "death" stood beside him.

Molly turned back but the runner was gone.

Seventeen

McCADE LIT THE latest in a long series of cigars and let his eyes drift along the line.

Phil stood three people back, talking with a down-at-the-heels roid rat, but McCade passed over him. It might or might not pay to have an open friendship. Time would tell.

The line stretched the length of the hall, wound its way down three flights of rickety wooden stairs, and out into the poorly lit street. The vid ads said, "All you can eat and a hundred credits a day." There were plenty of takers.

McCade shifted his weight from one foot to the other and stared at a graffiti-covered wall. Like most of the real estate bordering HiHo's spaceport, this building was waiting for a really heavy-duty lift-off to shake it down.

He was tired. Very tired. Things had moved along rather quickly after the interview with Nexus. The boys were freed, and just as McCade feared, they knew nothing about the girls.

But the stories the boys told about life on a pirate ship made McCade's blood run cold. Had Molly been though the same sort of thing? Was she going through it now? Or was she dead? Some of the boys hadn't made it. Pitiful little bundles ejected out of a utility lock as if they were so much garbage.

Looking at the boys' emaciated and sometimes scarred bodies, McCade saw Molly in his mind's eye.

So as he hugged the boys, and did his best to answer their

questions, McCade was close to tears. Pong had caused all this pain, all this misery, and Pong would pay.

But in order to punish the pirate he'd have to find him and that's where Captain Lorina Dep-Smith came in.

She was reluctant to talk at first, but after five minutes of private conversation with Phil, she became suddenly voluble.

In talking to Dep-Smith it became quickly apparent that she was little more than a hired hand, useful for running errands to places like Nexus, but not privy to Pong's long-range plans.

She did possess one piece of useful information however, something Pong could hardly deny her, and that was her next destination.

After leaving Nexus, Dep-Smith was headed for a planet called HiHo, where she'd load elements of a mercenary army and receive further instructions. She didn't know where the army was headed, or why, but she knew Pong would be in command.

So after giving the matter some thought and discussing it with his crew, McCade came up with what he hoped was a workable plan. Since they didn't have enough money left to send the boys home on a chartered ship, they'd cram them aboard the *Void Runner*. Rico was still recovering from his wound, but was healthy enough to act as pilot, and Maggie would handle everything else.

Meanwhile, McCade and Phil would sign aboard Dep-Smith's ship as replacements for the crew that Rico and Maggie had killed, and work their way to HiHo. Once dirtside the pair would join Pong's newly formed army and look for an opportunity to snatch him. Their plan had a lot of potential flaws, but it was better than nothing.

One of the potential flaws surfaced right away. Though appropriately threatened, and simultaneously bribed, they couldn't trust Dep-Smith further than they could throw an Envo Beast.

Once aboard her ship, and en route to HiHo, they were almost entirely at her mercy. The ship carried a crew of twelve, which meant they were outnumbered six to one if it came to blows, and given Dep-Smith's smoldering resentment, the battle could come at any time.

So, between Dep-Smith's efforts to make sure that they got

all the ship's most unpleasant jobs, and the fact that they were cooped up with ten sociopaths, the two of them got very little sleep. Regardless of the shifts they were assigned, one was awake at all times, blaster in hand, waiting for the attack that never came.

McCade yawned. A wooden door slammed open and a burly man with the look of a professional noncom stepped outside. There were no badges of rank on his brand-new camos and he didn't need any. The man had "sergeant" written all over him. In spite of the fact that they were only five feet away from each other, the noncom yelled "Next!" as if McCade were at the other end of the hall.

Having spent hours waiting to hear that word, McCade wasted little time stepping inside. The door slammed closed behind him. McCade found himself standing in front of a large med scanner. It came close to filling the room.

The sergeant appeared at McCade's elbow. He wore his hair high and tight, had bushy eyebrows, and the beadiest eyes McCade had ever seen.

"Lose the stogie, and listen up. You will take five steps forward, enter the med scanner, and follow its directions. Having done so, you will take six additional steps forward and assume a brace. Major Mike Davison will ask you some questions. You will answer them honestly, completely, and with the respect due an officer. Do you understand?"

McCade dropped the cigar into a spittoon and heard a hiss as it hit the water. "Yeah, Sarge, I understand. Five plus six, and a brace. Major Davison. Straight scoop and no bull."

The sergeant gave a slight nod, as if acknowledging someone he knew, and jerked a thumb toward the scanner. "Good. Hit it."

McCade took five steps forward. The med scanner came to life and closed in around him. It was like standing in a small closet. It was completely dark outside of the single red light located directly over his head.

"Stand completely still."

McCade obeyed the machine's orders and felt a number of artificially warmed pads make contact with his body. The bounty hunter was completely immobilized once they were in place.

A minute passed. Waves of white light rippled up and

down as the machine scanned his body in layers, starting with McCade's skin and working its way through all of his internal organs.

There was a whirring sound as the pads were withdrawn.

"Place your hands in the lighted receptacles."

McCade saw a pair of lighted slots appear in front of him. He did as he was told. His hands slid into a warm jellylike substance that held them firmly in place.

McCade flinched as needles drew blood from both of his index fingers.

"You will feel a pinprick in each index finger," the machine said belatedly, "stand by."

McCade swore softly and withdrew his hands.

The red light went out and the machine parted in front of him. There was a doorway ahead and a rickety old desk just beyond that. A porta comp sat on top of the desk and a man in crisp camos lounged behind it. He looked up at McCade's approach.

Major Davison had black hair, even features, and a neatly trimmed beard. The latter marked him as a merc since anything more than a neatly trimmed stash was forbidden to Imperial officers. Like his noncom, Davison wore brand-new camos.

Remembering the sergeant's instructions McCade took six steps forward, popped to attention, and rapped out his name. Or in this case the name he chose to be known by. "Sir, Blake, Roland, reporting as ordered, sir."

Davison was silent for a moment, looking McCade over, tapping his lips with a silver stylus.

The whole thing took McCade back to his days at the Terran Naval Academy, and his frequent visits to the cadet captain's office. Like then he was careful to keep his eyes focused on a spot one foot over Davison's head.

"So," Major Davison said softly, "a vet. Good. We need experienced people. We've got enough plow boys out there to start an award-winning farm. But experienced at what? Give me your last outfit, slot in the TO, and rank at separation."

"Yes, sir. Imperial navy, sir, special ops, lieutenant commander."

That was false of course, but McCade had known a Roland Blake in his navy days, and he might be a lieutenant commander by now.

Davison's eyebrows shot upward. "Special ops? Lieutenant commander? Explain."

McCade kept his eyes on the dirty green wall. He had a story prepared for this situation, a story that was partly his, and partly that of an officer he'd heard about. "I refused a direct order and was court-martialed, sir."

The officer leaned backward in his chair. "And the order was?"

"We were retrieving a recon team, sir. I was in command. If the indigs spotted the team and engaged, I had orders to lift without them."

"And you ignored those orders."

"Yes, sir."

"And the recon team?"

"Killed in action, sir."

"And the consequences of your decision?"

"Substantial damage to my ship, sir."

"So you were wrong?"

"No, sir."

Davison smiled. "You'd do the same stupid thing all over again?"

"Yes, sir."

Davison nodded thoughtfully. "You interest me, Blake. I like officers who are loyal to their people, but I won't stand for disobedience."

Davison's hand jerked forward and the silver stylus flashed by McCade's head to stick quivering in the wall beyond. The bounty hunter remained motionless.

The merc smiled. "Sorry about that . . . but you'd be surprised how many of the vets who come through that door have lost their nerve." Davison leaned forward slightly.

"I'm going to ask you three questions. If you are what you claim to be, you'll know the answers."

McCade felt his heart beat a little faster. Davison was no dummy. It was clear that he'd been an Imperial officer himself. Would McCade know the answers?

Davison looked thoughtful. "Who commands Naval Intelligence?" '

McCade came close to laughing. Finally, his old enemy and sometimes friend would do him some good! "Admiral Walter Swanson-Pierce."

The merc smiled. "Good. The second question. What is the motto inscribed on the plaque in front of headquarters on Terra?"

McCade's throat felt dry. "Headquarters," meant headquarters for Naval Intelligence, and the fact that he knew the answer was pure luck.

> "The first to see,
> The first to hear,
> The first to know,
> The first to die."

Davison nodded. "Excellent. Here's the last one. Everyone who works special ops is given a life-long code name . . .what is yours?"

McCade swallowed hard. A life-long code name? He'd never heard of that, but NI had lots of secrets, and code names were the sort of nonsense they loved. Still . . . McCade took a chance.

"Sir, I have no life-long code name."

"I'm glad to hear it," Davison said cheerfully, "because as far as I know, no one else in NI does either. At ease, Blake, and welcome to the brigade." Davison got up from behind the desk.

"Sorry I can't give you something equivalent to your last rank, but I do have a slot for a captain, and who knows? If a sufficient number of people die you might move up!"

McCade shook Davison's hand, replied that captain was just fine, and started toward the back door. He stopped and turned around. "One question, sir . . . is there a chance that you'll assign me to something like special ops?"

Davison pulled the stylus from the wall and wiped plaster off the needle-sharp tip. "It's too early to say for sure, but the idea had crossed my mind."

McCade gave mental thanks. The plan was working. An assignment to special ops would keep him out of the trenches, give him more freedom of movement, and a better chance to get at Pong.

"Yes, sir. I'd like that, sir. There was a variant in line behind me. He's big and looks like a Terran bear. Ex-recon if I'm not mistaken, sir. If you decide to create a special ops team, he'd make a good officer or senior noncom."

Davison pushed the button at one end of the stylus and watched the lethal-looking tip vanish inside the barrel.

"Thanks, Captain, I'll keep him in mind. Don't get wasted tonight. We'll be up at 0500 trying to turn this herd of dirt technicians into an army."

McCade grinned. "Yes, sir. Thank you, sir." McCade let himself out as another potential recruit stepped in.

The back door gave access to a hall, where a bored-looking trooper ascertained that McCade had been accepted, and directed him to an office down the hall.

Once in the office a civilian clerk asked McCade dozens of questions and dutifully typed the bounty hunter's lies into his computer.

And then, because McCade was an officer, a lance corporal took him down two floors into a warehouse area. It was filled with row after row of tables, each heaped high with different kinds of gear, each manned by a uniformed trooper. A long line of recruits was shuffling its way through the tables stuffing gear into camo-covered duffel bags.

With the lance corporal leading the way McCade was allowed to practically zip through the line cutting an hour-long process down to fifteen minutes.

The newbies looked resentful and the pros looked bored. Officers took care of each other. Always had and always would.

After that it was a few steps outside to a waiting command car, a bumpy ride to a well-lit camp, and total collapse on a folding camp bed. It felt heavenly. He was asleep in seconds.

The next few days were extremely busy. Everyone worked long hours. The goal of putting the entire brigade together within a month had seemed impossible at first but was actually starting to happen. In spite of Davison's comments to the contrary, most of their recruits were *not* fresh off the farm and had some sort of previous military experience. As a matter of fact most were fairly well trained.

That, plus a masterful job of organization by their XO, a legendary merc named Colonel Mary Surillo, had made the impossible seem increasingly likely.

The brigade was coming together in a huge field outside HiHo's main city of Ness. Thanks to the season, and a stretch of especially good weather, conditions were as good as they could be.

Just as he'd hoped, McCade was given command of a special ops team with Phil as his senior noncom. The team consisted of twenty-six men and women, all with recon or equivalent experience, which was good because McCade had none at all.

Interceptor pilots don't spend much time snooping and pooping dirtside, but like Phil, McCade did belong to Alice's militia and had picked up the basic infantry tactics in the process. So the trick was to hide his lack of knowledge behind a seemingly taciturn exterior and rely on his junior noncoms to structure most of the team's training.

Unfortunately *their* idea of a good time was to run the perimeter of the base yelling "One, two, three, four, I love the Marine Corps," while carrying an unarmed surface-to-air missile on their shoulders. Or like today, running over every hill in sight, dressed in class II combat gear.

Although McCade had considered himself to be in fairly good shape at the onset of training, he now knew differently. His lungs were on fire, his heart was trying to beat its way out of his chest, and it felt as if someone had filled his legs with solid lead. This in spite of the fact that the troops around him looked fresh as a daisy. Still under the pretext of giving *them* a break, McCade ordered a halt.

They stopped just below the summit of a sizable hill. Even McCade knew better than to do that at the top of the hill where they'd be outlined against the sky. The team scattered before Phil could yell, "One grenade would get you all!" and settled in smaller groups.

Trying to hide his desperate need for more oxygen, McCade turned his back on them and used a pair of mini-glasses to scan the valley below.

Seen from a distance the camp consisted of orderly looking streets, each crossing the others at right angles, and lined with identical pop-up shelters. The shelters were inflatable and capable of housing a full platoon of troops.

Spotted here and there were vehicle parks, supply dumps, landing pads, training areas, com trailers, and other less identifiable installations.

And surrounding the whole thing was a computer-designed

perimeter. It took into account the lay of the land, the distance between it and the hills, the areas of deepest shadow, indigenous life forms, the consistency of the soil, and much, much more.

As a result the perimeter seemed to jig and jag in what looked like random patterns but weren't. Every foot of the perimeter was not just guarded, but guarded with the weapons and personnel perfect for that particular spot, making it damned hard to penetrate.

Very professional, very high tech, and very strange. A computer-designed perimeter was something McCade would expect from the Imperial Marines, but not from a mercenary outfit thrown together by a pirate.

McCade moved his glasses across the camp. He saw rows of brand-new armored personnel carriers, hover tanks, missile launchers, supply trucks, and a lot of snappy-looking troopers.

Now that he thought about it, McCade realized that it wasn't just the computer-designed perimeter, *everything* was top-of-the-line brand-new. The camp and everything in it looked like something a child would set up on the floor of their bedroom. It was too damned perfect.

Not only that but most merc outfits were specialists, ground pounders say, or tankers. Hardly any of them had the resources to assemble a miniature army with everything from infantry all the way up to heavy armor.

McCade lowered his glasses. Why? Why had Pong spent so much money on a picture-perfect army? And speaking of Pong, where was the bastard anyway, and when would he take command? Soon. It had to be soon.

McCade found a half-smoked cigar in an outside pocket of his body armor. He sucked it into life and blew smoke out toward the valley below. He thought about Molly and whispered to himself, "Hang in there, honey. I'm getting closer."

Eighteen

MUSTAPHA PONG WAS frustrated. The planet Salazar was the last place in the universe that he wanted to be. Especially given his many business deals, his army forming up on HiHo, and the war brewing on Drang.

Of course that was the problem, the war on Drang, and the question of who would win it. Because the 56,827 wanted a full-scale, human-fought war, and because they wanted Pong to accept a personal role, it was important to stack the deck as much as he could.

Pong looked out the window. It was winter. Snow fell steadily from a lead-gray sky, swirling through the aircar's headlights, to cover the city of Segundo with a cloak of white. It was beautiful.

Pong longed for the cold kiss of a snowflake on his cheek, the bite of frigid air, and the wonderful silence that snow brings with it.

Then, after a brisk walk in the snow, a glorious retreat into the yellow warmth of a good cafe. The kind he stood outside of as a child, peering in through steam-fogged windows, marveling at the wonderful things that people ate.

"And unless you pay attention that's exactly where you will be," the Melcetian reminded him tartly, "on the outside looking in."

"And so what?" Pong asked resentfully. "As long as there's blood in my body, what do you care?"

"My, my," the mind slug replied sarcastically, "touchy aren't we? But let's discuss that. You made a lot of promises to the 56,827. In essence you promised them the entire human race. How will they react should you deliver something less? How much blood will you give me then?"

The Melcetian was right. There was a lot at stake and this was no time to make mistakes. Pong forced himself to concentrate.

Things were heating up on Drang. For years now a combine of large corporations had been gathering power, buying off as many elected representatives as they could, and working to counter the rest with an army of paid lobbyists. Now things were coming to a head and everyone knew it.

The combine officials were determined to fight rather than surrender what was left of the government. So, with hostilities about to begin, and both sides looking for an advantage, Pong found himself in the perfect situation.

In order to satisfy the 56,827's desire to witness a war, he was offering a brand-new, first-rate army at a bargain basement price. Both the world government and the combine wanted his help in the worst way.

And after careful consideration of both alternatives, Pong had decided in favor of the world government. The combine was strong, but according to Pong's intelligence the government was just a little bit stronger, and more likely to win.

In a few short minutes the aircar would land, Pong would meet with representatives from Drang's government, and the deal would be done.

Shortly thereafter he would make the short hop from Salazar to Drang, take command of his brand-new army, and win the ensuing war. Then, with backing from the 56,827, the boy from the slums of Desus II would turn the Empire on its head.

"Ah, such dreams," the mind slug said acidly. "And should they come true, what then? The new Emperor will be a slave to the 56,827, that's what."

"Perhaps," Mustapha Pong thought back, "or perhaps it will be the other way around."

"Ah," the Melcetian said amusedly. "Even more delusions of grandeur."

But even as the alien formulated the thought it also injected a chemical reward into Pong's bloodstream. The mind slug knew that the resulting physical pleasure would reinforce the human's ambition and encourage him to act on it.

Suddenly Pong felt warm and happy. He turned to look at Molly. He'd given her a red ball. She was playing with it and staring out the window.

Molly had been quiet, almost taciturn since their visit to the alien ship, and Pong was sorry that he'd taken her along. 47,721 scared her, that was clear, but there was something more as well. Something she refused to talk about. The ball, made from emergency hull sealer, had been by way of an apology.

Pong turned back to the window. This time there would be nothing more frightening than some government bureaucrats to deal with, and if the meeting went quickly, maybe they could sneak away for a walk through the snow. Maybe they'd stumble across a toy store and Pong could buy Molly something nicer than a ball made of sealant.

Up ahead a fancifully sculpted high-rise towered over all the rest. It was covered with black glass and surrounded by an invisible force field. Just part of the elaborate security measures required by both sides.

The pilot murmured something into her mic and the force field went down long enough for the aircar to slip inside and settle toward the carefully cleared roof.

The aircar touched with a gentle thump and a hatch slid open. A blast of cold air entered and brought a few snowflakes with it. Molly moved her finger under one and urged it to land. The snowflake shied away and fell toward a leather-covered seat. The snow reminded her of Alice.

Pong had to bend over to make his way out of the car. It was a single step to the ground. The fur-lined coat was custom-tailored to accommodate both Pong and the mind slug. The coat felt good as Pong pulled it close around him.

Raz and three of Pong's best security people took up positions around him. Raz wore the top half of some black body armor as a concession to both the situation and the weather. Like the others he was heavily armed.

Pong turned to help Molly out of the aircar. She looked cute in the brown hat and matching fur coat. She smiled briefly and it warmed Pong's heart. He subvocalized.

"Is everything clear?"

"We swept it twice, boss," Raz replied. "It's clean as a whistle."

Pong nodded. "Good. Let's get this over with."

With Molly at his side and guards all around him, Pong marched through a dusting of snow to the roof-top lobby. Doors swished aside and a uniformed security guard snapped to attention. Pong waved a hand in acknowledgment before coming to a halt in front of an open lift tube.

Raz and a tough-looking woman stepped aboard, waved detectors through the air like wizards casting a spell, and nodded their permission.

Pong stepped aboard and turned around. The doors closed and the platform started to descend. The inside walls were alive with vid-art. Color swirled. Abstract shapes appeared, melted, and merged to become something else.

Pong didn't like it. He preferred art that had substance and definition. Something you could count on.

The platform came to a smooth stop and the doors hissed open. The security guards got off, detectors scanning, weapons ready to fire.

A tall man with a long solemn face waited patiently for the security team to complete its inspection. He wore a formal-looking robe with gold trim and a high collar. The man bowed as Pong stepped out of the lift tube.

"Citizen Pong. We are honored. My name is Ethan Mordu, Drang's envoy to Salazar, and host of today's meeting. I apologize for our rather wintry weather."

Pong delivered a small bow. "The honor is mine. As for your weather, I find it quite refreshing."

Mordu smiled and looked down at Molly. "What a pretty little girl. Your daughter perhaps?"

Pong placed a possessive hand on Molly's shoulder. "No, though I'd be proud if she were. Molly, this is Envoy Mordu."

Thanks to her mother's position on the planetary council Molly had been to any number of formal occasions and knew the drill. She gave a slight curtsey, the kind reserved for minor diplomats, and considered throwing herself on Mordu's mercy.

Molly wondered what he'd do. Nothing probably, and that plus the L-band cinched tight around her head cautioned silence.

The two men made small talk as they walked down the wide shiny hall. The walls were paneled with a light-colored native wood. They glistened with wax.

Molly liked the way her heels made a clicking sound on the hardwood floors and tried a couple of surreptitious variations. Nobody seemed to notice.

Then the clicking sounds disappeared as they passed through large double doors and entered a large, well-carpeted room. Two well-dressed women and a man stood to greet them. Except for a circular table, and some comfortable-looking chairs, the room was otherwise empty.

Molly waited for Pong to introduce her, curtseyed in turn, and drifted away as the adults began to talk.

Each wall was completely different. One was hidden by a curtain of rich-looking fabric, another consisted of floor-to-ceiling glass, and the third boasted an enormous holo tank. But it was the last wall that caught and held Molly's attention. It featured a heroic mural.

The painting showed a man, woman, and child in the foreground, and behind them a colony ship that was already being stripped of useful metal. The mural incorporated lots of detail, including some of Salazar's most famous wildlife, and Molly studied it while the security team inspected the room.

Pong shrugged apologetically as Raz looked behind the curtain. "I'm sorry about that, but you know how security people are, once they get going there's no stopping them."

The others nodded sympathetically, well aware that the security people were following Pong's orders, and not in the least insulted. They would've taken similar precautions had positions been reversed.

Once Raz had signaled his satisfaction with security, Pong chose a seat with his back toward the holo wall, and wasted little time getting down to business. Molly took a seat right next to him with the security team fanning out behind.

Under normal circumstances the conversation would have centered around price, but given the fact that Pong was offering his army at cost, the discussion went off in another direction.

Not knowing of Pong's relationship with the 56,827, or their existence for that matter, Drang's officials assumed that his low asking price equated to ulterior motives. Pong was after something, but what was it? The mineral rights presently held by the combine? A role in Drang's government? What?

The officials needed answers to these questions and more before they signed a formal agreement.

Pong understood these concerns and knew how to handle them. The key was to show a little greed, but stop short of scaring them and breaking the deal. In other words it should be a rather enjoyable process that ended up the way Pong wanted it to.

So as the adults plunged into their negotiations Molly eased her way out of the chair next to Pong and drifted away. The guards ignored her.

First Molly looked out the window, wrote her name on the slightly fogged glass, and watched the snow fall. But the snow reminded Molly of home, of Mommy, and made her hurt inside.

She walked across the room, running a finger along the smooth surface of the holo tank, and over to the mural. It was a truly wonderful painting, full of interesting detail, and bright clean color. It absorbed Molly's interest for a full five minutes.

Then, without conscious thought, the ball left Molly's hand and bounced off the floor. The carpet absorbed the sound. She caught it and looked toward the adults. No reaction.

Molly smiled and bounced the ball again, and again, and again, until it hit the toe of her boot and hopped away. Molly followed as the ball headed straight for the drape-covered wall and rolled underneath.

Molly looked at Raz but the bodyguard was looking in another direction. She checked the other security people. Ditto.

As Molly turned back something strange happened. The ball rolled out from under the curtain, and just as it did, Molly saw the tip of a highly polished boot. There was someone behind the curtain!

Curious, Molly waited for the ball to reach her, and bent to pick it up. Now she saw more boots, at least six in all, suggesting three people. Molly straightened up and pretended interest in the ball.

Why would people hide behind the drape? And where had they come from? Molly remembered how Raz had pulled the curtain aside and looked behind it. She'd seen no sign of a door. A secret passage then! Like in the books she'd read.

Something cold fell into Molly's stomach. Suddenly she knew that the people shouldn't be there.

Forcing herself to walk very slowly, Molly ambled toward the table and took her seat next to Pong. Except for a glance in her direction the adults took little notice.

Trying to hide her action Molly tugged on the side of Pong's tunic.

Pong felt Molly pull at his tunic and felt annoyed. Couldn't she see that this was the critical moment? In a minute, maybe two, he'd call for closure. And given the way things were going there was little doubt that he'd get it.

Molly tugged again. Pong forced a smile. "Excuse me. You know how children are. This will only take a moment."

Pong turned toward Molly. His voice was an urgent whisper. "Damn it, child, can't you see this is the wrong time to bother me?"

Molly bit her lip. Was she wrong? Was there some simple explanation for the people behind the curtain? Would Pong know that and be angry with her?

"I dropped my ball," she whispered, "it went behind the curtain. Someone kicked it out to me. When I bent over I saw three pairs of feet."

Pong started to say something irritable, stopped when he realized what Molly had said, and turned slightly pale. He subvocalized and smiled as he turned toward the officials.

"Wouldn't you know it? She needs a bathroom."

Then all sorts of things happened at once. Molly found herself on the floor, Raz and the others sprayed the curtain with stun beams, and a man fell forward bringing the entire drapery down with it. Then two more men toppled over, weapons falling, bodies hitting the floor with a soft thump.

At that point Pong's security team shouted orders, one of the officials pulled a blaster, and fell facedown when Raz stunned her. The woman's head hit the conference table with a loud thud.

A few seconds later and Raz had guards on the secret passage and the room's main entrance. Reinforcements would get a big surprise.

Silence descended on the room. Pong was on his feet. During the confusion a small slug gun had materialized in his hand. The barrel was touching the inside of Ethan Mordu's right ear.

Mordu looked distinctly uncomfortable.

Pong caught Raz's eye, nodded toward Mordu, and removed his gun from the diplomat's ear. Turning toward Molly he bent to help her.

"Are you alright, child? Sorry about throwing you down but there wasn't much time. What you did was very brave."

Molly didn't *feel* brave. She felt cold and shaky inside.

Pong turned his attention to Mordu and the two other officials who sat frozen in their seats, hands on top of the table, faces etched with fear. "So, were the assassins just an option, or were they the entire plan?"

The officials looked at one another but remained silent.

Pong shook his head sadly. "Come, come. No need to be modest. It was a good plan and would've worked except for my little friend here."

Mordu cleared his throat. "The assassins were an option. In case negotiations broke down."

Pong nodded understandingly. "I understand. Quite sensible. Always have a backup."

Pong smiled. "Of course it helps if the backup works."

Raz put a hand to his ear as if hearing something. "The aircar is almost here."

Pong pulled on his coat and looked around the room. "Excellent. You may prepare our exit."

Raz swiveled toward the window and squeezed the trigger on his automatic weapon. The slug thrower made a roar of sound.

Molly held her hands over her ears as the window shattered and fell in a shimmery cascade of glass. She staggered as air rushed out through the opening, taking loose pieces of paper with it. An alarm sounded out in the hall.

Then the aircar appeared and hovered just outside the window. It looked huge and somewhat ominous with its flashing beacons and ugly-looking guns.

"So," Pong yelled over the whine of the aircar's drives, "that brings this meeting to a close. In just a moment Raz will say good-bye as only he can."

Something about the way Pong said it, and the look on his bodyguard's face, told Molly what would happen. The moment Pong climbed aboard the aircar Raz would kill them. She pulled at Pong's coat.

"Don't kill them! What good will it do? We survived. That's the important thing."

Pong frowned, started to say something, and changed his mind. He looked at each official in turn. "This is your lucky day! The child is right. Killing you will accomplish nothing. But when my army comes, and pulls your government down, remember this moment. You brought this end upon yourselves."

A cold wind entered the room, picked up some papers, and threw them down. Snowflakes settled toward the top of the conference-room table.

Pong took Molly's hand and led her toward the aircar. "Come on, child, let's go for a walk in the snow."

Nineteen

"HAMMERFALL LEADER, THIS is hammerdrop one."

McCade chinned his mic. The drop module was only slightly larger than his combat-equipped body. He could smell his own sweat. "Hammerdrop leader. Go."

"We are five to the zone. Repeat, five to the zone. Stand by."

McCade swallowed hard. In less than five minutes he and his special ops team would fall through Drang's atmosphere, pray that their drop mods would hang together long enough to get them below the government's radar, and hope that their electronic countermeasure gear was as good as the sales literature claimed it was. If not, they'd be easy targets for the government's air defense battalion.

McCade chinned the team freq. "Hammerfall leader to hammerfall team. We are minus five and counting. Auto sequence and sound off."

McCade flipped a switch and pushed a button. There was an armored box under his seat. Inside the box was a minicomp. It ran an auto check on the module's systems, found everything to its liking, and lit a green light on the instrument panel.

Meanwhile the special ops team checked in.

"Mod one . . . green board."

"Mod two . . . green board."

"Mod three . . . green board," and so on, until all twenty-four men and women had checked in. Two members of Mc-

Cade's team had turned up at sick call. Some kind of virus. Lucky bastards.

"Roger," McCade replied. He eyed the digital readout in front of him. "Prepare for drop. One-thirty-six and counting."

Time became plastic and seemed to stretch. The readout worked its way down with frustrating slowness until there were fifteen seconds left. At that point Major Davison's voice came over both command and team freqs.

"Hammerdrop one here. We're in the zone. Ten, nine, eight, seven, six, five, four, three, see you dirtside, hammerfall team! Good luck!"

McCade was thrown violently sideways as the egg-shaped module shot out of the port launch tube and began its journey toward the planet below.

McCade couldn't see them, but knew that eleven modules had followed his, with twelve more to starboard. Phil's would be last. The variant would assume command if McCade were killed.

The team was heading dirtside two rotations prior to Pong's main force so it was important to avoid detection. There was no point in providing the government with an early warning. That's why the techs had gone to the trouble of installing an expensive launch system in a tramp freighter. After it had dropped McCade's team into the upper atmosphere the ship would land and unload a legitimate cargo.

The module jerked as it hit a slightly thicker layer of air and McCade felt the temperature start to climb.

Outside the tiny passenger compartment layer after layer of ceramic skin was burned away as the egg fell. And as the layers of protective material became increasingly thin, more and more heat was conducted inside.

Eventually, after the module had fallen through all of Drang's interlocking radar nets, the hull would disintegrate and a parachute would open. At that point McCade would float gently to the ground.

Or so the techies claimed. Needless to say none of them had tried it.

McCade's vision blurred as the module began to vibrate. He strained to see the instrument panel and couldn't. The egg tumbled end over end, stabilized when the mini-comp fired the module's steering rockets, and fell like a rock toward the reddish orange planet below.

Strange things went through McCade's mind. Unconnected memories of places that he'd been and things he'd experienced. He remembered Sara, Molly, and his long-dead parents. He thought about Molly's birthdays, and how many he'd missed over the years, always assuming that there'd be more.

McCade blinked sweat out of his eyes and whispered a prayer he hadn't used since childhood.

The module began to shake and shudder again. Pieces flew off. Air pushed its way in through the holes, roared around McCade's head, and spun the module like a top. Blackness appeared where the instrument panel had been just moments before. The rest of the hull leaped away in chunks, broke into smaller pieces, and spread itself out over twenty square miles of desert.

The chair, with McCade still in it, continued to fall. And fall, and fall, and fall.

The chute? Shouldn't it be open by now? Scooping air and slowing his fall? Something must be wrong. It was time to pop the reserve chute. McCade had flipped the protective cover up and was closing his fingers around the lever when the main chute opened. It made a loud cracking sound.

Air filled the chute and McCade felt as if it was pulling him upward. The force of it pushed him down into the chair's padding. Things slowed. The chair twirled under a canopy of fabric.

Still on duty, the mini-comp used radar to make a tightly focused sweep of the terrain below. It located the best place to land and activated a pair of servos.

Lines grew taut, air spilled from one side of the chute, and McCade felt himself slide toward the ground. He braced himself. The chair fell away a few seconds later. With less weight pulling down on it the chute slowed even more.

There was a distant thump as the mini-comp blew up and took the chair with it.

Air rushed around McCade's face. He was worried. Sure, the mini-comp had aimed him in what it thought was the right direction, but mini-comps could be wrong. What if he landed on some rocks? In a river? Right on top of a missile battery?

McCade strained to see the ground but couldn't. There was a scattering of lights to the right, many miles away, but only blackness below. Should he switch to night vision?

The ground came up with unexpected suddenness. McCade's legs absorbed most of the impact and he managed an awkward roll. He scrambled to his feet. How the hell were you supposed to roll wearing body armor and a day pack? Who thought of this stuff anyway?

McCade hit the chute release before a sudden gust of wind could pull him off his feet. He touched a pressure plate on the side of his helmet and watched a ghostscape appear around him.

Most of the things around him were a sickly green, except for the rocks, which retained enough of the daytime heat to show up as fuzzy red blotches.

McCade spilled the last bit of air from his chute, gathered it into his arms, and looked for a place to hide it. A black patch between a pair of red blotches suggested a crevice. McCade walked over and found that the chute fit with room to spare. A loose rock went on top.

Good. Now for the team. Where were they? And was everyone okay?

McCade removed the small tac comp from his combat harness and flipped it open. He touched some buttons and a map appeared. It looked weird via night vision but was still readable. A glance told McCade that he was located just fifteen miles west of their target. Not bad.

His position was marked by a red star with a scattering of blue dots all around. Twenty-three in all according to the data summary at the bottom of the tiny screen.

McCade frowned and pushed another button. The map vanished and was replaced by words:

> Subject: Zemin Mary Ann
> Serial number: NB965471
> Status: KIA, Drang
> Cause: Module Failure
> Disposition: Explosive Disintegration
> Threat Factor:.001

McCade swore softly. He had liked Zemin, in fact, with a couple of exceptions, he liked the whole team. Zemin had been cheerful, competent, and their best electronics tech. There were others, each member of the team was qualified in at least three specialties, but none of them was Zemin. There had been only one Zemin and she was dead. Dead in a stupid war, on a stupid planet, in a stupid universe.

McCade cleared the screen, touched a key, and looked around for a place to wait. Somewhere out in the darkness twenty-three men and women would hear a solid tone in their headsets and follow it to this position. If they had trouble tracking the tone, a quick check of their own tac comps would solve the problem.

McCade pulled a weapons check, found that his slug gun, blast rifle, and force blade were all where they should be, and retreated between a couple of boulders. With any luck at all his body heat would blend in with the warmth stored in the rocks and shield him from infrared detection..

McCade readied his blast rifle just in case. After all, there was always the chance that government troops had located him somehow, and were on the way.

Ten minutes of almost total silence passed before McCade heard gravel crunch under someone's boot. He grinned as a ghostly red blob appeared ten feet away and looked around. It was Martino, easily identifiable due to the launch tube strapped to his back, hoping to catch McCade by surprise.

Moving carefully McCade picked up a small rock and tossed it in Martino's direction. It made a soft thocking sound as it bounced off the mercenary's helmet. Martin spun around, auto thrower ready to spit lead, and swore when he saw McCade. "That wasn't very nice, Skipper . . . I damn near messed my pants."

McCade chuckled. "Sorry . . . I couldn't resist. Besides, it isn't nice to sneak up on your CO."

Martino grinned unashamedly. His teeth looked green.

The two men repositioned themselves in the rocks and waited for the rest of the team to show up. They came in ones, twos, and threes, whispering the password prior to closing on the rocks. It was like a ghostly echo out of the night, "Hammerfall, hammerfall, hammerfall," until all were present. Everyone was okay outside of some bumps and bruises.

Phil came in third from last. He checked to make sure the team had established a defensive perimeter and huddled with McCade. "Too bad about Zemin."

"Yeah," McCade replied. "I hope it was fast."

"Yeah," Phil agreed somberly. "I hope so too."

McCade flipped his tac comp open and pushed a series of buttons. Because the entire area was flat the tac comp dispensed with contour lines and gave him what amounted to a simplified road map.

The target showed up as a pulsating orange square. According to the tac comp it was some fifteen miles to the east. That would be the lights McCade had seen from the air.

The mission itself was relatively simple. The team would cross fifteen miles of desert, infiltrate the town of Zephyr, and find one particular home. And according to McCade's information, that should be relatively easy.

The home belonged to one Nigel Harrington and by all accounts it was huge. A mansion really, spread all over two acres of land, and as eccentric as its owner.

It seemed that Harrington was the patriarch of the entire Harrington clan, and taken together they owned Harrington Industries, the very heart of the combine.

The combine feared, and Pong agreed, that the moment his fleet showed up government forces would try to take Nigel Harrington hostage. The old man would provide considerable leverage. And because he lived in a small town, far from the combine-dominated cities, it would be easy to do.

Over and over Nigel Harrington's sons and daughters had pleaded with the old man to stay with them, and over and over he'd refused. Zephyr was where his wife was buried and Zephyr was where he'd stay.

The family had reinforced the mansion's small security force but couldn't do much more than that without alerting the army unit stationed in town.

So it was McCade's job to reach the mansion, defend it for the better part of two days, and keep Nigel Harrington alive. Of more immediate concern however was the fifteen miles of desert between him and the Harrington mansion.

The first ten miles looked relatively easy. Open desert mostly, crisscrossed with dry riverbeds and dotted with unmanned oil pumps. The original source of the Harrington family fortune.

Closer in things got more complicated. There was a five-mile-deep defense zone around the town, ostensibly created to defend against raids by the nomadic indigents, but actually placed there because the Harrington family wanted it to be. Like all wealthy families the Harringtons lived in fear of thieves, kidnappers, and assassins. Between the efforts of their well-bribed government representatives and their army of lobbyists, the proposal for the Zephyr defense zone had sailed through the parliament.

Now, however, their government-funded defenses might work against them. In addition to fortified positions and motorized patrols, McCade and his team would have to deal with an unknown number of robo sentries. These were of some concern not only because of their heavy armament but due to their sensors as well. The team would have to be very, very careful during that last five miles.

"Well," McCade said, "time to move out. We've got fifteen miles of desert to cross and about six hours left to do it in. When morning rolls around, and the sun comes up, the desert will turn into a frying pan. Not only that, we'll be visible for miles around."

Phil nodded soberly. The very thought of all that heat made the ice-world variant start to sweat. "Right, Sam. What do you want?"

McCade flipped the tac comp closed and attached it to his harness. "Put Evans and Kirchoff on point, with Abu Rami running the left flank, and Stobbe guarding the right. I'll go first and you ride drag."

Phil nodded and whispered into his mic.

Three minutes later the special ops team was up and running. They were spread out to lessen casualties in case of an ambush, or land mine, but thanks to the enhanced optics built into their visors still in sight of each other most of the time. Radio traffic was kept to minimum and all-out speed was sacrificed to a ground-eating jog. Every now and then the team would top a slight rise and see lights in the distance. They got brighter all the time.

Time passed and McCade fell into a comfortable rhythm. Thanks to the conditioning on HiHo he felt pretty good. His boots made a steady crunch, crunch in the loose gravel. His breathing was deep and steady. His pulse pounded evenly through every vein and artery. In spite of Molly, in spite of what lay ahead, it felt good to be alive.

Twenty

MUSTAPHA PONG WAS awake although his eyes were closed. He heard the swish of the hatch sliding open followed by the click of boots on the metal deck. He recognized the step as belonging to Raz. "Yes?"

"The Harrington party has come aboard, sir."

Pong opened his eyes and blinked in the light of the overhead spot. It felt good to be back aboard his ship safely ensconced in the privacy of his own cabin. He hated the prospect of making small talk with the Harringtons but it had to be done. They'd hired his army, and as representatives of the combine had a right to see what they'd paid for.

Pong nodded. "Thank you, Raz. Show them into the ward-room. I'll make my entrance after they've had some time to stew."

Long accustomed to Pong's ways, Raz nodded and with-drew.

Pong closed his eyes. He directed a thought toward the mind slug. "Show it to me again."

The alien gave the Melcetian equivalent of a sigh. Pong nev-er seemed to tire of the fantasy and demanded to see it at least once or twice a day. The mind slug secreted some chemicals, waited for them to take effect, and projected the appropriate thoughts.

Color swirled in front of Pong's eyes, paused, and gradually took shape. A vision emerged, an omnipotent vision such as

God might have, in which entire solar systems and galaxies were little more than pieces laid out on a table of black marble.

Here and there Pong saw bursts of light as stars were born, black holes as others collapsed, and collisions so monumental that entire planets were turned into clouds of cosmic debris.

But these were trivial events, no more important than a spring rainstorm on Desus II. Of more importance was the vast sweep of sentient activity. He could see it drifting across the blackness like star dust, succeeding here, failing there, all according to chance and the work of a few unusual minds. Minds like his.

Well, not exactly like his, because Pong could see the possibility of order within the chaos. He could conceive of something greater than the stars themselves. A single civilization, with him at its center, reaching across known space and beyond, to wrap all races and cultures in a single embrace, an organism so big, so powerful, that it would live for a million years.

Yes, that was a vision worth working toward, worth sacrificing to. Humans, Il Ronnians, and, yes, the 56,827, all of them would kneel to Pong.

The chemicals ebbed from Pong's system and his eyes snapped open. The vision had the effect of reenergizing him. Now he was ready to deal with trivial annoyances like the combine and its somewhat arrogant leadership.

Pong got down off of his thronelike chair and headed for the hatch. It swished open at his approach. Raz and Molly waited outside.

Ever since the assassination attempt Pong had insisted that Molly be with him at all times. Pong had always liked and respected the little girl, but this was something more than that, an almost superstitious belief that she brought him good luck.

After all, since Molly's abduction from Alice Pong had yet to suffer a single defeat, and she had literally saved his life. Surely it would be wrong to ignore such an obvious talisman.

Pong smiled at Molly, and she smiled back, but it was polite and somewhat distant. Oh, how he hungered for a real smile! The kind he saw on those rare occasions when she was swept away by the joy of the moment. Like the precious hours they'd spent walking the streets of Segundo, the aircar hovering above them like a guardian angel, Raz practically dancing in his eagerness to get Pong off the planet.

Those had been magic moments during which Molly had forgotten herself, and her parents. Yes, her parents were the problem, and one with which he would eventually deal. Perhaps Molly's mother had been killed in the attack on Alice. If not, a hired assassin could finish the job.

As for the almost-legendary Sam McCade, well that might be a little more difficult, but where there's a will there's a way. The trick would be to kill Molly's parents in such a way that their deaths could never be traced to him. And then, with that accomplished, arrange for Molly to find out. She'd be sad for a while, but children are resilient creatures and recover quickly. With all hope of being reunified with her parents gone, Molly would gravitate to him, and Pong would see those smiles a good deal more often.

Yes, just two more of the many small details that must eventually be dealt with. Pong took Molly's hand and together they walked down the corridor toward the ship's wardroom.

Pong cut it extremely close. By the time he entered the wardroom Marsha Harrington, the most senior of the Harringtons present, was just short of a boil. No one kept her waiting on Drang, and by God no one should keep her waiting here either, especially some jumped-up mercenary general. Her escort, a rather junior officer named Naguro, had done his best to stall but had run out of small talk five minutes before.

So as Pong entered the room, Marsha Harrington turned her somewhat beefy body his way and was just starting to speak when he preempted her.

"Citizen Harrington, this is an enormous honor. I knew the president and chief executive officer of Harrington Industries was brilliant . . . but I had no idea that she was beautiful as well."

Being far from beautiful, Marsha Harrington flushed at this unexpected compliment and found herself completely disarmed. Pong was entirely different from what she'd been led to expect. Quite pleasant in fact, and, aside from the grotesque alien draped across his shoulder, dangerously handsome. She found herself babbling like a schoolgirl.

"The honor is mine, General Pong. May I introduce my brother Howard, and my cousin Nadine?"

Howard, a rather sallow man in his mid-thirties, gave a stiff bow, and Nadine, a dissipated-looking creature in a custom-tailored Harrington Industries business suit, nodded. She looked at Pong like a rancher judging a prize bull. "Charmed."

Pong smiled. "Likewise I'm sure. Hello, Lieutenant Naguro, it's good to have you with us."

Naguro, a nervous little man, nodded jerkily and did his best to fade into the background. Pong, and the rainbow-colored thing on his shoulder, made Naguro sweat.

"Now," Pong continued, "if you'll take a seat around the table, we'll review the additional forces now at your disposal. With the landing only two rotations away I'm sure you'll agree that time is of the essence."

The next two hours were so boring that Molly had a difficult time staying awake. Aided by a long series of holos, Pong droned on and on about ships, troops, equipment, logistics, and drop zones. And if he wasn't talking, then it seemed as if Marsha Harrington was.

Making the situation even worse was the fact that the wardroom was extremely spartan. Outside of the occasional holos there was nothing to look at.

The only interesting moment came about halfway through the presentation, when Boots, Lia, and two of the girls entered the room with trays of refreshments. Boots had been out of the brig for some time now . . . and made no secret of her hatred for Molly.

Molly could understand that, but still hoped to make friends with Lia and fix things with the others.

Molly smiled, hoped for some sort of friendly response, and was quickly disappointed. The girls ignored her, while Lia put on a show of exaggerated deference, and hated Molly with her eyes.

So Molly just sat there, staring miserably at the floor, wishing she were dead. Didn't they realize how she felt? Couldn't they see that she was a slave too? Subject to Pong's slightest whim?

No, Molly realized, they couldn't. The fact that they served while she did nothing had blinded them to the way things really were. Finally, after what seemed like an eternity, the girls left the room.

"And so," Pong said, plucking a grape and popping it into his mouth, "that completes our review. The government's forces are strong, but so are yours, and with the addition of my troops the advantage is ours."

Marsha Harrington nodded agreeably. Pong's presentation had compared favorably with the reports of her own intelligence apparatus. Not only that, but the mercenary had kept self-serving exaggeration to a minimum. She liked that. There was only one question left.

"An cxcellent presentation. Thank you, General. One more question before we leave. Can you tell us anything about my father? With hostilities only hours away, and his home almost completely unprotected, we can't help but worry."

Pong did his best to look appropriately concerned. He searched his memory and came up empty. Damn. There were so many things to track. The mind slug filled the gap. Pong seized the information and put it to use.

"Of course. I'm pleased to report that a special operations team under the command of Captain Roland Blake has landed on Drang and is en route to your father's home. They should reach the mansion within the next few hours."

Marsha Harrington beamed, while her brother nodded dutifully, and her cousin examined perfect nails. "Thank you, General Pong. I can tell we are in good hands. To a successful campaign." She raised her wine glass.

Pong smiled and raised his wine glass in return. "Yes. To a successful campaign."

Twenty-one

MCCADE AND THE rest of his team were spread out along the edge of a dry riverbank. Five miles of reddish desert stretched away in front of them, the last five miles before their objective, and the most dangerous of all.

The problem was that they were quickly running out of time. They'd been forced to hide twice, once when the soft rumble of engines filled the air, and again when spotlights made tunnels through the night. They'd escaped on both occasions but paid a price in time.

Now a jagged line of light had crept its way across the horizon and separated earth from sky. The bushlike plants that dotted the desert had begun to stir, waking from night-long hibernation, to creep up and out of the river bottoms.

Within an hour or so they would line the top of the riverbanks like a silver hedge, soaking up energy with their shiny leaves and storing it against the cold of night.

Later, when temperatures started to soar, they would retreat to the river bottoms and the shade cast by high-cut banks. From there the plants would sink tap roots down toward the water hidden deep below.

Which is fine for the plants, McCade reflected, but doesn't help us at all. When the sun comes up we're dead.

McCade flipped up his visor and took a look through the binoculars. He panned from left to right. Nothing. It made him nervous. Where were the robo sentries they'd briefed him on? There weren't many, that was true. Maybe four or five in the entire Zephyr defense zone. But given the fact that they stood nearly three stories tall, and carried enough armament to destroy a light tank, how many did the government need? One would be enough.

Well, robo sentries or no, they couldn't wait any longer. McCade stashed the binoculars and activated the team freq.

"Okay, listen up. We've been lucky so far, but don't get overconfident. There could be all sorts of stuff up ahead. Keep your eyes open and pay attention. And if you notice something that stands about thirty feet tall, and has lots of weapons sticking out of it, don't hesitate to let me know."

There were chuckles followed by some rude comments.

McCade grinned. "Okay, let's hit it. Maintain your spacing, and watch where you put your feet."

"Yeah," Martino added wryly, "you could step in some deep do-do."

Nobody laughed.

McCade waved Evans and Kirchoff forward, gave them a few seconds to take the lead, and followed. After hours of running it was easy to slip into a ground-eating jog.

The desert was deceptively beautiful in the early morning light. A soft inviting palette of earth tones that gave no hint of the searing heat yet to come.

The ground was treacherous however, full of holes that could turn an ankle, and loose gravel that skittered underfoot.

But time passed and McCade began to relax. The town of Zephyr was clearly visible from every rise, a cluster of twinkling lights, shimmering in the distance. A peaceful sight reminiscent of small towns everywhere.

Then came a cracking sound. The force of the explosion threw Evans ten feet into the air. Her body cartwheeled and landed with a heavy thump.

Phil yelled, "Land mine!" over the team freq and everyone came to a sudden halt. A quick check confirmed that Evans was dead.

McCade swore under his breath. Another casualty. Another life gone in defense of what? Of the combine's right to line its pockets? What a waste.

The team hurried to pile loose rocks on top of Evans' body.

She'd get a formal burial after the main force landed if things went well.

A trooper named Slotman carried their only mine detector. He took the point and waved the wandlike device in front of him like a shaman seeking water. The rest followed, careful to stay in line behind him, slowed to little more than a fast walk.

McCade wanted Slotman to move faster but resisted the urge to tell him so. He scanned the horizon instead. Surely someone had seen or heard the explosion. What would they do? Send a patrol to investigate? Assume that a wild animal had set it off? All he could do was wait and see.

The first sign of trouble was a shard of reflected light. It came in low and from the left. McCade stopped and brought his binoculars to his eyes. What he saw scared hell out of him.

It looked like an insect at first, a metallic beetle, on long skinny legs. Slowly but surely it got to its feet, rising up from the hollow where it had been hidden, to turn in their direction. Light glinted off its shiny skin.

A robo sentry! Lying in ambush! McCade spoke into his mic. "We've got a robo sentry two thousand yards to the left! Stay behind Slotman and we'll run for the next riverbed!"

Blue light slashed past them and hit a large boulder. It exploded throwing superheated chunks of rock in every direction. Something stung McCade's cheek.

Slotman stashed the detector wand. He was running too fast for it to function effectively. He glanced back over his shoulder. The next member of the team was a full hundred feet behind him. It confirmed what Slotman already knew. *He* was the mine detector now. If he lived, the way was clear, and if he died, it wasn't. Simple but effective.

It got so that Slotman dreaded the impact of his boot hitting the ground, the necessity of lifting it up and putting the other one down. Would this be the one? The final footfall? A sudden flash of light followed by eternal darkness?

Blue fire ripped the ground ahead and something exploded. A mine! The robo sentry had triggered a mine! A mine he might have stepped on.

Slotman ran straight toward the patch of smoldering ground and pounded his way through it. The riverbed was just ahead. Slotman knew because the silvery bushes had aligned themselves along its edges and spread their leaves to catch the morning sun. Just a few more yards, a few more feet, and he'd be there.

Slotman dived through the plants and tumbled into the riverbed below. The rest of the team were right behind him. They half jumped, half fell into the bottom of the cut, and scrambled to find defensive positions.

What was the robo sentry up to? A bend in the riverbed blocked the view. McCade was in the process of scrambling back up the bank when a shaft of blue light hit the bushes. They absorbed part of the blast and reflected the rest, sending shafts of coherent energy in every direction. One skimmed the length of McCade's left arm and left a black scorch mark on his body armor.

Straining to keep his balance on the steep bank, McCade fumbled the binoculars to his eyes. The robo sentry was closer now, using the riverbed as a highway, its four podlike feet kicking up clouds of dust each time they hit. No wonder the machine hid. Otherwise people would see it coming from miles away.

All sorts of energy projectors, gun barrels, and launch tubes stuck out of the robot's shiny torso. One moved slightly and burped light. The section of riverbank in front of McCade became a thick liquid and dribbled downward.

McCade took the slope in a series of small jumps. "Martino! As soon as that monster comes around the bend nail it with your launch tube! And don't forget to move afterward!"

"That's a rog, Cap," Martino said, already hidden behind a large rock.

"Spread out," Phil ordered, "and fire thermal grenades when it comes into view."

The ground shook as metal pods hit one after the other and the robo sentry came into full view. A lot of things happened all at once.

Martino fired all five of his launcher's mini-missiles and sprinted for another boulder knowing that the robo sentry's tac comp would compute a reciprocal course and fire on his last position. He'd barely dived behind another rock when an auto cannon turned the first one into gravel.

Those armed with grenade launchers fired thermal rounds, not at the robo sentry itself, but out and away from the team.

They made a gentle pop and burned white-hot as they fell toward the ground. The thermals pulled two of the robo sentry's heat-seeking missiles away from the ops team and disappeared inside fiery explosions.

Meanwhile, boulders popped like party balloons as the robot's energy weapons probed among the rocks searching for life. Rock shrapnel screeched through the air and McCade heard someone scream.

Ignoring the danger, Abu Rami rested his long-barreled rifle on its custom-designed tripod, removed a magazine of hollow points, and inserted one filled with armor-piercing rounds. Rami looked through the electronic sight. The robot was huge and menacing. The sniper felt a sudden need to relieve himself. He struggled to remember the machine's weak points.

The robo sentry's ECM gear fooled three of Martino's five mini-missiles but couldn't confuse the other two. They were dummies, with no more intelligence than bullets have, flying where the launch tube had directed them to go. They exploded against the robot's belly.

The robo sentry's designers had anticipated such a possibility and armored the underside of the robot's torso. But while the missiles were unable to penetrate the robot's armor, they did spray chunks of hot metal in every direction.

One piece penetrated a joint, sliced through a cable, and cut power to both rear legs. Undeterred, the machine used its front legs to pull itself forward. There was a horrible screeching noise as metal was dragged over rock. Meanwhile the robo sentry continued to fire in every direction.

McCade was scared. It seemed as if nothing could stop the metal monster. Explosions rippled across its top surface as Martino fired another salvo of missiles. They didn't even slow the robot down. It just kept coming, dragging its useless legs behind it, a mindless killer.

Knowing it was a waste of time McCade fired his blast rifle and waited to die.

Abu Rami made a fine adjustment to his scope. Then, wrapping a finger around the trigger, he took a deep breath. Somewhere in the back of his mind Rami heard the hunting prayer his father had taught him. He let out half the breath, squeezed the trigger, and absorbed the recoil with his shoulder.

The armor-piercing bullet ran straight and true. It sped across the intervening distance, smashed through a thin-skinned sensor housing, and tunneled its way through the robot's tac comp. Denied all control the robot's weapons fell suddenly silent.

This didn't stop the machine from dragging itself forward however, metal screeching against rock, like a wounded beast returning to its lair.

One by one the team came out from their hiding places, somc with bloodstained battle dressings, all with shell-shocked expressions. For a moment everyone just stood there, staring at the wounded machine, amazed at how harmless it had suddenly become.

McCade felt something warm touch his cheek and realized that the sun had topped the edge of the riverbank. All around them the silvery bushes were root-walking to the edge of the bank and sliding downward. It was time to go and then some.

A quick check turned up the fact that while no one had been killed, a trooper named Banks was badly wounded.

Because the energy beam had cauterized the wound on its way through Banks' thigh there was very little bleeding, but it hurt like hell just the same. Phil gave him an injection. Banks was smiling sixty seconds later.

McCade found Abu Rami and thanked him for making the critical shot.

Rami listened politely, acknowledged the compliment with a nod, and turned his attention to the rifle. A thin layer of dust covered its outer surface. That would never do.

A stretcher was assembled from the pieces some of them carried and Banks was strapped onto it. It was difficult getting the stretcher up and over the lip of the bank but they made it.

They formed a column of twos and ran toward Zephyr. It was only two miles away. McCade could see the whitewashed buildings shimmering in the sun. With the enemy warned, and the sun up, there was no time for mine detectors or other niceties. McCade was gambling that the robo sentry worked along the inside edge of the mine field. If so, this area should be clear. If not, it was just too bad.

And now there was another danger as well, a danger they couldn't do a damned thing about. It lurked above them in the clear blue sky, or could, and might descend at any moment. A fighter, a chopper, an armed aircar, any and all of them could, and would, turn the team into chopped liver.

But when danger came it was on the ground. The first sign of it was a dust cloud coming straight toward them from Zephyr. Someone *had* noticed their run-in with the robo sentry and was coming to investigate. That pretty much ripped it, but if they were forced to surrender, McCade wanted to do it from a position of relative strength. Assuming that the government was willing to take prisoners, a proposition that was far from certain.

"There's company coming," Phil said laconically, the words jerking out with each breath.

"Yeah," McCade replied, "I see 'em."

Still running, the world rose and fell around him as McCade looked around. Outside of the oil pump off to the left there was no place to hide. "Okay, everyone, head for the oil pump, it's the only cover around."

They swerved and jogged toward the oil rig. A glance toward the growing dust cloud assured McCade that they'd make it in time. There was only one vehicle as far as McCade could tell, a troop carrier perhaps, or a military truck. Something big anyway, big enough to carry plenty of troops and a lot of weapons.

There wasn't much to the oil pump. Just a vertical mount, a steel crosspiece, and some shiny pipe that disappeared into the reddish soil. It went up and down, up and down, like a bird pecking at the ground. Standing next to it was an equipment shed and some empty oil drums.

The team spread out, found what cover they could, and got ready for their final battle.

The dust cloud was bigger now, much bigger, and McCade could see the vehicle that caused it. First he frowned. Then he brought the binoculars to his eyes, looked, and looked again. Then McCade recognized the conveyance for what it was and laughed.

A bus! A school bus, or crew bus, with a white flag flying from its antenna! It was big, lime green in color, and equipped with huge desert tires.

McCade triggered the team freq. "Hold your fire and stand by. This could be a friendly."

It could also be a trick, McCade thought to himself, and watched as the bus approached, then skidded to a stop. The enormous tires sprayed gravel in every direction. Now McCade could see the words "Harrington Industries" printed along the vehicle's dented flank.

A door hissed open and a man stepped out. He had white hair, a deeply tanned face, and an athletic body. The man was dressed in a short-sleeved white shirt, khaki shorts, and a pair of beat-up desert boots. He summoned them with a wave.

"My name's Harrington. You folks look like you could use a lift. Climb aboard, and let's get the hell out of here. We can expect a flight of T-40 fighters in about twelve minutes. Their base is a couple hundred miles away so it's taking them a while to get here."

McCade knew that it could still be some sort of an elaborate trick, but didn't think it was, and decided to take the chance. "All right, everybody . . . you heard the man . . . let's get aboard!"

Phil entered first, his ugly-looking submachine gun at the ready, making sure the bus was empty. It was, and he waved the rest of them forward.

Once the team was aboard, Harrington wasted little time in closing the door and accelerating away. McCade noticed the older man was wearing a headset, and from the speed with which they were traveling, McCade suspected that he had a means of tracking the T-40s. If so, they were coming on strong.

The bus swerved to avoid a rock and threw McCade against hard metal. He smiled. This was silly. Not only was Nigel Harrington a good deal different from the helpless old man that he'd imagined, the industrialist also showed every sign of rescuing his rescuers, and doing so with a good deal of panache.

Zephyr was clean and crisp up ahead, safe behind a carefully maintained wall, all curves and rounded corners. Then McCade saw the iron gate, the pillbox located next to it, and the troops spilling out of a government truck.

Harrington's voice boomed over the PA system. "They're on to me, so hang on, folks, we're gonna dent some government property!"

An automatic weapon opened up from the pillbox, but the gunner hadn't fired at a real target before, and put all of his slugs where the bus had been instead of where it was headed.

An officer waved her arms, mouthed some sort of order, and dived out of the way as Harrington accelerated toward the gate. There was a crash as the bus hit, a snow storm of shattered safety glass, and the stutter of hand-held weapons. McCade sensed rather than saw government troopers falling away as members of his team fired out through the windows.

Up front Harrington yelled, "Yahooo!" and put his foot down. The bus fishtailed around a corner, sideswiped a lamp-post, and screeched its way up a well-kept boulevard.

Just then three barely glimpsed somethings roared overhead, shaking the bus with their combined slipstreams.

"That's the T-40s," Harrington yelled happily, "they can't fire on us without hosing the entire neighborhood! Most of my neighbors are government officials. Silly bastards!"

McCade made eye contact with Phil a few rows back and on the other side of the aisle. The variant shook his head in amazement and smiled. It was easy to see why Harrington Industries had been so successful.

The aircraft made one more pass during the time it took for the bus to wind its way down some residential streets and roar toward a pair of massive gates. They opened like magic and closed behind the bus as it bounced inside and slid to a screeching halt.

McCade was impressed with what he could see through the broken windshield. In the foreground were carefully planned rock gardens, thoughtfully interspersed with desert plants, and crisscrossed by well-swept walkways.

Farther back was the mansion itself, a huge rambling structure, all of which was blindingly white.

Harrington tried to open the vehicle's door and found it wouldn't budge. Not too surprising, since it had sustained a good deal of damage during the crash and was badly twisted.

A heavily armed security guard, dressed in a paramilitary uniform with a Harrington Industries logo stitched to his breast pocket, managed to pry the door open with a crowbar.

They unloaded Banks first, with the rest of the team tumbling out after that, and McCade last. Nigel Harrington was there to greet him. There was a smile on the older man's face. His grip was dry and firm.

"Captain Blake, I presume. Welcome to my home. I received word of your arrival a few hours ago."

Harrington gestured toward a tall spindly tower that soared up from the corner of the mansion. "Margaret had that built, God bless her soul. Used to sit on the observation deck and paint. I saw the whole battle from up there. Nasty business that. Could've been worse though. The night patrols were in and the day patrols were getting ready to go out. Idiots don't have enough brains to overlap their patrols. Be surprised if we don't whip the whole government in a week."

McCade thought Harrington's projection was more than a little optimistic but didn't say so. "We sure appreciate your help, sir, we owe you one."

Harrington waved the comment away with a smile. "Not for very long. I'll be owing you pretty soon."

Harrington looked around at his mansion, the gardens, and the pristine grounds. "I wonder how much of this will still be standing two days from now."

Three fighters flashed by overhead, their wings almost touching, the roar of their engines nearly drowning Harrington's last words.

McCade watched the fighters go. Afterburners glowed red as they stood on the tails and screamed toward the sky. He met Harrington's eyes. "That's hard to say, sir, but one thing's for sure, now's the time to dig in."

Twenty-two

AT EXACTLY 0300 Mustapha Pong gave an order and death fell toward the planet Drang. It came in the form of drop modules, assault boats, bombs, missiles, and beams of pure energy.

And as Pong struck, so did the combine, quickly securing generous landing zones for the invading forces.

But the government forces were tough and, thanks to good intelligence, well prepared for the attack. They'd known since Salazar that war was inevitable, and that Pong would side with the combine. So they gave ground, but did so grudgingly. Every LZ was contested, every target defended, and every victory paid for in blood.

The night was full of fire. Assault boats blossomed into flowers of flame, aerospace fighters exploded, and cities glowed reddish orange. Death was everywhere.

As in most wars Drang's civilians came in for a large share of the suffering. There was no way to protect them against a damaged assault boat cartwheeling out of the sky, a pod of misdirected bombs, or a heat-seeking missile that couldn't tell the difference between a residential power grid and a military one.

But thanks to a common need to win popular support, both the government and the combine avoided civilian targets as much as possible.

And because both sides wanted to live on the planet when

the war was over, they refused to use nuclear weapons. Of course the fact that nuclear war was grounds for intervention by the Emperor might have had an impact on their thinking as well. Neither group wanted to live on a planet governed by Imperial Marines.

So, some five hours after the attack had begun, Pong was quite satisfied with the way things had gone. His forces had suffered casualties, but nothing unexpected, and thanks to the excellent leadership provided by Colonel Surillo, 81.7 percent of the primary objectives had been taken. A high score indeed.

Pong had watched the first hours of the battle from orbit with 47,721 at his side. A special booth made of one-way glass had been set up inside the flagship's situation room to protect the alien's identity.

Just one leak, one whisper of a previously uncontacted race, and Imperial intelligence would be all over the place. That would be inconvenient, and potentially disastrous as well, since Pong's plan depended on surprise.

Forewarned is forearmed, and if the Empire knew about the 56,827, there was a fairly good chance that they could win the ensuing war. Regardless of what the aliens believed, Pong knew his fellow humans were a tough lot and capable of amazing stubbornness. Not only that, they were also a good deal more technologically sophisticated than the 56,827, and mean as hell when threatened.

No, Pong thought to himself, I mustn't let that happen. Victory depends on a surprise attack by an absolutely ruthless race using weapons the Empire hasn't seen before. It would start when the moon-sized alien ship dropped out of hyperspace into near Earth orbit and cut loose with everything it had. A few hours later man's ancestral home would become little more than charred rock.

The Emperor would be killed along with his entire family, the seat of Imperial government entirely eradicated, and the home fleet destroyed. The rest of the Empire would burst like an overripe fava fruit, split into warring factions, and finish the process Pong had started.

And then, with some key victories over the Il Ronn, and a few other space-faring races, a new order would be born. A new order conceived by *him*.

"By *us*," the Melcetian put in waspishly.

"Of course," Pong responded impatiently. "That goes without saying."

"It better," the mind slug replied, but thought better of it, and slipped Pong some soothing chemicals.

Completely unaware of Pong's thoughts, or his interchange with the Melcetian, 47,721 shifted in his seat. It was of 56,827 manufacture and served to cradle the alien's backward curving midsection. Both of its outward bulging eyes were swiveled forward in order to follow the action.

The privacy booth included three sophisticated holo tanks, twelve different video monitors, and a sophisticated com set.

Using video supplied by hundreds of spaceships, assault boats, drop modules, combat vehicles, and individual troops, a rather sophisticated computer had woven it all together to provide them with a live blow-by-blow account of the battle.

So skillful was the computer's manipulation of incoming information that it took on the quality of a holo drama, complete with ongoing characters and running subplots.

More than once Pong and 47,721 were watching when a particular video source disappeared from the screen and never returned. Often there was natural sound, explosions, or screams followed by silence.

Each time Pong was conscious of the fact that real men and women had just died, yet because it was little different from watching a well-executed holo drama, it didn't seem to mean much.

Not to Pong anyway, although 47,721 grew somewhat agitated during the scenes of personal combat, and his toe claws had left scratches in the surface of the durasteel deck.

All around the booth there was the quiet murmur of com traffic, an occasional burst of static, and the gentle hiss of air-conditioning. All of it comfortably distant from the battle that raged below.

But not for long. In a few minutes Pong would depart for the surface where he would take personal command of his troops and prove his worthiness to the 56,827. Silly but necessary. He turned to 47,721.

"So, we are well on the way to victory. In a few weeks, a month at the most, our work will be done. In the meantime I must join my troops."

A long rope of saliva drooped out of the alien's mouth parts ınd plopped to the deck. "Yes, numberless one. You have lone well. I shall remain here for a while and monitor the ›attle before returning to my ship."

Pong delivered a small bow of acknowledgment. He eyed the ıood and cape arrangement thrown over the back of 47,721's hair. It would protect the alien's identity between the situation oom and the shuttle. The crew was curious, but so what. With he exception of Molly, none of them had seen anything more han the outside of the alien's spaceship. And for all they knew, : was an asteroid transformed into an elaborate habitat and rewed by Lakorian swamp dancers.

Pong cleared his throat. "Do you need anything before I ›ave?"

The alien was quiet for a moment, as if giving the question is full and undivided attention. "Yes, as you know, our sucess stems in part from the care with which we prepare for attle."

Sure, Pong thought to himself. If you never take chances ou never lose.

Out loud Pong said, "And quite right too."

"So," the alien continued, "I will take the juveniles along vith me as I return."

The 56,827 had made their desire for some human children nown early on, and Pong had saved some from the slave ıarkets of Lakor specifically for that purpose. And up till ow he'd never dared to ask why.

But flushed with the successful attack on Drang, and more onfident of his position, Pong decided to indulge his curiosity.

"Of course. I will have the children prepared. May I ask ›hat you'll do with them?"

The alien's reply was matter-of-fact. "Of course. Some of ır more sophisticated weapons kill by disrupting the enemy's ervous system. However, due to the fact that neural systems ary from species to species, it is necessary to fine-tune our ›eapons prior to battle. Some of the juveniles will be used ›r that purpose. Others will provide an interesting variation › our rather monotonous shipboard diet."

Pong shuddered. Although well aware of the 56,827's preference for dinner on the hoof, it was something he'd tried to ;nore. On one occasion they'd invited him for dinner and it ad taken weeks to get over it.

Pong thought of the slave girls who'd been captured with Molly. What a horrible way to die. Still, a deal's a deal. He would give the necessary orders.

As for Molly, well, she was safe. Remembering her fear of 47,721, Pong had ordered Molly to remain in his cabin while the alien was aboard, and during his trip dirtside as well. Much as he enjoyed Molly's company, Pong knew it would be dangerous on Drang, and wanted to protect her. He stood to go.

"The juveniles will be ready, 47,721. May your hunts go well."

"And yours," the alien replied politely, before returning his attention to the video screens. A small city was on fire and he didn't want to miss it.

Twenty-three

"INCOMING!" THE VOICE was an unidentifiable croak in McCade's ear.

He dived behind the wreckage of a once-graceful water fountain. Like everything else in and around Nigel Harrington's home, it had been reduced to little more than twisted metal and shattered masonry. The mortar shells made a loud cracking sound as they marched across the driveway and rock garden leaving large craters behind. The barrage ended as suddenly as it began.

"Here they come!" This time McCade recognized the voice as belonging to Phil. He rolled over and poked the brand-new assault rifle up and over a chunk of broken duracrete. There was no shortage of weapons and ammunition thanks to Nigel Harrington's underground arsenal.

But what good are weapons if you don't have troops to fire them? Only twelve members of McCade's team were still alive. They, plus the five surviving members of Harrington's security force, were all that stood between the industrialist and the government troops that were trying to capture or kill him.

The air was full of dust and smoke. A couple of dozen dimly seen figures sprinted through the wreckage of the main gate. Their armor was covered with powdery white dust. It puffed away as they ran.

Auto throwers stuttered, energy weapons burped, and a grenade went off as the government troops came straight at him.

McCade fired in ammo-conserving three-round bursts, methodically working his way from left to right, watching the soldiers jerk and fall. He cursed them for coming, for running at him through the smoke, willing them to turn and flee.

But they kept on coming, their bullets dancing through the rubble around him, screaming incoherent war cries.

The deliberate *thump, thump, thump* of a heavy machine gun came from McCade's right, and he watched as geysers of dirt exploded upward next to the troops and then among them.

Bodies were thrown backward, loose weapons flew through the air, and the *thump, thump, thump* continued. Continued, and stopped, when there was nothing left to kill.

McCade dropped down and rolled over onto his back. The sky was partially obscured by drifting smoke. Then a momentary breeze blew it away and he saw contrails crisscrossing the sky. The battle for Drang was well under-way.

McCade wondered how the battle was going, who was winning, and who was dying.

He thumbed the magazine release and fumbled for another. The bounty hunter didn't even look as he shoved it home. The magazine made a loud click followed by a clack as the bolt slid forward.

"Fighters! South side, six o'clock low!"

McCade looked to his left and swore. What was this? Their seventh sortie that day? Their eighth? He supposed it didn't matter much. About five or six hours after the team arrived the government had evacuated the rest of the neighborhood and called for an air strike. The planes had been strafing and bombing the hell out of the place ever since. The entire neighborhood had been leveled.

McCade rolled to his knees, scrambled to his feet, and sprinted for a bolt hole. It had been a basement window once, but it was no more than a hole now, one of the many passageways they maintained in and out of Harrington's underground shelter. All around the mansion others were doing the same thing. They didn't need orders. The planes came and you hid. It was as simple as that.

McCade heard the roar of the approaching planes and the growl of their mini-guns. The black hole was just ahead. He dived through it and landed on the mattress placed there for that purpose.

The world outside was suddenly transformed into a hell of exploding rockets, bursting bomblets, and flying lead. Wave after wave of death flowed across the land churning the rubble and sending up great clouds of smoke and dust. The noise was almost deafening.

McCade put his hands over his ears just as the voice came through his tiny receiver. "Blake . . . Harrington here. They won't attack as long as the planes are here. Come on down for a minute."

McCade got to his feet and staggered out of the small storage room and into a richly paneled hallway. He followed that for thirty feet or so and came to a heavily armored door.

McCade turned his face so the security camera could get a good look at him and was rewarded with a loud click. He pulled on the door and it came open.

A wide set of stairs led downward. McCade pulled the door closed and made his way down the stairs. Cool air rose to meet him, along with the smell of fresh coffee and the odor of cooking.

Built to protect the Harrington family from everything up to and including nuclear war, the shelter was much more than the name would imply.

Powered with its own fusion plant, and stocked with five years' worth of supplies, it included all the basic necessities and then some.

Harrington's sentient servants and house bots had retreated underground along with him. So, as McCade entered the large sitting room, everything was sparkling clean and a maid was in the process of serving coffee. The thick rugs, modernistic furniture, and expensive art all gave the impression of relaxed luxury.

One entire wall, the one that almost screamed for a window, was given over to a huge vid screen. It was filled with a shot of dramatic-looking boulders, some stunted greenery, and a crystal-clear pool of water.

Like the view from a picture window it was absolutely static, except for small details like an eight-legged reptile scampering over the surface of a sun-warmed rock, and a bird skimming the surface of the water in search of insects.

McCade assumed the shot was live, piped in from somewhere out in the desert.

Harrington wore light body armor, still dusty from a stint on the surface a half hour before, and marked here and there with impacts from flying debris. The industrialist was a damned good shot and had done his share of the fighting and then some. How old was he anyway? Sixty? Seventy? Whatever the industrialist's age he was tough as hell. Harrington gestured toward a comfortable chair.

"Excellent work up there, Captain Blake. Have a seat. Nancy, coffee and cigars for my guest."

A middle-aged woman who looked more like an executive secretary than a maid nodded pleasantly and went to work. Within moments McCade had a humidor full of expensive cigars at his elbow and a coffee cup in his hand. It made an unbelievable contrast with the surface. McCade took a sip of coffee, it burned his tongue.

"You wanted to see me, sir?" It felt good to sit down and rest, but McCade couldn't leave his team for very long.

Harrington touched a remote. The desert scene disappeared from the huge vid screen and was replaced by a wide shot of the Harrington compound. A line of explosions marched through the debris as a plane roared by overhead. Harrington turned the sound down.

"No need to worry, Captain. Most of my vid pickups have been destroyed, but as you can see, I still have one or two left. They're still at it, and as long as they are, your team is safe."

McCade nodded and lit a cigar.

The older man waited until the cigar was drawing satisfactorily and smiled. "I used to enjoy them but was forced to quit. Even with anticancer shots and all that other medical hocus-pocus old age eventually has its way."

Harrington waved a hand. "But enough of that. I have good news. The initial battle is winding down. Your forces have landed and in most cases linked up with the combine. Within an hour, two at most, Zephyr will be in friendly hands."

It *was* good news. McCade knew he should be happy but wasn't. Half his team were dead, and the outcome of the war didn't matter to him. What mattered was a little girl, and a woman on another planet. He forced a smile.

"I'm glad to hear it, sir. The truth is I'm not sure we could've held for another day."

Harrington nodded. "No, I think not."

McCade grabbed a handful of cigars, stuck them in a breast pocket, and got to his feet. "Thanks for the news, sir. I'll go topside and tell the team."

Harrington nodded and watched him leave. A tough-looking man, a soldier from all appearances, but something more as well. Something more complicated than a hired killer. But what? Just one of the many questions he'd never get an answer to.

It was actually more like five hours before a flight of the combine's fighters swept in to control the sky and soften up the government's ground forces, and two hours after that when a flight of choppers landed and disgorged two companies of Pong's best infantry.

First they surrounded what was left of the Harrington mansion, then they swept through the town of Zephyr and secured that as well.

McCade was sitting on a chunk of garden wall smoking one of Harrington's cigars when Major Davison found him. Although it was clear from the condition of his armor the other officer had been in or near the fighting, he looked disgustingly fresh.

"There you are! I've been looking all over for you! Nice job, Blake, damned nice. So nice that the old man wants to shake your hand. Fred's too."

Frederick Lambert was the name Phil had taken.

McCade raised an eyebrow. "The who?"

"The old man, the general, Mustapha Pong himself."

McCade's heart beat a little bit faster. Finally! A chance to meet Mustapha Pong! Maybe he'd know Molly's whereabouts, and even if he didn't, there was a score to settle. A *big* score.

McCade stood up and flicked the cigar butt away. "The old man. Yes, sir. Ready when you are, sir."

The wounded had been flown out minutes after the combine swept in, but McCade found the others and thanked them one by one. Martino, Abu Rami, Kirchoff, and a few others were completely untouched. Then, with Phil at his side, McCade climbed aboard the waiting chopper and watched Zephyr shrink below him.

Then, stretching out on a pile of cargo nets, McCade went

to sleep. Davison shook him awake two hours later.

"Rise 'n' shine, Blake. This is brigade headquarters. Before we came it was a nice little hell hole called Foley's Folly, and don't ask, because I don't know why they called it that."

McCade yawned, stretched, and sat up. Over on the other side of the chopper Phil did the same.

Without the breeze blowing back through the open hatch it was hot, damned hot, and McCade's mouth was dry. Not only that, his neck hurt from sleeping on the cargo nets, and he smelled like rancid vat slime.

Davison grinned. "Well, Blake, I hope you feel better than you look, cause you look like hell."

McCade got to his feet. He squinted toward the hatch. The sun was high in the sky and the glare off the desert was incredible. "Thanks for the pep talk, sir, I feel better now."

Davison laughed and waved them toward the hatch. "Come on, Captain, Sergeant, let's get you cleaned up. We can't parade you in front of the general looking like that."

The sun fell on them like a hammer as they stepped down onto the fused sand. Engines roared all around them, as insect-like choppers took off and landed, their rotors blowing sand sideways forcing McCade to turn his head.

Once off the landing pad Davison ushered them into an open combat car. The vinyl seats were hot as hell. Phil looked terribly uncomfortable, panting heavily, his fur matted with sweat.

A private sat behind pintle-mounted twin-fifties, looking bored and doing her nails. She didn't even glance their way. The driver was a cheerful-looking corporal. He had bright brown eyes, black skin, and a gold earring in his right ear.

"Welcome aboard, sirs. Where to?"

"The O club and step on it," Davison replied.

McCade was thrown backward as the car spun away, spraying a nearby work party with sand and reinforcing all the negative images they already had regarding officers.

The corporal liked to drive combat cars, and saw each errand as an opportunity to hone his skills. As a result the trip from the helicopter pad to the O club was transformed into a high-speed sprint through an imaginary combat situation, with piles of camo-netted cargo modules standing in for tanks, and rows of inflatable tents representing troop carriers. This made the trip fast but somewhat terrifying as well. McCade was thankful when the car skidded to a stop in front of a large tent. A steady stream of officers was coming and going through the front entrance.

Davison thanked the corporal, turned his face away to avoid the inevitable spray of sand, and waited for the combat car to clear the area. He turned to Phil.

"Here . . . pin these tabs to your armor. I put you in for lieutenant and we'll assume it's been approved. Can't have sergeants in the O club . . . might contaminate the beer or something."

Phil laughed, did as Davison requested, and followed the major inside. It was soothingly dark, redolent of smoke and beer, and filled with the low mumble of conversation. There were thirty or forty folding tables, about half of them filled.

Davison led them to the bar, bought a round of beers, and watched as they chugged them down. Phil chased his with a full pitcher. When it was gone the variant wiped his muzzle with the back of a furry hand, belched, and said, "Thank you, sir, that hit the spot."

With their thirst quenched, Davison sent them to the rear of the building where they stripped down and entered the male showers. There was no such thing as cold water, but it felt wonderful to stand in a steady stream of tepid water, and let it wash away days' worth of desert grime.

McCade soaped and rinsed three times before he felt really clean.

Phil, always given to singing in the shower, did so, his prodigious baritone filling the area with sound. At least one officer thought about asking Phil to stop, but caught a glimpse of the variant's bulk, and decided to let it go. A few minutes later they had the showers to themselves.

Finally, two bars of soap and many gallons later, they emerged much refreshed and ready for the new uniforms that Davison had waiting. Phil's was an extra large, triple X, and barely fit.

Davison nodded approvingly when they joined him at the bar. "Better . . . much better . . . and just in time too." The major glanced at his wrist term.

"We're due to appear in front of the general at 1730. The general's not much for handing out medals and that sort of thing, but he's got the combine to consider, and Marsha Harrington is real pleased about the way you took care of her father. So the heroes are about to receive their just due, along with some other fortunates who had the good sense to save a combine factory. We're off."

It was a shock stepping out of the air-conditioned O club into the late afternoon heat. Fortunately for them the HQ bunker was a short distance away. It was more than a bunker actually, being a fairly good-sized freighter, which had been landed in a specially prepared ravine and buried under tons of rock and sand. The result was a hardened command post that was nearly invulnerable to attack.

The entrance was inside a small tent some fifty yards from the command post itself. It was heavily guarded. All three were subjected to an identity check and asked to surrender their weapons prior to admission.

Up to this point McCade had been looking forward to a confrontation with Pong, unsure of exactly how things would go, but determined to make something happen. Now, stripped of his weapons and surrounded by Pong's personal troops, that seemed suicidal. But thanks to the fact that Pong had never seen him before, he could accept the medal and leave. After that he'd get together with Phil and make a new plan.

Somewhat comforted by this analysis McCade turned his attention to following Major Davison through the underground tunnel. The walls were made of fused sand and chem strips lighted the way. The exaggerated zigzag of the tunnel was no accident. Each corner represented a place where defenders could take cover while their attackers were forced into the open. It was very professional.

There was another identity check once they reached the ship's lock, followed by a pat down, and a trip through a standard metal detector.

Phil's durasteel teeth and claws set the detector off right away and caused quite a stir. Finally, after much arguing and explaining by Major Davison, they were allowed to pass.

A junior rating led them through the freighter's interior to a specially modified cargo hold. Half the space was filled with banks of com gear and people, most of whom were milling around a centrally located tac tank. It shimmered and swirled with distant battle.

Folding chairs had been set up in the other half of the hold and most of them were already filled. The occupants looked tired and extremely bored.

"A bunch of ground pounders," Davison whispered, "you know, the ones who saved the factory."

McCade nodded and took one of the few empty seats. Phil sat beside him.

Five or ten minutes passed during which nothing seemed to happen. Then a hatch hissed open and a man stepped through. A rather pleasant-looking man with a Melcetian mind slug riding on his shoulder. The alien rippled with reflected light.

McCade felt adrenaline pour into his system. His heart beat like a trip-hammer.

Mustapha Pong! The man who had stolen his daughter, wounded his wife, and murdered his friends. Where's Molly? What have you done with her? McCade wanted to scream it, and was half an inch out of his chair when Phil touched his arm.

"Not now, Sam. Not here. We'll get our chance, but not now."

The voice was calm, logical, correct. McCade fell back into his chair and looked around. Had anyone noticed? No, not as far as he could tell anyway.

The room had grown quieter, whether from Pong's presence or actual orders, McCade couldn't tell. A stern-looking woman in perfect body armor nodded to Pong and turned toward the small audience. She had heavy black eyebrows, a predatory nose, and a stern mouth. The woman cleared her throat.

"Hello, I'm Colonel Mary Surillo. It's my pleasure to welcome you to brigade HQ. Being mercs, we don't give out a lot of medals, but when we do they really mean something. Each one of the medals given out today comes with a cash award."

The ground pounders gave a cheer and Surillo nodded approvingly. "That's right . . . the stuff we fight for. Here to present your awards, and to congratulate you on behalf of the combine, is General Mustapha Pong."

Surillo nodded toward Pong and took a step backward.

Pong produced a smile, stepped forward, and let the mind slug feed him what he needed to know. "Thank you, Colonel, it's a pleasure to be here. As I give your names please stand up. First I'd like to recognize Major Elroy, Lieutenant Deng, Private Hoskins . . . "

Pong's voice became a dull drone as he listed the ground pounders, their sterling service on behalf of the combine, and their various rewards.

McCade watched the pirate's face, wondering how such evil could lurk behind those banal features, and wishing he could do something about it right then.

McCade felt a nudge from Phil and realized that their turn had come. The ground pounders had taken their seats, and Pong was about to speak.

"And that brings us to our next set of winners. Captain Roland Blake and Second Lieutenant Frederick Lambert, please stand."

McCade stood, as did Phil, and Pong had just launched into a description of what they'd done when a loud squawk came from the other side of the room.

McCade looked just in time to see Captain Lorina Dep-Smith step out of the crowd, belly jiggling, and point a pudgy finger in his direction. Her voice cut through the noise like a knife through soft butter. "Roland Blake my foot! That's Sam McCade!"

Twenty-four

MOLLY HUDDLED IN one corner of Mustapha Pong's vast cabin, half asleep, half awake. She was fantasizing about home, reliving a wonderful afternoon when she, Mommy, and Daddy had gone up to Uncle Rico's summer place for a picnic. Everything was cozy and warm inside the cabin, while outside the snow fell thick and heavy, covering the world with a layer of white frosting.

There had been a big blazing fire, lots of good food, and the pleasant drone of her parents' voices. There was nothing exciting about the trip, nothing special, just the warm fullness of being cared for and loved.

Molly remembered how it felt to have Daddy throw her into the air, while Mommy cautioned him to be careful and smiled from the other side of the room. Oh, what she wouldn't give to be back there, reliving that moment, feeling strong arms around her.

A tear trickled down Molly's cheek and she wiped it away as the hatch hissed open. There were loud footsteps as someone walked into the center of the room and stood in the cone of light that bathed Pong's chair. A knot formed in Molly's stomach when she saw who it was. Boots! What was she doing here? Molly cowered in the corner and hoped the woman would go away.

Boots laughed, a horrible cackling sound, full of hate and satisfaction. "So! Hiding in the corner, eh? Get out here!"

Molly did as she was told, wondering what was going on and wishing Pong would appear. He didn't.

Two quick steps and Boots had her by an ear, pulling Molly along, towing her through the hatch and down the corridor. It hurt, and just to emphasize that fact, Boots gave her ear an extra jerk every once in a while.

Molly bit her lip, determined not to cry, and looked around for help. Crew members passed them in both directions. Where was Pong? Raz? Surely they'd help her. But no one came to her rescue or even looked especially interested. Slaves, even ones favored by Mustapha Pong, were still slaves.

Bit by bit it became clear that they were headed for the launch bay, and sure enough, when Boots came to a halt it was outside robo lock four.

The hangar had been depressurized so that shuttles could come and go freely, but a limited number of accordianlike robo locks allowed direct access to high-priority vessels, and it seemed Molly was destined for one of those.

Aha! Molly felt suddenly better. Pong had sent for her. Boots would put her aboard his shuttle, and that would be that.

But that hope was snatched away when the rest of the girls were herded into the area, all nineteen of them, with Lia leading the way. The older girl had a sneer on her face.

"Well, look who's here! Little Miss Privileged. What's the matter, Molly, did Pong get tired of wiping your nose?"

Molly ignored her and did her best to figure out what was going on. It wasn't just her. They were taking *all* of the girls off ship. Why?

Boots counted noses. "Well, that should be the lot of them."

"Yup," the other crew member agreed, checking his porta comp, "let's get 'em on board. Chow's in twenty minutes. We wouldn't want to be late."

Boots shoved Molly toward the lock. "Get moving, brat . . . it seems Pong came to his senses. We're well rid of you."

Molly stumbled, caught herself, and stepped into the lock. She felt an emptiness inside. Pong had sent her away. It shouldn't matter, but it did.

Molly knew Pong was a horrible man, knew he was capable of destroying entire planets to get what he wanted, and liked him anyway. She shouldn't but she did. He'd been kind to her, or as kind as he knew how to be, and seemed to like her. That's why Molly felt betrayed. What had she done to displease him? Why was Pong sending her away?

A tremendous wave of self-pity rolled over Molly as she groped her way through the dimly lit tube. It wasn't fair! Why her? Why?

The question found no answer as Molly knew it wouldn't. She saw a dimly lit lock up ahead. The light had a lavender hue. It reminded Molly of something she couldn't quite put her finger on.

She entered the lock along with Boots and five other girls. There wasn't room for more. Much to Molly's relief Lia was back toward the end of the line.

Boots hummed as the lock cycled through, and was so pleased with the occasion that she allowed Molly to slip by untouched.

It was dim inside the shuttle and it took Molly's eyes a moment to adjust.

Then Molly's heart jumped into her throat. She saw dirt where the deck should be, vegetation to either side, and a lavender sky overhead. The shuttle was a smaller version of the moon-sized ship! The ship that belonged to the horrible aliens!

Molly whirled and headed for the lock. She shouted, "Run! Run!" but it did no good. The other girls stayed right where they were; Boots cuffed her on the side of the head and kicked her as she went down.

Molly struggled as Boots dragged her toward the shuttle's stern, doing her best to tell others what was waiting for them, screaming with frustration when they ignored her.

An openhanded slap sent Molly reeling as the rest of the girls poured into the small compartment and a metal gate slammed into place. Boots stood on the other side of the gate and grinned. Molly grabbed the bars and shook them.

"Let us out . . . please let us out . . . they plan to kill us!"

But Boots laughed and disappeared into the near darkness of the corridor. Hands pulled Molly away from the bars and held her while Lia moved in front of her.

"Now listen, and listen good. You're going to shut up and do as you're told! We're tired of being abused while you sit around playing princess. From now on you'll do what *we* say when *we* say to do it. Understand?"

Molly jerked her arms free and looked Lia in the eye. "I understand all right . . . I understand that you're an idiot! Do you know where we're headed? And what will happen once we get there?"

Some of the other girls looked interested, but Lia crossed her arms and spat the words out one at a time. "No, and you don't either! Now shut up and sit down!"

Molly shrugged and looked for a place to sit down. Information is power, and by bottling it up, Lia hoped to control the situation. It was stupid and immature but effective nonetheless.

A quick look around confirmed Molly's earlier impression. The shuttle contained a miniature biosphere, but unlike the mother ship's, this one seemed limited to plants and insects. Not enough room for higher life forms, she supposed.

A half hour passed during which the other girls wondered at their alien surroundings and ignored Molly.

Then came a rustling sound, followed by the whir of a hatch closing, and the slow swish of something moving their way. Molly had a pretty good idea of what it was and moved toward the rear of the compartment, while the other girls jostled one another trying to see.

Then 47,721 stepped out into the half-light. He was hidden by a black cloak, but looked ominous enough to elicit a collective gasp and start a general movement away from the gate.

Molly shuddered. She saw some drool hit the dirt by the creature's feet and knew it was one of them. The alien moved its head as if looking at each one of them individually.

Then, with a grunt that might have meant anything, it turned and left.

Eva, one of the younger girls, was first to speak. She was short, chubby, and plainly terrified. "Wha-what was that?"

Molly started to answer but Lia held up a restraining hand.

"Don't be so xenophobic. It doesn't matter what's under the cloak. We all know that biological form flows from environmental conditions. There's nothing to worry about."

Eva and the rest of the girls didn't look so sure, but Lia's domineering approach left no room for dissent, so they remained silent.

Molly smiled. You had to give Lia credit. Her answer sounded good, and would've pulled an "A" back in school, but didn't answer Eva's question. Worse than that, it left all the girls ignorant of what was coming.

Anyone who was standing, and that included Lia, fell as the shuttle moved up and away.

There was a long slow period of acceleration, followed by what felt like nothing at all, as the ship reached cruising speed. Molly waited for the momentary nausea that often signals a hyperspace jump but it didn't come. It seemed the alien mother ship was relatively close by.

Molly wrapped her arms around her knees and rocked back and forth. There was nothing to do but wait. She couldn't help but dwell on her first exposure to 47,721, and his inquiry about "the juveniles." The alien wanted human children. Why? And what for?

Time passed, exactly how much was hard to say, since none of the children had a watch. But judging from how hungry Molly was when the shuttle started to slow, she figured it had been six or seven hours, maybe more.

The knot in her stomach grew larger and larger.

Finally, after what seemed like an eternity, the ship settled into place with a discernible thump.

All of the girls watched the gate and, in spite of Lia's insistence that everything was okay, looked very apprehensive. All of them wondered the same thing: What now?

Time passed and Molly heard movement, a shuffling sound from the corridor. Then 47,721 appeared. The cloak was gone now and even Lia whimpered with terror. All the girls took a step backward. The gate slid open as if by magic. Molly tried to disappear.

The alien entered the cell, drool plopping into the dry dirt, and looked at each of them in turn. The process seemed to last forever. Then, with his decision made, 47,721 raised a bony finger and pointed at three of the girls in quick succession.

"Come." The word grated its way out of the translator that hung around its neck.

All three of the girls whimpered and looked at Lia. She forced a smile. "Go ahead . . . I'm sure it'll be okay."

Molly wanted to scream, "Don't do it! Don't go!" but knew it wouldn't do any good. 47,721 would take them away regardless of what she or Lia said or did.

Karen, Suki, and Niki looked back over their shoulders as they stepped into the corridor, and 47,721 shuffled along behind. All four were quickly lost to sight. The gate slid closed.

Molly heard the hiss of equalizing pressure as the lock cycled open. The gate slid open five minutes later. The message was obvious. They were free to go.

The girls looked at Lia. She smiled. "See? I told you not to worry. We can leave anytime we want."

Molly opened her mouth to speak but closed it when Lia looked her way.

Satisfied that she had the situation under control, Lia did her best to look confident, and stepped into the corridor. The other girls followed. Molly waited for someone to give her orders, and, when they didn't, stayed right where she was.

Once they were gone, Molly tiptoed through the leafy corridor and found that a durasteel hatch barred the way to the control compartment. She palmed the lock. Nothing. 47,721 was a lot of things but stupid wasn't one of them.

Unable to see any advantage to staying on the shuttle alone, and afraid that one or more of the aliens might show up, Molly left the ship. Making her way through the lock and down a ramp, she found herself in the same landing bay as before. There was no sign of the others.

Stepping up to the same lock that she and Pong had used, Molly touched a heat-sensitive panel and waited for the hatch to cycle open.

Once inside she saw that one of the girls had lost her comb. It lay on the deck in a pool of alien goo. Molly didn't blame her for leaving it there.

When the opposite hatch whirred open Molly stepped out to find that everything was as before, with the possible exception of the sky, which seemed a little bit brighter. A little earlier in the simulated day perhaps.

Everything was the same. The path, the hill, the strange-looking trees at the top.

Lia and the others had followed the path partway to the top where they stood huddled together looking around. Molly knew how they felt. She also knew that they should scatter, hide wherever they could, and hope for some sort of miracle. Perhaps the runners would help them.

Lia grew visibly tense as Molly approached and did her best to look commanding. Molly expected some sort of comment on her late arrival but was ignored instead.

"All right," Lia said importantly, "let's spread out and see what's going on. Marsha, check out the tree things toward the top of the hill; Eva, take a look at those boulders. I see some holes down there and we might need some shelter."

Eva started downhill but Molly grabbed her arm. "Don't do it, Eva . . . there's some sort of creature living in those rocks."

Lia gave an exasperated sigh. "Here we go again. I thought I told you to shut up? Ignore her, Eva. There's nothing to worry about."

"Oh, yeah?" Molly asked. "Well watch this."

So saying she picked up a rock and threw it toward the boulder. Nothing happened.

Molly stared downhill in openmouthed amazement. Where was the black thing?

"See what I mean?" Lia sneered. "Molly lies like a rug."

With a show of nonchalance, the older girl stuck her hands in her pockets and strolled downhill. Molly ran after her and grabbed Lia's arm.

"Don't do it, Lia! I've been here before. Something lives in the boulders, honest!"

Lia jerked her arm away and walked even faster than before.

Molly threw another rock hoping that the monster would reveal itself. Still nothing.

Unable to do anything else Molly stood and watched. Maybe Lia was right after all. Maybe the creature had gone somewhere else.

Then, without any warning whatsoever, the black thing lashed out and dragged Lia into its hole. There was a scream, a horrible crunching sound, and total silence.

Molly just stood there for a while, staring at the spot where Lia had disappeared, unable to accept what she'd seen. Poor Lia. She'd been mean and nasty but didn't deserve to die for it.

Molly turned and made her way back up the hill. The girls gathered around. Molly had been elected to lead them without a word being said. Some were crying and all of them looked scared. Molly forced a smile.

"Come on, kids. We've got a friend around here somewhere. Let's find him."

Twenty-five

THEY TRIED TO run but it was hopeless. Within seconds McCade and Phil were surrounded by gun-toting military police. There were at least fifteen weapons aimed at them. Not even Phil could beat odds like that.

As he turned toward the front of the room and Mustapha Pong, McCade felt a tremendous sense of disappointment. To come so far, to be so close, and lose. It didn't seem fair.

Mustapha Pong smiled. He felt good. Very good. He'd waited a long time for this moment.

The Melcetian, who saw the human tendency to gloat as a complete waste of time, stirred slightly. "We have a lot to do . . . so keep it short."

Pong ignored the alien and moved forward.

The ground pounders got up and left. They didn't know what was going on and couldn't care less. They had their bits of brass, some money to spend, and were well satisfied. How stupid when the universe was full of larger and more important goals.

The MPs shifted slightly in order to make room. Pong was careful to stay well out of reach. "Sam McCade. So, we finally meet. I should've killed you when I had the chance."

McCade remembered the moment well. He'd been searching for the Il Ronnian Vial of Tears, and along with some others had been standing on the surface of an asteroid. Pong's cruiser had hung over them like some omnipotent God while the pirate's voice boomed into their helmets. "Which one of you is Sam McCade? Raise your right arm."

McCade had raised his arm and a spear of white light had flashed down to pin him against the ground. But instead of an energy weapon, it was a spotlight, and McCade had lived. Up till now anyway.

McCade forced a crooked smile. "You'll have a hard time getting any sympathy from me."

Pong smiled indulgently. "A sense of humor . . . I like that in a dead man. Tell me something. If we hadn't invited you here ourselves, what then?"

McCade shrugged. "I would've found some other way to get here."

Pong nodded agreeably. "Of course. You're resourceful if nothing else. Well, I'm glad things turned out as they did. I'll feel better knowing that you're adding some much-needed nutrients to Drang's soil. It'll be my little contribution to the planet's ecology."

McCade knew that Pong was hoping for a reaction and refused to provide it.

Pong laughed and walked away. He hadn't gone more than five feet before he stopped and turned. "Oh, and one more thing. My compliments on your daughter. Molly's a wonderful little girl. I plan to raise her myself. Just thought you'd want to know."

Rage boiled up from deep inside and McCade threw himself in Pong's direction. If only he could wrap his hands around the pirate's throat and kill that evil brain, his own death would be worthwhile.

But the MPs grabbed McCade and beat him with their rifle butts until blessed darkness pulled him down.

There were moments, brief episodes, when McCade floated to the surface. He felt rough hands pick him up, heard coarse voices give unintelligible commands, and saw shapes move around him. Then came movement and a constant bumping up and down as he hovered somewhere between light and darkness.

And there was pain, a dull throbbing in the back of his head, and something more as well. Another pain that was sharp, like an animal's bite, and came at regular intervals. What could it be? This intermittent pain that came between him and peaceful darkness?

It was curiosity as much as anything that caused McCade to open his eyes and look around.

He was in the back seat of an enclosed military vehicle, either a command car, or something very similar. There was desert outside. The same desert Pong planned to bury him in.

McCade turned his attention to the vehicle's interior. A driver and a guard sat up front, and directly behind them were two MPs on fold-down seats. They faced backward and looked mean as hell.

The woman seated directly in front of him wore a ruby stud in the side of her nose and the skin along the left side of her face had the patchy look that comes with a recent skin graft. Like the pro she was, the woman had her side arm out and pointed to one side. If the weapon fired accidentally, the slug would hit the door instead of her partner.

The second guard was handsome in a sort of sallow way, his dark brown eyes darting here and there like little animals, searching for something to eat. Every once in a while he would reach up to tug on his left earlobe. Like the first guard his weapon was drawn and aimed to the side.

This amused McCade because both guards could have aimed their guns at him. If the car hit an unexpected bump and the guns went off, so what? They planned to kill him anyway so why worry?

They were pros, that's why. Regardless of uniforms the guards were hired killers. It would be a mistake to kill him accidentally and they didn't make mistakes.

McCade felt a sharp pain in his right arm. What the heck was that anyway? Carefully, letting his head drift with the motion of the car, he looked to the right.

And there, in all of his furry majesty, sat Phil. His wrists were chained together in front of him, but there was just enough slack for the variant to cheat them left, and prick McCade's arm with the tip of a durasteel claw. Phil saw the subtle movement of McCade's head and his eyelids drooped downward in silent acknowledgment.

Now McCade understood. The pain was Phil's way of bringing him around. The variant was ready to make his move but wanted McCade conscious when he did it. Overpowering the guards would be extremely difficult, doing it alone would be close to impossible.

McCade moved slightly, almost imperceptibly, checking to see what kind of restraints they'd placed on him. Handcuffs and leg irons. Good. No nerve shackles, thank Sol.

The vehicle shook violently as the driver pushed it through a series of chuck holes. McCade swayed, apparently in response to the motion, and fell forward in the woman's lap. By doing so he blocked both her handgun and legs. That's when Phil went into action.

With twenty-five percent of the opposition momentarily immobilized, the variant brought his feet up and kicked as hard as he could. Because guard number two had turned to look at McCade, Phil's boots hit him in the side of the head and snapped his neck like a dry twig. The ice-worlder caught the man's body as it slumped forward, felt for the gun, and couldn't find it.

McCade was having trouble too. Still woozy from the earlier beating, and something less than a hundred percent, it was hard to keep his opponent under control.

First she tried to throw him off and, having failed at that, brought her forehead down on the top of his head. Darkness swirled and threatened to roll him under.

The weapon! She'd try to use it. McCade's hands found hers and fought for the gun.

The driver heard the commotion in the back, saw it from the corner of his eye, and stood on the brakes.

As the command car started to slow, the third guard yelled something incomprehensible and looked for an opportunity to fire. With the vehicle skidding, and the bodies swaying to and fro, it would be easy to hit the wrong person.

The driver, a rather ruthless individual known to his friends as Snake, saw the flaw in this approach and said so. "Shoot, you idiot! Shoot *all* of them!"

Unfortunately for Snake, the third guard wasted precious seconds analyzing the order and understanding the logic behind it.

So, by the time the guard had made the decision to obey and had started to squeeze the trigger, Phil had located the second guard's gun and freed it. There was no time to bring the weapon up, align it with the third guard's face, and fire, so the variant did the only thing he could. He pointed the gun toward the front of the vehicle and squeezed the trigger.

The weapon made a dull thumping sound as the slugs ripped through the second guard's already dead body, the thin partition behind it, and hit guard number three in the abdomen.

Guard number three looked surprised. Something hurt. What the hell was going on? Then he toppled over and crashed into Snake just as he brought the command car to a complete stop.

Meanwhile, with the gun trapped between them, McCade and guard number one were still struggling for control. She had wiry little fingers and they moved in and around McCade's to pull the trigger.

McCade felt the weapon jerk under his hand and felt the impact of a slug punching its way through his left arm. Damn! McCade twisted the gun barrel in what he hoped was the right direction and felt the weapon go off again.

The woman stiffened, tried to say something, and slumped sideways.

Phil swore as Snake bailed out of the driver's side door, slipped, fell, and got up running.

The variant flexed massive muscles, snapped the durasteel chains on cuffs and leg irons, and tried the door. It was locked and the handle came off in his paw.

It took a moment to find the key card in guard number two's pocket, slide it into the proper recess, and push the door open. Once outside Phil saw that the driver had a huge head start. A really well-aimed shot might bring him down, but why bother? They were free, and that was the important thing.

Now, with the adrenaline draining away, McCade's arm was starting to hurt and he felt dizzy. He tried the door and found it was locked. He was just getting ready to search for a key card when Phil pulled it open from the outside.

McCade swayed and Phil grabbed him. There was blood all over the place. "Whoa, Sam, you took one through the arm. Sit down and keep some pressure on it while I look for a first-aid kit."

McCade did as he was told and felt a little better. His arm still hurt but the dizziness began to fade. He heard a flight of aerospace fighters scream by overhead.

The restraints fell away at the touch of the electronic key that Phil had retrieved from guard number one's pocket. McCade rubbed his left wrist where the handcuffs had chaffed his skin.

Phil found a well-stocked first-aid kit under the driver's seat, cut McCade's sleeve off, and examined the wound. The bullet had passed through the fleshy part of the bicep and missed the bone. Both the entry and exit wounds were reasonably small.

The variant cleaned both holes, ignored the things McCade said when he poured half a bottle of antiseptic over them, and used butterfly strips for closure. The strips weren't as good as sutures but were better than nothing.

After that it was a simple matter to apply self-sealing dressings, bind them in place with gauze, and slap an injector against McCade's good arm. The bounty hunter couldn't feel the antibiotics going to work, but the pain killers made a big difference, giving McCade a warm fuzzy glow. He stood up and rotated his left arm.

"Good work, Phil, I feel good as new."

"Well, you aren't," the variant replied sternly, "so don't get carried away. You could do a lot of damage to that arm."

McCade nodded absently as he fumbled around for a cigar and eyed the horizon. They were exposed as hell, sitting right in the middle of the open desert, only miles from Pong's HQ. The camp was a clearly visible smudge from which a variety of aircraft came and went on their various errands. A makeshift spaceport sat slightly to the south, clearly marked by fingers of flame as ships landed and took off.

McCade found a cigar butt and lit it. The words came out with puffs of smoke. "Phil, we need to tidy up. Take what we need, lose the bodies, get our act together. We'd look real suspicious to a patrol or a recon drone."

The variant nodded, as if expecting something of the sort. "And then?"

McCade's eyes narrowed. "You heard him, Phil. The bastard has Molly. You can do whatever you want . . . but I'm going after her."

Phil snarled. "You mean *we're* going after her. I'm her godfather remember?"

McCade nodded soberly. "I remember. But the odds aren't very good. You've done more than your share already."

Phil gave a disapproving snort. "What a lot of bull. Let's clean up. We've got work to do."

Two hours later the command car rumbled up to the outermost checkpoint and came to a stop. The spaceport was a temporary affair, little more than fused sand and a collection of prefab buildings.

It boasted some impressive defenses though, at least three rings of them, and the checkpoint was the first. It was little more than a break in the huge antitank ditch that surrounded the complex. A ditch that had been sown with mines, was preregistered with Pong's computer-controlled artillery, and could be flooded with burning fuel.

The corporal was reluctant to step out from under the square of plastic that protected her from Drang's sun. She bent over to look in the driver's side window and eyed the tabs pinned to McCade's collar. The bounty hunter had ripped his right sleeve off to match his left, a practice that was nonreg, but winked at in Drang's heat. He figured the battle dressing was safe enough this close to the front. A transport rumbled into the sky behind her. She waited for the noise to drop off. "Good afternoon, sir. Can I have your pass please?"

McCade smiled reassuringly. "Of course. Here it is."

So saying McCade gave her the plastic card that they'd recovered from guard number three's body. Phil had seen him use it as the command car made its way out of the main compound two miles to the north. With any luck at all the card, and the password that went with it, would work here as well. Their plan depended on it.

But what if the spaceport used different codes? Or the driver had warned Pong's MPs? Or a million other possibilities?

The sentry smiled politely. "Thank you, sir. I'll be back in a moment."

As the woman walked toward her rectangle of shade, and the computer terminal that rested there, McCade eyed the boxy-looking vehicle that sat a few yards away. He could hear the hum of its auxiliary generator and found himself staring into all four of its automatic cannons. Just one word from the sentry and those black holes would burp sudden death. Within seconds he and Phil would become little more than meat frying on what had been a command car.

"Sir?"

McCade jumped. The sentry had approached from his side this time. She handed his card through the open window. "You're cleared all the way through. Today's password?"

"Trident."

"Thank you, sir. Have a nice day."

McCade croaked something appropriate, and for the first time noticed how pretty she was.

The vehicle jerked as Phil stepped on the gas, then rolled through the checkpoint, and roared toward the next checkpoint.

Though even more formidable than the antitank ditch, the second and third lines of defense were even easier to pass through, since they'd already cleared the computer checkpoint.

In each case Phil simply slowed down, growled the password, and was waved through. In fact, the worst danger came from the hover truck convoys that were headed in the opposite direction. The trucks were heavily loaded with supplies and highballing for the front more than ninety miles away.

They took up two thirds of the gravel road and their fans stirred up miniature dust storms that peppered the command car's windshield with flying debris. The dust made it hard to see, and by way of adding insult to injury, the drivers took great pleasure in hitting their air horns.

McCade breathed a sigh of relief as the command car rolled off the access road and into a large parking area. Another convoy was forming up and a small army of specialized robots was whirring back and forth as they loaded the last few trucks. They looked strange in their desert camouflage, like huge insects, gathering food for their nest.

The combined noise of hover truck engines, auto loaders, and spaceships was almost deafening.

In the middle of all this, striding about on a stiltlike walker, was a stocky-looking officer. His face was concealed by a bulbous command helmet. From the way the officer moved, and the robots scurried around him, he was obviously in command.

McCade was still debating the merits of asking the man for information when the decision was made for him. The officer took two giant steps and blocked their way. His voice boomed out of twin loudspeakers mounted on the exoskeleton's ten-foot-long metal thigh bones. Noisy though the area was he had no difficulty in making himself heard.

"Hey, you in the command car! What the hell are you doing in the middle of my loading zone?"

Based on the officer's belligerent tone, McCade assumed

he carried lots of rank, or was some kind of a mean S.O.B. It seemed like a good idea to humor him either way.

McCade triggered the command car's PA system. "Sorry, sir . . . we've got an important package for General Pong. Could you direct us to his ship?"

A beam of red light shot out from the walker to touch a distant ship. McCade did a quick count and found it was sixth in a row of eight. The light vanished.

"You see that?"

"Yes, sir."

"That's the general's ship. Now get the hell out of my way before I load your car on a truck and send it to the front."

"Yes, sir."

Phil tromped on the gas, swerved around a train of power pallets, and scooted onto the burn-blackened surface of the spaceport itself. Here there was even more activity as maintenance crews swarmed over ships, robotic fuel hoses snaked their way between pieces of equipment, and ground vehicles dashed in every direction.

McCade hoped the hustle and bustle would help cover their activities.

They passed ship after ship, boxy-looking freighters for the most part, until Pong's lay just ahead. It looked like a greyhound sitting among mongrels. Slim and obviously fast it crouched low on its landing jacks as if ready to leap off the ground at any moment. The main lock was open and a short set of metal stairs reached down to touch the ground.

Seeing the command car, and assuming it contained at least one officer, the single sentry popped to attention and delivered a rifle salute. He wore light armor, a combat helmet with the visor pushed back, and looked very warm. The sun was blistering hot, and the heat radiated off the surrounding ships, plus that reflected off the surface of the landing pad itself, made things even worse. Sweat rolled off the sentry's farm-boy face.

The command car screeched to a halt and McCade jumped out as if in a big hurry. The sentry knew his lines. "Sir, this is a class-three restricted vessel. Please present your class-three authorization code."

McCade summoned an officer-type frown. "At ease, Private. Tell me, is the general aboard?"

"No, sir," the sentry answered uneasily, "but he's due soon."

Good! McCade felt downright jubilant. Things were definitely looking up. The sentry was their only remaining obstacle.

McCade smiled disarmingly. "Excellent. I made it just in time. I have an important message for the general's pilot. Is the pilot aboard?"

The sentry remembered the somewhat arrogant cyborg who'd gone aboard earlier and shuddered. He didn't like cyborgs. "Yes, sir, the pilot's aboard, sir, but no one goes aboard without the correct code."

McCade nodded understandingly. "Of course, but this is an emergency. Why don't *you* go aboard, tell the pilot I need to see him, and enjoy some of that nice cool air-conditioning? That way you obey orders, I get the message through, and there's no harm done. I'll stand guard in the meantime."

The sentry's face worked along with his thoughts. This was a difficult situation. This was a captain and therefore a deity. The private didn't wish to offend such a lofty being. But lofty or not, the captain was minus the necessary code, and other even higher gods must be taken into consideration. Their commands left no room for doubt. What about the captain's proposal? Surely that was permissible.

The sentry would enter the ship, careful to enjoy the air-conditioning for as long as possible, and find the pilot. The pilot would emerge, get the emergency message, and everything would be fine.

The sentry grinned. "That should be fine, sir. Shall I leave my blast rifle with you?"

McCade peered at the name embroidered just above the sentry's left-hand breast pocket. "Good idea, Platz. That way I'll have something a little more potent than my side arm in case there's trouble."

Platz looked worried and McCade realized his mistake. "Not that there will be any trouble mind you." McCade waved toward their surroundings just as a Destroyer Escort roared into the sky. "I mean what could go wrong in the middle of all this?"

Platz looked relieved as he removed his helmet, placed it on the stairs, and handed McCade his blast rifle. "There you go, sir . . . I'll be right back."

The sentry's boots made a clanging sound as he climbed the metal stairs.

McCade looked at the command car and nodded toward the hatch.

Phil slipped out of the vehicle, winked at McCade as he started up the stairs, and disappeared into the lock.

McCade did his best to look sentrylike as he surveyed his surroundings. So far so good. The nearest ship was a reentry-scarred freighter. A group of techs were busily relining a tube with help from a sturdy-looking robot. They were completely uninterested in McCade's activities.

But then, just as McCade turned back toward the ship, he saw movement on the northern perimeter of the spaceport. It was a command car, newer than his, and flying some sort of pennant from a long whip-style antenna. The car was moving like a bat out of hell and heading straight at him. It didn't take a genius to figure out who was in it. Mustapha Pong himself!

In spite of Drang's oppressive heat McCade felt suddenly cold. What to do? He couldn't run, not with Phil trapped inside, and he couldn't just stand there either.

McCade heard a burst of static followed by some unintelligible gabble. The sentry's helmet! They were calling Platz and warning him of Pong's arrival. And unless they got some sort of answer, and got it real soon, all hell would break loose!

McCade picked up the helmet, slipped it over his head, and pulled the visor down. The mirrorlike surface would cut the glare and would make him faceless besides. A female voice blasted both ears. "Platz! Wake up, you idiot! The general's on the way."

McCade chinned the radio on. "I read you. The general's on the way. Sorry . . . I had my helmet off for a moment."

"Yeah?" The voice came back, "Well, keep the damned thing on. You okay, Platz? You sound different."

"Just the heat I guess," McCade mumbled. "I'll be fine."

"If you say so," the woman replied doubtfully. "I'll bring you something to drink when I make my rounds. Take a salt tablet."

The radio clicked off and McCade snapped to attention. All he could do was pray that Pong didn't notice his officer's tabs, or try to speak with him.

The command car came to a dignified halt. Pong got out, said something inaudible to the driver, and hurried toward the lock. The Melcetian didn't like direct sunlight and urged him on. Pong didn't even give McCade a second glance as he made his way up the stairs and disappeared into the lock. The moment Pong was gone the command car pulled away and headed toward one of the spaceport's prefab buildings.

McCade took one last look around to make sure no one was watching, slipped up the stairs, and entered the lock. It was well lit and, outside of some racked space suits, completely empty. Good. McCade palmed the control panel and heard the outer door close behind him.

As he waited for the inner hatch to open, McCade removed the helmet, put it on a bench, and drew his slug gun. It had been the property of guard number one and it felt good in his hand.

The inner hatch whirred open allowing a blast of cool air to fill the lock. Trying not to expose any more of his body than was absolutely necessary, McCade peeked into a long, narrow corridor and found himself looking straight down the barrel of a gun. A big gun in a furry paw. McCade gave a sigh of relief and stepped out of the lock.

"What are you trying to do? Give me a heart attack?"

Phil held a massive finger up to his muzzle and jerked his head toward the ship's bow. McCade nodded and followed along behind as the variant moved up the corridor.

Suddenly Phil paused, held up an enormous paw, and opened a door. McCade looked inside. Instead of the emergency equipment the locker was supposed to contain there was Platz, bound, gagged, and trying to signal McCade with his eyes.

McCade smiled, winked, and closed the door. Thanks to Phil the sentry was safely out of the way.

From there the two of them eased their way up the corridor and paused outside the hatch marked Control Compartment. Pong was clearly visible. He and a humanoid-shaped cyborg were busy reviewing some data on the ship's navcomp.

McCade took one last look around, verified that no one was in sight, and got a nod from Phil. The variant had checked, and outside of the cyborg and Pong, they had the ship to themselves.

McCade stepped into the control compartment and cleared his throat.

Pong turned, clearly startled.

McCade pointed his gun at the pirate's chest and smiled. "Remember me? Surprise!"

Twenty-six

MOLLY SQUIRMED HER way to the top of a low rise and peered through low-lying vegetation. A small valley was spread out in front of her, the same one she'd seen before, but from the opposite side. Although the light was dim Molly could see the gathering of boulders where the black thing lived, the hill where the strange-looking trees grew, and a small discontinuity that could be the lock. Molly was too far away to be absolutely sure.

"I'm hungry," Eva whined from beside her. "When do we eat?"

The question was unfair and made Molly angry. She forced the anger down. Leaders who squelch stupid questions suppress intelligent ones as well. At least that's what Mommy said. Molly tried to keep her voice even and calm. "We'll eat when we find food."

Eva didn't say anything but her discontent was obvious. Remembering field trips in school, Molly had asked the girls to pick buddies and spread out. If a member of the 56,827 showed up, they had orders to run in different directions and meet back at the lock. At least some of them would survive and the buddy system would help them deal with whatever dangers they encountered.

The plan had a flaw however. After everyone had chosen their buddies, and registered their choices with Molly, Eva was left over. Which meant that Molly was stuck with her. Still another benefit of leadership.

Molly scanned the valley again. She'd chosen this position because it was away from the lock but not too far away. Until such time as she could make contact with the runner named Jareth, or another of his race, Molly had no way to navigate. The lock represented a reference point and their only chance of escape.

Eva began to say something just as Molly saw movement. She held a finger to her lips and shook her head. What was it? Jareth? One of the 56,827?

The answer came with blinding speed. Jareth, or another just like him, emerged from some tall grass and ran. He, she, or it was extremely fast. No wonder they referred to themselves as "runners."

But if the runner was fast, so was the horrible-looking thing that followed, and it was closing the gap with a series of tremendous leaps.

The runner changed direction, angled off to one side, and headed for the protection of a thicket. But there were low-lying rocks barring the way and tall grass slowed it down, so the pursuing alien drew even closer. There was no doubt about the outcome anymore. 47,721, or one of its brethren, was going to win.

That's when the runner did something strange. It stopped, turned, and waited for death to come. And come it did, with such unrelenting violence that Molly couldn't watch. Her eyes met Eva's.

"Did you see that?"

Eva's eyes were big as saucers. She nodded slowly.

"Good. That's what I've been warning you about. That's what they look like without a cloak. Get the others. Bring them up here in pairs. I want them to see what we're up against."

Eva did as she was told, running down the slope and notifying the nearest pair of girls. They laughed, giggled, and gave Molly curious looks as they followed Eva up the slope, crawling the last few yards. Then they looked, gasped with horror, and ran down the hill. Some were crying and others looked like they wanted to throw up.

Molly didn't blame them. By now the creature the runners referred to as "death" was consuming its prey.

Molly remembered the way the runner had stopped and turned toward certain death. She knew hardly anything about the runners, but that single action spoke volumes. It communicated intelligence, bravery, and a tremendous dignity. She would remember it for the rest of her life, short though that might be.

When the last pair of girls had returned from the top of the slope Molly convened a council of war. The dim sunlight had almost disappeared, suggesting that a period of complete darkness was about to begin. The girls were tired, hungry, and scared. But their attitude toward Molly had undergone a radical change. When Molly spoke they listened.

"All right. You've seen what we're up against. The 56,827 use the runners for both crew and food. There's little doubt what they have in mind for us. Our only chance is to get help from the runners. If you see a runner, an alien that looks different from the one you saw aboard ship, let me know right away."

Molly looked around. She could practically hear what they were thinking. Since the aliens eat sentients, and number 47,721 took Niki, Karen, and Suki away, did that mean what they thought it meant?

Molly swallowed hard. "I know you're hungry, but the artificial sun's going down, and there isn't much we can do until it comes back up. Blundering around in the dark could be extremely dangerous. Stay with your buddy and get some sleep. Four of us will be awake at all times. Does anyone have a watch?"

There was silence for a moment, then a girl named Linda spoke up. "Sasha does . . . she stole it aboard ship."

Sasha had dark hair and flashing black eyes. She started to deny it but Molly held up a hand. "Good going, Sasha. You and Carla take the first watch along with Eva and myself. We'll wake the next group in three hours. Any questions? No? Okay, let's get some sleep."

The night passed slowly. It was quiet for the most part, with only occasional stirrings by unseen animals, and the usual absence of wind. Once, about halfway through Molly's watch, it rained. It was warm and felt good.

The rain stopped fifteen minutes later just as suddenly as it had begun. Molly wondered if it rained at the same time every night. She suspected that it did.

Finally it was Molly's turn to sleep but she found that difficult to do. There were so many things to worry about, so many people depending on her, and so many things to go wrong.

Molly remembered her mother's parting words. "Never give up hope. No matter where they take you, no matter how long it takes, Daddy will come. He'll hunt them clear across the universe if that's what it takes. Be ready. There'll be trouble when Daddy comes, and he'll need your help."

But Molly had survived so much, and waited for so long, that rescue didn't seem possible anymore. If Daddy were coming, surely he'd be here by now. Maybe he was dead and Mommy too. There was no way to know.

Eva was sound asleep, sucking her thumb. Molly raised her head and took a quick look around. There was no one close enough to hear so she allowed herself to cry.

Deep sobs racked her body, until the need for them had passed, and then, as Molly wiped her face with a shirtsleeve, she found that one of Eva's chubby little arms had found its way around her middle. The other girl didn't say anything, but she'd heard, and was offering what little comfort she could.

It felt warmer with Eva snuggled up beside her and Molly fell asleep.

Molly awoke to a feather-light touch. With it came awareness of where she was and her eyes flew open. Alien eyes stared at her from only inches away. Molly started to push herself away but stopped when she realized who and what it was. The alien was seated next to her and wore a complicated vest.

"Jareth? Is that you?"

The triangular head moved slightly. "Yes, it is I."

"Do you remember me?"

"Of course. That is why I approached you rather than one of the others."

The others. Molly got up on her knees to look around. It was lighter now, and although some of the girls were up and around, none seemed aware of Jareth.

He seemed to read her thoughts. "Do not be angry with them. They kept watch as well as they know how. This is, how do you say it, my 'home,' and I am good at hiding."

Jareth dangled something from bony fingers. It took Molly a moment to recognize what it was. The L-band! Her fingers flew to her head, and sure enough, the explosive device was gone.

"I hope you do not mind," Jareth said apologetically. "But

this is a dangerous device, and should not be worn around your head."

"No," Molly replied gratefully, "I'm happy to get it off. How did you know it was dangerous?"

Jareth blinked. "I knew."

Molly tried another approach. "How did you disarm it. Wasn't that dangerous?"

The alien made a sign. "Not very damned likely."

He reached into one of his multitudinous pockets and pulled out a tiny box. "This produced an electronic signal that entered the trigger mechanism, neutralized it, and withdrew."

"Thank you," Molly said solemnly. "It might've killed me."

"Death is bad," Jareth agreed evenly.

Molly thought of the other runner, the one who'd been eaten. "I . . . we . . . saw a member of the 56,827 chase one of your people."

Jareth made some sort of a sign with his left hand. "Yes. That was Mizlam. It was her turn to die."

Molly frowned. "Her turn to die? What does that mean?"

Jareth cocked his head to one side. "Did I say it improperly? I meant that others have died in the past and this was Mizlam's turn."

Molly had forgotten how frustrating Jareth could be. "So you take turns dying?"

"Yes," the alien replied. "Oldest first, youngest last. Izliak is next, followed by Threma, followed by Dorlia."

Molly searched the alien's face. It bore the same expression. "Why? Why do you take turns?"

Jareth made a complicated gesture with his left hand. "Because it is fair."

Molly remembered how Mizlam had died, turning to face death, meeting it with dignity. She shook her head in amazement. "I admire you and your people, Jareth. You are strong and brave."

When Jareth blinked, Molly saw that his eyelids were almost transparent. "Thank you."

Molly gestured to the surrounding area. "Can you help us?"

"I will try," Jareth replied. "What do you need?"

Molly sat up and wrapped her arms around her knees. "We need water, something to eat, and a way to defend ourselves from the 56,827."

Jareth seemed to consider her request. "Water is easy, and the food also, if you can eat what we do. I cannot satisfy your last request however. There is no defense against death."

Molly searched the runner's face and found no information in the alien features. "Jareth, I don't understand. Your people built this ship, you run it, surely you have a knowledge of weapons."

Jareth made a hand sign. "The knowledge yes. This entire ship is a weapon. A weapon so powerful it can destroy entire planets. But we cannot operate such weapons."

"Can't? Or won't?"

Jareth blinked. "There is no difference. We cannot, and we will not use such weapons. Our ancestors rose to sentience by running faster, thinking better, and organizing more effectively than their enemies. We are and always have been vegetarians. We have no experience at killing things. More than that we have a—how do you say?—a revulsion? A dislike for violence which prevents us from using it on others. Killing isn't fair."

Although Molly had read about pacifists in school, she'd been exposed to violence all her life and couldn't imagine doing what she'd seen Mizlam do. All of her training, all of her experience, suggested that the runner should've fought to the death no matter how hopeless that might be. Molly respected the runners, and their beliefs, but was personally unwilling to give up her life without a struggle. She frowned.

"I understand, Jareth, but our races are different, and humans *are* willing to use violence. Most of them anyway. Is there anything that prevents you from giving us weapons?"

Jareth cocked his head to the other side. "Weapons? Are you and your companions old enough to use them?"

Molly grinned. "On the planet I come from everybody's old enough to use them. We have no choice."

Jareth wiggled his fingers. "What kind of weapons?"

Molly shrugged. "Small stuff, you know, slug guns and blasters."

"Slug guns? Blasters? What are those?"

"Small hand-held projectile and energy weapons."

Jareth blinked. "I have no personal knowledge of such weapons but will ask the others. There is water nearby, I will show you where and bring you food."

Molly nodded solemnly. "Thank you, Jareth. And there is something else as well."

"Yes?"

"The 56,827 took three of our kind. They are somewhere aboard ship. Could you help us find them?"

Jareth stood, causing some of the girls to scatter. "We will try. But remember, little one, if they are alive, it is for a short time only."

Molly nodded. She understood all too well.

Twenty-seven

MCCADE FELT BETTER and worse than he had in a long time. Better, because he was closing in on Molly, and worse, because the medication had begun to wear off, he was tired, and his arm had started to throb.

McCade forced the fatigue aside and squinted through a haze of his own cigar smoke. Drang was a brownish ball that filled half of the main screen, and there, miles ahead, light winked off Pong's flagship.

In fifteen minutes, twenty at most, they'd be aboard. McCade imagined Molly rushing into his arms and tightened his grip on the blaster he'd taken from Pong's arms locker. Sol help anyone who got in his way.

The control room was comfortable to the point of being luxurious. There was the soft glow of instrument lights, the steady hiss of air through carefully located vents, and the comfort of the leather acceleration couches. A rather pleasant compartment except for the tension that filled the air.

The cyborg occupied the pilot's position, her plastiflesh face completely impassive as she conned the ship, her metal-ceramic composite fingers dancing over the keys.

And beside her, with weapon drawn and fangs showing, sat Phil. The variant watched the pilot the way a cat watches a mouse, conscious of her slightest move, ready to pounce if she tried to escape.

The com set buzzed softly. The cyborg looked at Phil. The

variant nodded. She pushed a button. A male voice flooded the compartment.

"CF warship LC4621 to approaching vessel. Provide today's recognition code or be fired on."

The cyborg glanced over her shoulder at Pong. The pirate looked at McCade, the bounty hunter nodded his permission, and the pilot pressed a key. Then she read off a series of numbers and touched another key.

There was silence for a moment followed by the male voice. "Acknowledged. Out."

McCade made a note of the abrupt tone. The shuttle had lifted in something of a hurry, and a whole barrage of inquiries had followed them into space, making it clear that Pong's staff knew something was amiss. The dead guards, the missing sentry, and the massive violation of lift protocols had made sure of that.

Yes, a reception committee would be waiting aboard Pong's ship, but with the pirate as a hostage, McCade thought he could handle it. Would *have* to handle it.

Pong sat on McCade's right just behind Phil. The pirate was uncharacteristically silent. The reason was simple. Pong was scared for the first time in years.

It was McCade's eyes that frightened him the most. They were like cold, hard stones. He saw no weakness there, no sign of the greed, fear, and lust for power that Pong usually saw in others, or in himself for that matter. No, this man could not be bought, intimidated, or tempted.

Pong wondered if he was going to die. He directed a thought toward the Melcetian.

"Well? I notice you missed this development. What do you suggest we do now?"

The mind slug had oozed its way toward Pong's right shoulder, gradually putting more and more of the pirate's body between itself and danger, already plotting what to do if its present host was to die. The alien's reply was caustic.

"First of all, I believe it was *you* who insisted on raiding this man's pathetic planet for reasons of revenge, and *you* who insisted on turning his offspring into some sort of personal mascot. So, if you wish to place responsibility, look no further than yourself.

"As for what to do now, well that seems quite simple. I

suggest that you give this man what he wants as quickly as you can. Why sacrifice all of your hopes, all of your ambitions, to the rather understandable desire of a father to rescue his child?"

Pong thought it over. In the strictly logical sense the Melcetian was correct. He should use the girl to buy his way out, allow them to escape, and forget the whole thing. There were worlds, nay, an entire universe to conquer. Why let this get in the way?

The answer was pride, and more than that emotion, things the Melcetian knew very little about. Yes, he'd look like a fool if he allowed McCade to take Molly away, but worse than that, he'd lose something he treasured. Molly herself. She was more than a good-luck charm.

Molly was the one person Pong could rely on to say what she thought, to be herself, to accept him as he was. And because Molly was a child there was no need to worry about her true motives, her allies, or her ambitions.

Pong knew she didn't like him all that much but so what? Affection would come with time. No, logic or no logic, Pong wasn't ready to surrender Molly to her father. Not yet anyway.

McCade watched Pong's flagship grow steadily larger until it ran off the edges of the screen. What had been little more than a white dot, had slowly transformed itself into a rectangle, and then into a large hatch. He could see the gleaming deck within, a variety of smaller spacecraft, and the stutter of alignment beams.

The cyborg fired the ship's retros, and McCade felt the shuttle slow as three delta-shaped fighters arrowed out of the larger vessel's bay and accelerated away. Then, with a tiny increment of thrust from the main drive, the pilot moved them forward.

McCade admired her touch. The *Arrow* seemed to float inside the launching bay, where the retros slowed her again, and the ship settled gently toward the durasteel deck. It touched with an almost-imperceptible bump.

Outside the shuttle a huge pair of external doors slid steadily closed. McCade watched them on two of the control compartment's smaller vid screens. When the bay was sealed Pong's crew would pump an atmosphere into the bay allowing the shuttle's passengers to disembark without space armor. A routine courtesy extended to Pong? Or part of a trap? McCade grinned. The second possibility seemed the most likely. Once the doors were closed the shuttle would be immobilized. The time had come to make some preparations.

Thirty minutes passed before McCade was ready to leave the *Arrow*. During that time the bay was pressurized and fifty or so heavily armed crew members had taken up positions around the shuttle. They wore reflective armor and looked like toy soldiers.

Raz stood in front of them, chest almost bare to the frigid air, his face expressionless as the lock whined open. He had snipers stationed at various points around the hangar. They'd kill the bounty hunter and his furry friend the moment they emerged.

There was a gasp of surprise as Mustapha Pong stepped out. He had gray repair tape wound around his head, and more than that, something taped to his left temple. A blaster! A blaster bound to the bounty hunter's right hand by a ball of tape! Even if the sharpshooters managed to kill McCade before his brain sent a message to his right index finger, the weight of his falling body would apply pressure to the firing stud and send a bolt of energy straight through Pong's head.

Raz brought a small radio up to his lips. "Don't fire! I repeat, don't fire!"

All over the bay fingers came off firing studs and weapons were lowered.

Seeing this McCade gave an internal sigh of relief. He felt the tension ease a little. So far so good. Now for the next step. His voice carried well within the open bay.

"Hi there, everybody . . . let's keep this nice and simple. You've got some children aboard, slaves taken from a planet called Alice. I want them, and I want them now."

McCade pushed the blaster against Pong's head. "How 'bout it, Mustapha? Got anything to add?"

The pirate glared at McCade and turned his attention to Raz. The bounty hunter's blaster left Pong with very little choice. "Do as he says. Bring the girls here. Be sure to include the one called Molly."

Raz nodded stiffly, started to turn, and stopped when a petty officer touched his arm. There was conversation. Raz turned back. "I'm told the girls were taken off-ship, sir, on *your* orders."

"He's right," the Melcetian reminded Pong, "you gave them to 47,721.".

Now Pong remembered. He'd given the alien some of the snotty-nosed kids . . . but not Molly. He'd never agree to that. Someone had gone into his quarters and taken her! Anger sent blood pounding through Pong's veins.

"Find the person or persons who put the children aboard the shuttle! Bring them here!"

McCade felt something heavy fall into his stomach. Taken away? Shuttle? He'd missed her again? When would it end?

Raz nodded. "Yes, sir." He said something into his radio and four guards jogged toward the nearest lock.

There was movement to McCade's right and a flash of light. Someone screamed and a body fell. Phil's voice boomed through one of the shuttle's external speakers.

"Stay where you are. As you can see, the secondary lock is well protected, and there's no point in getting killed."

And they *had* seen. Smoke drifted up and away from the crumpled body. Nobody moved.

Eight extremely long minutes passed before the guards returned. They dragged a man and woman between them. The woman was crying, begging for mercy, and doing her best to blame everything on her companion. The man was silent, looking around, trying to understand.

Then the woman saw Pong, the blaster, and the man with the cold gray eyes. The whimpering stopped as Boots searched for a way out. Pong was in trouble. Could that work in her favor?

Pong ignored the man and focused his attention on Boots. She'd been in charge of the slaves and she'd been punished for allowing Molly access to the Navcomp. A motive perhaps?

Pong's voice was soft and reasonable. "Boots, isn't it?"

Boots nodded, pleased that Pong remembered. Things were looking up.

Pong smiled. "The man with the blaster pointed at my head is looking for the children that were aboard this ship. Did you put them on a shuttle?"

Boots did her best to look innocent. "Yes, sir, I was ordered to, sir."

Pong nodded understandingly. "Of course. Now tell me,

Boots, did you have orders to load *all* of the slave girls? Or was there an exception?"

Boots frowned as if trying to remember. This is where it got tricky, but Pong's phraseology, plus his tone, suggested a way out. "I don't remember any exceptions, sir."

"I see," Pong said sympathetically. "And did you happen to remove the slave girl known as Molly from my quarters? And having done so, load her aboard the shuttle along with the others? This man would like to know."

Boots did her best to look rueful. "Yes, sir, now that you mention it, I did, sir, it was my understanding we were to load *all* of the girls."

Pong looked thoughtful and McCade felt silly holding the blaster to his head. Pong had taken control of the situation and it seemed as if their positions ought to be reversed.

"I see," Pong said calmly. "Well, Boots, that's too bad. I left Raz in charge, and if your information is correct, then the whole thing's *his* fault. Tell me, Raz, was it your fault? No? I didn't think so. So here's what I want you to do, Boots. Go get your space armor, suit up, and get the hell off my ship."

"But I'll die!" Boots wailed. "I'll run out of air!"

"Probably," Pong agreed, "but not before you get a good look at Drang. A nice long look. Consider it my little gift."

Boots tried to run but the guards caught and dragged her away.

Unable to turn his head because of the blaster, Pong swiveled his eyes toward McCade. "I know where Molly is. She's in great danger. We could be there in a few hours."

McCade was surprised. Why so cooperative? A trap? Then it hit him. What Pong had said about raising Molly was true! The pirate liked her! More than that, wanted her for himself!

McCade felt a lot of things, jealousy and fear foremost among them. Pong liked Molly. Did she like him? Had she changed? And what about the danger Pong referred to?

Pong cleared his throat. "Time is of the essence, McCade. We need to leave *now*. I suggest that we bring some of my troops."

McCade shook his head. He believed Molly was in trouble, but wasn't about to bring any of Pong's troops. There was no way that he and Phil could control additional people. "No troops. Tell them to clear the bay and open the outer doors."

Pong did as he was told, and the double doors slid open fifteen minutes later. The doors were still in motion when the cyborg took *Arrow* out. Phil ran the sensors at maximum sensitivity but no one followed.

With the tape undone, and everyone back in their former positions, McCade was about to ask Pong some questions when an unexpected hand touched his shoulder. "Coffee, sir?"

McCade spun his chair around to find Platz standing there with a tray of coffee containers. He looked rumpled but otherwise no worse for wear.

Phil grinned. "Platz is out on good behavior. It was a bit cramped in that storage compartment."

McCade nodded and accepted a container of coffee. "Thank you, Platz. Sorry about this, but you were in the wrong place at the wrong time."

Platz shrugged and offered Pong some coffee. It was sealed in a zero-G bulb making it useless as a weapon. "That's okay, sir. Phil explained what's going on, and I hope you find your daughter."

McCade smiled and turned toward Pong. "Which brings us to you. Where's Molly? And what sort of danger is she in?"

Pong didn't hesitate. He told McCade about the 56,827, their ship, and their so-called death experiments. It was true that 56,827 were his secret weapon, but he couldn't save Molly without admitting their existence. If things went the way he hoped, McCade would die aboard the alien ship, and if they didn't, well, those were the breaks.

The Melcetian listened but made no attempt to interfere. The alien had computed all of the most likely outcomes, and while it still had hopes for Pong, was ready to find itself a new host if necessary. Number 47,721 might make a good candidate. Disgusting, but completely ruthless, and sufficiently ambitious. Yes, the best plan was to lie low, and see where the advantage lay.

As the bounty hunter listened to Pong's description of the 56,827, their planetoid-sized warship, and his plans to take over all of known space, McCade was more and more amazed. Not only did the pirate propose murder on a scale hitherto unknown, he did it with the calm, measured prose of a businessman describing plans to enter a new market, or an architect discussing his latest design.

If not actually insane Pong was the next closest thing to it. It showed in Pong's total selfishness, his complete lack of empathy for others, his inability to see them as anything more than pieces in some elaborate game.

Although the pirate liked Molly, and was clearly determined to save her, the other girls meant nothing at all. Only Molly had something to offer Pong personally, so only she was real.

Although McCade had encountered a large number of sociopaths during his days as a bounty hunter, Pong was the worst by far. Still, if he wanted to save Molly, he'd need more information and that meant playing along.

"It's an amazing plan, Mustapha, and if anyone could pull it off, you could. There's something I don't understand though. If you want to help Molly, and these aliens are friends of yours, why is she in danger?"

For the first time during their conversation Pong looked slightly embarrassed. He cleared his throat. "Well, I don't approve mind you, but the 56,827 have some rather unpleasant ways. For one thing they insist on performing what they call 'death experiments' on a representative sample of the sentients they plan to fight, and for another, they are rather actively carnivorous."

It took McCade a moment to decode the last part of Pong's statement, and when he did, the bounty hunter was incredulous. " 'Death experiments'? 'Actively carnivorous'? Does that mean what I think it does?"

Pong refused to meet McCade's eyes. "Yes, I'm afraid it does."

McCade's eyes narrowed as he leaned forward, his hands working in and out of fists, only inches away from killing Pong then and there. "You mean you took little girls, Molly included, and handed them over to be tortured? Or eaten? Or both?"

Phil growled, a long, low rumble that made Pong's blood run cold, and Platz gave an involuntary gasp of surprise.

Pong knew death was extremely close. He also knew that McCade wanted some sign of sorrow, of contrition, so he provided it. "I'm sorry, I really am, and I tried to protect Molly. Things went wrong, that's all. It wasn't my fault."

Only the need to get aboard the alien ship and find the children kept McCade from wrapping his fingers around Pong's throat and choking the life out of him. McCade forced himself to lean back in his seat. His eyes were little more than slits and his hands shook with suppressed rage. Once they reached the alien ship, once the children were safe, Pong would pay for the things he'd done. And if they arrived too late, if . . . McCade forced the thought away. Silence fell on the control compartment and time slowed to a virtual crawl.

Twenty-eight

McCade and Phil stood watches, two hours on, and two hours off. When he wasn't on duty McCade slept and, in spite of his bone-deep fatigue, dreamt of monsters that ate little girls.

But the rest did him good, and that, along with another round of medication from Pong's well-stocked first-aid kit, put him in reasonable shape by the time the alien ship filled the screens. He was surprised by the ease with which the *Arrow* was permitted to approach and enter the larger vessel's bay.

Pong shrugged. "The 56,827 have a simple policy. Admit the *Arrow* and destroy anything else."

McCade thought about what life would be like under such rulers and shuddered. It reminded him of the larger problem. Even if they found the children, and managed to neutralize these aliens, there was the rest of them to worry about. But first things first.

McCade spent the next twenty minutes quizzing Pong about the 56,827, the interior of their ship, and anything else he could think of. Good intelligence is absolutely critical when you're forced to fight on enemy ground.

By the time the shuttle landed inside the bay McCade and Phil had added blast rifles to their already extensive armament, agreed to let Platz come along on the condition that he was unarmed, and rigged up some leg shackles that would slow Pong down should he attempt to run.

When the ship was secure, they wasted little time locking the cyborg in the head and cycling out into the bay.

There was no sign of the 56,827, or the children either, so they headed for the ship's lock. It was already open. McCade stepped inside, found it empty, and motioned for the rest to follow. They did and the hatch closed behind them.

McCade lit a cigar and blew smoke toward the inner hatch. Pong stared straight ahead, face impassive, mind churning through his options.

Phil smelled something foul, something he'd never encountered before, and allowed his lip to curl away from durasteel fangs. A growl came from deep inside his massive body.

The Melcetian shimmered, throwing light in every direction as it repositioned itself on Pong's shoulder, and monitored the human's thoughts.

Platz looked around as if seeing a lock for the first time, saw a comb lying on the deck, and bent to pick it up. But there was some kind of goo on it so he let it lay.

The hatch whirred open and McCade stepped through. He held his blast rifle up and ready to fire, but saw nothing more threatening than a dim lavender sky and an alien landscape. There were rocks, strange foliage, and some distant trees. Or things that *looked* like trees anyway. The others followed.

McCade was just about to ask Pong where the dirt path led when there was a stirring in some nearby bushes and the sound of a hesitant voice.

"Citizen McCade? Is that you?"

McCade's heart leaped into his throat. "Yes! Who's there?"

"We are," the voice answered, and one by one a group of bedraggled little girls emerged from the bushes. McCade inventoried each dirt-smudged face until a small group stood in front of him and Molly was nowhere to be seen. McCade bit his lip. He recognized some of the children but not all.

The girls looked from McCade to Phil and back again. The same one, a girl named Linda if he remembered correctly, spoke again. "Is it really you? You came for us?" Her upper lip trembled.

McCade managed a smile. He wasn't sure, but he thought that Linda's father was dead, buried below the permafrost on Alice. A tear ran down his cheek. McCade got down on one knee. He bit back the desire to ask about Molly and forced himself to wait. "Yes, it's really us, and we came for you."

The girls cried, threw themselves at McCade and Phil, and bombarded them with questions. "Is my mommy all right? Did you find my brother? Can we go home now?"

Platz beamed and Pong whistled through his teeth. Finally, when the pirate couldn't take it anymore, he said, "Save it for later, McCade . . . where's Molly?"

McCade peeled two little girls away from his chest and held a finger to his lips. "He's right. There'll be lots of time to celebrate. Where *is* Molly? Are there any others?"

The story spilled out in fits and starts, first from one girl, then from another, until McCade had the whole picture. It seemed three of the girls had been taken away by one of the 56,827, presumably for the "death experiments" Pong had mentioned, and Molly, with help from a friendly alien called Jareth, had gone after them.

And then, about three hours after Molly's departure, another member of the 56,827 had swung through the area. Hunting, exercising, the girls weren't sure what. But they had orders to scatter and proceeded to do so. The alien lingered for a while, then left. After that it was a relatively simple matter to regroup around the lock as Molly had instructed them to do, and that's where they were when McCade arrived.

As McCade listened he was conscious of Molly's leadership role, and found himself alternating between pride and fear.

McCade held Linda by both shoulders. "Do you know where Molly went? Can you show us which direction?"

Linda nodded. "Jareth showed her the way. He said he wouldn't fight but he gave Molly some sort of gun."

"A gun? Molly has a weapon?"

Linda nodded again. "Yes, she said you'd taught her how to use it."

McCade remembered putting an empty meal pak on a snow-covered rock, helping Molly to wrap cold little fingers around the grip of a blaster, and watching as blue light burped past the rock to hit the scrub beyond. He tightened his grip on Linda's shoulders. She winced and he let go.

"Show us, Linda, show us where Jareth and Molly went."

Linda turned and started down into the valley. The others followed as Linda made a wide detour around the boulders where Lia had disappeared, took them past the pile of still bloody bones where the runner called Mizlam had faced death, and climbed the slope beyond. When Linda reached the top of the hill, she looked back to make sure the others were with her, and disappeared from view.

By the time McCade topped the hill, and had started down the other side, Linda was already at the bottom of the slope pointing at a rock.

"That's where they went, Citizen McCade . . . and they never came back!"

McCade came to a stop in front of the rock and looked quizzically at Linda. "They went where?"

"Under the rock," Linda answered impatiently. "It lifts up."

McCade bent over, got a grip on the rock, and pulled. It came up with surprising ease. And no wonder, since one glance at the rock's underpinnings showed that it was hydraulically assisted. The rock concealed a rather standard maintenance tube.

It made sense when McCade thought about it; biosphere or not, the ship would require maintenance, and as a member of the crew this Jareth character would know his way around.

Metal rungs extended straight down, rungs spaced farther apart than would be comfortable for humans, and disappeared into darkness. Molly had climbed down those rungs and ended up where?

McCade wasted little time. "Okay, Phil. Take Pong's restraints off. We've got some climbing to do. Platz, come here."

The trooper obeyed. His open-featured face radiated trust. "Yes, sir?"

McCade held up his blast rifle. "What would you do if I gave you this? Would you shoot me and ask Pong for a bonus?"

Platz didn't even blink. "No, sir. I'm not stupid, sir. If something happens to you, the general will kill me and try to keep all of this secret."

Pong raised his eyes heavenward but didn't attempt to deny it.

McCade nodded and handed Platz the rifle. "You've got that right. I'm leaving you in charge of the girls. Take them back to the lock. If you see any of the 56,827, shoot to kill. Wait for three hours, if we aren't back by then, put the girls on the ship and get the hell out of here.

"Take them to the nearest Imperial Navy base and ask for Admiral Swanson-Pierce. They'll give you lots of guff but hang in there. Use my name a lot. Walt will show up eventually, and when he does, tell him I promised you ten thousand credits. The same for the pilot. He'll make it good, and get the girls home to boot."

Platz listened with a look of complete amazement, as did Pong, who raised one eyebrow. "You've got some interesting friends, McCade. I suspect I underestimated your influence."

McCade turned toward the pirate. "Shut up and listen. I'm going into the maintenance tube first. You're second, and Phil's third. Just one wrong move and we'll kill you. Got it?"

Pong shrugged. "Got it." For the moment he had no choice but to do what McCade said, but figured the 56,827 must be well aware of their uninvited guests, and would make an appearance sometime soon. That would be his chance.

"Good," McCade replied. "Okay, girls, do what Citizen Platz says, and I'll see you in a little while."

The girls looked doubtful, many wishing that he would stay, but waved gamely as Platz led them away. McCade was pleased to see that the soldier held the blast rifle at port arms and was watching both his flanks.

McCade checked to make sure that his remaining weapons, a hand blaster and a slug gun, were secure, and lowered himself into the tube. Pong followed, as did Phil.

Sensing a certain amount of mass and movement within the tube, a distant computer turned on the lights. The lights were circular like the passageway itself, and came at roughly ten-foot intervals, as did the tiny rivet-sized surveillance cameras that fed video to alien eyes.

Looking down between his feet, McCade could see lights stretching away for what seemed like forever. He continued downward.

Their boots rang on the metal rungs, and the farther down they went, the warmer it became. Four or five times they went by intersections where horizontal tubes connected with their own, and on two occasions they heard the sound of rushing water, as if some sort of large conduit paralleled their tube.

The intersections were troublesome, since Molly and Jareth could have used any one of them, but each of the horizontal tunnels had a fine layer of dust at the bottom, and as far as

McCade could tell none of them had been used for a long time.

Then, just when McCade was sure they were descending into hell itself, the tube grew suddenly cooler and continued that way until it bottomed out.

Here too the dust came in handy, clearly showing the scuff marks where Molly and her alien companion had headed toward the right, showing McCade where to go.

McCade was cautious now, sensing they were close to something important, glaring at Pong to make sure that the pirate understood.

This was more a corridor than a tube, and dark at the other end. McCade slid forward, his left hand maintaining contact with the bulkhead, his right wrapped around the comforting weight of the slug gun.

From Pong's description of the 56,827 a weapon with some stopping power would be best. The problem with energy beams is that they tend to go right through the target without producing any hydrostatic shock. Not very good if your opponent is large and has lots of inertia.

Lavender light flooded the corridor. By the time McCade's eyes had adjusted, and his brain had processed the new information, the alien was in motion. It came straight at him and the bounty hunter responded automatically.

The slug gun made an enormous booming sound within the close confines of the corridor. McCade could see where the hollow points hit, punching their way through the alien's thin exoskeleton and blowing huge chunks of flesh and bone out of its back. Although it didn't seem possible the alien kept on coming.

McCade fired again, and again, expecting each slug to put the creature down, but it just kept coming, staggering with each impact, but refusing to die.

Finally, when a slug cut through the second of its redundant spinal cords, the alien tripped, fell forward, and slid almost to McCade's feet. He jumped backward as the alien's still dying nervous system caused it to jerk and snap.

Turning, McCade found Pong plastered against the bulkhead, and beyond him, Phil looking down at a second crumpled body. It had a hole the size of dinner plate burned through its bony chest. Goo drooled from its mouth.

The variant caught McCade's look and gestured upward. The aliens had known where thcy were and attempted to box them in.

McCade started to sidestep the body, felt his foot hit something, and heard it skitter away. Light bounced off a shiny object. McCade bent to pick it up. An energy weapon of some sort, the butt felt awkward in his human hand, but there was still no doubt as to its function.

McCade held it up for Pong to see. The pirate nodded. "It's like I told you before. The 56,827 like to hunt, and while willing to use weapons when they have to, consider them demeaning. Especially where personal combat is concerned."

McCade smiled grimly. "Yeah? Well guess what . . . from now on they're gonna be known as the 56,825."

McCade thumbed the magazine release on his slug gun, slammed a fresh one into place, and pulled the hand blaster too. The aliens were damned hard to kill. He'd need every weapon he had.

They eased their way around the dead alien and headed for the hatch at the end of the corridor. Just before they reached it McCade grabbed Pong and pushed him forward. "Time to earn your keep, old sport . . . open that hatch."

Fear ran through Pong's body like an icy stream. Anything could be, and probably was, waiting beyond that door. Pong considered begging but knew it wouldn't work.

As Pong crouched low and reached up toward the control plate, he felt the Melcetian ooze down as far as it could. The miserable piece of worthless fecal matter was using him as a shield!

Pong's hand touched the heat-sensitive plate and the hatch slid open. They waited for a barrage of slugs and energy beams but it never came.

McCade felt his heart beat just a little bit faster as he eased his way forward and peeked through the door. He found himself looking into some sort of equipment room, where metal catwalks turned and twisted through a maze of metal pipes, and the air seemed to shimmer with radiated heat.

McCade looked at Phil, got a nod in return, and stepped out onto a catwalk. The response was almost instantaneous. Two aliens stepped out from behind a cluster of pipes and opened up with energy weapons. One of the beams cut through a piece of conduit at McCade's elbow and showered him with sparks.

McCade fired the slug gun five times in quick succession, saw each of them jerk, and burned them down with the blaster before they could charge.

McCade heard Phil roar something incoherent, and turned to find the variant firing down the tube way, his blast rifle stuttering blue death.

As the bounty hunter added his fire to Phil's, three more of the aliens struggled forward and died in the combined fire of three weapons.

"Behind you!"

McCade spun around on Pong's warning just in time to find one more creature charging him. The bounty hunter emptied the slug gun into the alien's head, just barely destroying the thing's brain before the insectoid body hit and bowled him over. It took the alien a moment to flop around and die.

McCade crab-walked backward to get away, scrambled to his feet, and checked his weapons. Then, with a new magazine in the slug gun, and a fresh power pak in the blaster, he was ready once again.

With Pong following close behind and Phil bringing up the rear, McCade made his way through the maze of pipes to another opening.

Once again Pong was forced to open the hatch, and once again there was a lack of reaction.

They waited for a full minute. Still nothing. McCade motioned for the pirate to step through the door. Pong started to balk, but the bounty hunter waved his slug gun, and the pirate changed his mind. He stepped through the door and looked around.

"McCade! There they are! There's Molly!"

McCade came through the door in a low crouch, weapons in his hands, eyes searching for trouble. He found himself in a large circular area. It had a crude dirt floor, a source of lavender light high above, and at least twenty tunnels spaced equidistantly around its walls. Each was identified with some sort of pictograph. Maintenance tunnels? Private entrances for the super-territorial aliens? It made little difference.

And there, right at the room's exact center, was some sort of cage. It contained three or four children and a type of alien McCade had never seen before. The one called Jareth?

The thought was pushed aside as his eyes met Molly's and he heard her voice. "Daddy! Watch out . . . "

But the warning came too late.

Strong arms wrapped themselves around him, immobilizing both of his weapons. McCade heard Pong laugh, and knew the pirate had seen the ambush, but failed to give warning.

The bounty hunter felt both handguns ripped away and heard a growl from behind as Phil struggled with assailants of his own.

Within seconds both of them were completely immobilized. There were two of the aliens controlling McCade, and no less than four struggling to hold Phil.

There was a scraping sound and McCade turned to see an alien walk out of a tunnel. There was a translator hung around his neck, and when the creature stopped, the device swung back and forth. The alien addressed itself to Pong.

"So, numberless one, you come bringing death with you."

Pong shook his head and forced a smile, forgetting that it had no meaning for 47,721. "I was forced to come and bring them with me. That one, the creature that looks like me, was searching for his daughter."

"Daughter?"

"One of the juveniles. One of those," Pong said, pointing at the girls. "She is his—how do you say it?—progeny."

47,721 swiveled toward the cage. "Which?"

Pong frowned. He didn't like the way this was going. "The one with the black curly hair. But what difference does that make?"

47,721 didn't answer. It walked over to the cage, undid the latch, and opened the door. Jareth placed himself in front of the children, but 47,721 brushed the runner aside. Long heavily clawed fingers locked themselves around one of Molly's arms and pulled her from the cage. She struggled but it made no difference.

"Pong!" McCade shouted. "Don't let him touch her! You said you cared about her, you said you liked her, how can you stand there and let this happen?"

Pong took a hesitant step forward. "Leave her alone, 47,721. You can have the rest, but leave that one alone."

The alien paused deliberately, Molly still clutched with one hand. "You forget yourself, numberless one. I do as I wish, and since I'm hungry, I shall eat. A meal that will not only satiate my hunger, but teach this human a lesson."

Pong saw Molly, the obvious terror in her eyes, and tried to take another step forward. But the Melcetian wouldn't let him. The mind slug projected emotions into his head and poured chemicals into his bloodstream.

Pong found that each motion took tremendous effort. It was like walking underwater or in heavy gravity. The mind slug's nervous system had been integrated with his for years now, and the alien had developed a tremendous amount of control, more than Pong had ever imagined.

"Let her die!" the Melcetian screamed in Pong's mind. "You're throwing away everything I worked for, everything I wanted, all for a stupid child!"

The words echoed through Pong's brain as he willed himself forward. What was it the mind slug had said? "I?" As in "everything *I* worked for, everything *I* wanted."

And suddenly Pong knew something he should've known long before, that his "I" and the Melcetian's "I" were entirely different. This was no partnership, no sharing of similar ambitions, this was slavery. The alien was, and always had been, his master.

Reaching deep into some hidden reservoir of energy Pong found strength and used it to hurl himself forward. He felt his hands close around 47,721's neck, and saw Molly spin away as the alien turned its attention to him.

Pong felt something tear deep inside his body as the Melcetian pulled itself loose. The mind slug had waited until the last moment before separating itself, hoping that Pong would come to his senses, and now it was too late.

A terrible agony lanced through Pong's nervous system. He screamed, and as he did, the mind slug screamed too.

47,721 gloried in the feel of his razor-sharp hand claws slicing through alien flesh. His first few strokes cut the soft shiny thing to ribbons and the next cut deep four-inch channels through the human's upper torso. Then with a single darting motion of his oblong head, 47,721 administered the *Natawkwa*, or killing bite. A sticky red fluid sprayed across 47,721's face and he gave thanks for the hunt. There would be much meat when this was over.

Then, as the killing rage began to fade, 47,721 saw that

things had changed. The hairy thing, the one the humans called a variant, had broken loose. 47,721 dropped Pong's remains in order to watch. His venturing companions would make short work of the human.

Phil had waited, hoping to avoid going into full augmentation, knowing he'd be worthless for days afterward. But when the alien grabbed Molly, and Pong threw himself forward, Phil knew there was no choice.

The variant activated certain triggers planted deep within his subconscious, felt chemicals pour into his bloodstream, and saw the world around him slow. His reactions were speeded up, his muscles chemically augmented, his entire body a murderous machine.

Now a single jerk from Phil's arms was enough to free him from his alien guards. A spinning kick and one went down, its leg broken at the joint, screeching loudly. Another kick broke its neck.

The others rushed him, confident of their superior strength, eager to give the *Natawkwa*.

Phil roared his approval, rammed a fist through the first one's chest, and pulled something out.

A whitish fluid sprayed everywhere as Phil grabbed another alien by the skull and turned it around. The creature dropped like a rock.

The variant felt something slice through fur and flesh and turned to grab it. As he hugged the alien to his chest, Phil felt bones crunch and heard organs pop.

"You want a fight?" the variant roared. "You want combat? Well how's this!"

So saying Phil lifted the already dead alien up over his head and bounced it off a bulkhead.

In the meantime Molly had been sent tumbling head over heels. As she hit the cage it knocked the wind out of her. Molly struggled to breathe as the alien did something horrible to Pong. Blood spattered on her boots.

Then Molly saw Phil break loose from his guards and spin-kick one of them. Meanwhile Daddy was struggling to break free.

Molly saw a gun, one of Phil's knocked loose in the struggle, slide across the packed earth. She dived forward and felt it heavy in her hands.

Daddy shoved and kicked but to no avail. One of the 56,815 still had hold of his arm. Molly tried to aim but was afraid that she'd hit Daddy instead of the alien. She ran forward and pressed the muzzle against the alien's torso. The slug gun practically jumped out of her hand when she squeezed the trigger. It made a muffled bang.

Mortally wounded, the alien let go and McCade yelled, "Molly! Give me the gun!"

Molly tossed the gun to her father and backed away as the remaining alien moved toward her. It staggered as McCade pumped four slugs into its back, took two more steps, and toppled onto its face.

Both of them stared at it for a second until Molly saw something over her father's shoulder and pointed. "Daddy! Behind you!"

McCade whirled to find 47,721 coming straight at him, a horrible-looking sight with saliva dripping from its jaws, and Pong's blood smeared all over its torso.

The bounty hunter brought the gun up in a two-handed grip, fired shot after shot into the alien's chest, and kept on firing as it slumped to the deck. He stopped when the gun clicked empty.

There was silence for a moment as all of them looked around, surprised to be alive and extremely grateful.

Then McCade was on his knees, with Molly in his arms, both crying and trying to talk at the same time.

Molly heard herself talking, heard herself say, "Oh, Daddy, Mommy said you'd come, but it took so long! And I was scared, and every time I did something it went wrong, and everything was awful. Is Mommy okay?"

And she heard her father reply, saying, "You did a great job, honey, and I'm sorry it took so long to find you. Yes, Mommy's fine, and waiting for you to come home. I love you, Molly. Thank God you're safe."

But years later, long after Phil had recovered, the remaining alien had been hunted down, and the effort to find their homeworld had begun, Molly would remember other things.

She'd remember the strength of her father's arms, the familiar smell of his clothes, and the fact that he'd crossed a thousand stars to find her. Molly was home.